D0040811

# Blood Retribution

## BY DAVID & AIMÉE THURLO

### ELLA CLAH NOVELS

*Blackening Song*
*Death Walker*
*Bad Medicine*
*Enemy Way*
*Shooting Chant*
*Red Mesa*
*Changing Woman*
*Tracking Bear*

*Plant Them Deep*

### LEE NEZ NOVELS

*Second Sunrise*
*Blood Retribution*

### SISTER AGATHA NOVELS

*Bad Faith*
*Thief in Retreat*

# Blood Retribution

A LEE NEZ NOVEL

DAVID & AIMÉE THURLO

A Tom Doherty Associates Book / New York

This is a work of fiction. All the characters and events portrayed in this novel are either fictitious or are used fictitiously.

BLOOD RETRIBUTION: A LEE NEZ NOVEL



This book is printed on acid-free paper.

A Forge Book
Published by Tom Doherty Associates, LLC
175 Fifth Avenue
New York, NY 10010

www.tor.com

Forge® is a registered trademark of Tom Doherty Associates, LLC.

Library of Congress Cataloging-in-Publication Data

Thurlo, David.
Blood retribution : a Lee Nez novel / David and Aimée Thurlo.—1st ed.
p. cm.
Sequel to: Second sunrise.
ISBN 0-765-30442-2 (acid-free paper)
EAN 978-0765-30442-1
1. Police—New Mexico—Fiction. 2. Government investigators—Fiction. 3. Navajo Indians—Fiction. 4. New Mexico—Fiction. 5. Werewolves—Fiction. 6. Smuggling—Fiction. 7. Vampires—Fiction. I. Thurlo, Aimée. II. Title.

PS3570.H825B57 2004
813'.54—dc22

2004049305

First Edition: September 2004

Printed in the United States of America

0 9 8 7 6 5 4 3 2 1

To librarians everywhere for providing us access to the twin worlds of information and imagination.

## ACKNOWLEDGMENTS

With special thanks to the dedicated law enforcement officers—regardless of the color of their uniforms—who protect and serve the citizens of New Mexico.

# Blood Retribution

# CHAPTER 1

*June 2002*

Hunting skinwalkers was risky at night, but what other choice did a vampire have? New Mexico state police officer Lee Nez, technically only half vampire, looked over at his companion, Diane Lopez, who was being bounced around the inside of the pickup like popcorn in a Dutch oven, struggling to maintain a safe hold on the barrel of her shotgun.

"Surprise me by trying to miss a bump here and there, will you?" Diane grumbled. "One more thump against the roof, and the button on the top of my cap will penetrate my skull." She'd come ready for action. Jeans, a loose T-shirt and dark jacket, and a black cap that kept her hair out of her eyes.

It was close to midnight and they were traveling through an isolated area of the Navajo Nation southwest of Shiprock, near Rattlesnake. "Hey, by Rez standards this is a *good* road." Complaining or making small talk was one way of putting up roadblocks against fear and hesitation. But Diane, a trained FBI agent, would make the right moves when the time came.

Lee remembered his father, a doughboy from World War I, telling him that the soldiers who claimed not to be afraid were either liars or stupid. The trick was learning how to make fear work for and not against you.

"This damn shoulder harness rubs a short woman like me right in the . . . wrong places," Diane continued. "Designed by a man, no doubt."

Lee chuckled. Developing a bad attitude now would serve to get them in the right frame of mind for the wet work ahead. They were hunting one particular Navajo skinwalker—a human witch capable of shape-shifting into a black jaguar. Killing wasn't a possibility—it was a requirement. Skinwalkers were evil by nature and had to be destroyed.

"Getting this woman just isn't going to be enough payback for me."

"I understand. She killed your partner." Lee kept his eyes on the road, swerving to avoid a long, narrow rut. His ability to see clearly in total darkness allowed him to drive without any headlights.

"Not very much prey around here for a skinwalker pack, is there? Or do they keep a low profile around their . . . dens?" Diane asked, doing her best to keep a watch out her side window, despite her lack of nightwalker senses. She'd brought a night-vision scope, but if she tried to use it now, she'd probably just end up with a black eye.

"They're very careful not to attract any attention. Other Navajos will shoot them if given the opportunity. At least we have a lead." He drove on, studying the dry terrain. "We're probably less than two miles from the Blackhorse house now. If we're lucky, my guess will turn out to be right and she headed here after escaping our dragnet."

"I hope she'll be in panther form when I see her again. That's the shape she took when she killed my partner and that's what I'd like her to be when I kill her."

"This one got away once and knows about some of my

abilities. I just hope she hasn't had time to share what she's learned with the others," he said. "Just remember their scent-tracking ability and that they'll be especially tuned in to my nightwalker blood. Since there's a slight breeze coming in from the west, we'll have to stay on the north, south, or east when we make our move."

"Right."

Lee stopped the SUV and turned off the engine. "A heads up: If skinwalkers are out here hunting, all bets are off. We won't be the hunters—we'll be the hunted."

They climbed out of the vehicle and took a long look around, weapons in hand, before moving any farther.

Lee's rifle was always loaded, but now he made double sure and flipped the safety off. The black panther they were after weighed at least a hundred and fifty pounds. Most skinwalkers he'd encountered in the past fifty-five years or so had preferred the endurance of a wolf, or the agility of a mountain lion. But the black jaguar could be a deadly hunter, especially on a night as dark as this.

Signaling her readiness, Diane gave him a nod, and they crossed a narrow dry arroyo, then walked in a northeasterly direction, parallel to the arroyo but on the east side. Fifteen minutes later they reached their destination. To the west stood a gray, stuccoed wood-framed house with a pitched roof. There was a simple corral constructed of peeled pine logs, and there were two steel water barrels beside the house, but as expected no animals were around. Fifteen feet from the front door was an old Ford pickup.

They moved closer, keeping watch, when suddenly a small dog started barking. Diane raised her shotgun, though it was still quite a reach at that distance with buckshot.

"Too small to be a skinwalker. That's the real thing," Lee whispered, lowering his own rifle.

The dog, a black Lab cross probably less than six months

old, had apparently been sleeping under the wooden porch. The young animal ran out toward them a little farther, then stopped, but continued to bark at the top of his lungs, throwing his head back with enthusiasm.

A light came on inside the house; then they saw an old Navajo woman standing just inside by the half-opened door. "Who are you? What do you want?" She was wearing a long flannel nightgown and was barefooted.

"Sorry, *ahdzah'nih*," Lee said, using the Navajo word for "ma'am" as he moved closer and held out his gold shield. "I'm a state police officer. We were looking for a woman in her twenties or thirties we heard lives here with a man named Darvon Blackhorse."

"He owns this house and has been letting me rent a room. The Navajo police came by looking for him a few days ago, too. But all I know is that my landlord said he was going into the mountains to tend his sheep. Maybe the woman you're looking for went with him. His sheep camp is north of Narbona Pass. I don't know any more than that."

"His cousin, Clarence Atso, is he here?"

"He comes and goes. I haven't seen him for a week now, maybe more."

"Thanks for the information, *ahdzah'nih*. Sorry to disturb you. Good night," Lee said. Then they began to walk away, back in the direction they'd come.

"Something hinky's going on here," Diane said quietly. "I can't see a skinwalker herding sheep—the animals would be terrified once they picked up the smell of a predator."

"I know. I just want her and whoever's in the house to think that we're leaving," Lee answered. "We'll be coming right back from the north. Maybe we can avoid the dog on the replay. He didn't smell us, so he must have heard or seen us. This time we'll be extra careful."

"What about the woman? How does she fit in? Any ideas?"

"She could be a hostage or a close relative protecting her kin. But my guess is that she's a skinwalker too—and an old, smart one. She could be the alpha female of the pack."

"And the puppy . . . it's just a dog, right?"

"Yeah. They probably use it just like we would, to keep watch. He's young enough to bond to whoever—or whatever—comes along, and they'd smell basically the same to him in animal or human form."

Once they were a few hundred yards from the house they circled around to the north, moving at a fast jog. This time as they crept toward the house, staying low to the ground, the young Lab neither saw nor heard them approach.

Lee got up close to the window and peered inside. Nobody appeared to be in the first of the two rooms. Diane, who'd looked in the window farther along the wall using her night scope, indicated that the room appeared to be empty too. There was an outhouse in the back, but the door was open and he could see it was unoccupied. They met at the corner of the house to discuss the situation.

"I saw the puppy curled up on the bed, asleep. If any humans are inside, they're in a basement or the attic," Diane whispered.

"The pickup hasn't moved. But they might have taken off—in animal form—while we were circling."

"Then they're stalking *us,*" Diane said quickly, and studied the ground. "Oh, crap. Those are multiple animal tracks."

Lee studied the large impressions, which led down the road. "We'll take the bait, as they expect. Let's follow them," he whispered.

Moving away from the house, they walked beside the road for a while, then angled closer to verify the presence of the animal tracks. Lee spotted a set immediately in the soft earth between the wheel ruts. "They've already split up. We have two sets of tracks heading east, and the tracks of one big cat, moving right down the road like it knows exactly where it's going."

"Toward our car," she said. "Those who went east will be able to pick up our scents. Part of their plan?"

"Yes. They'll probably stay to the east of the road, too, in order to keep that edge."

"Let's pick up the pace, then, and not give them too much time to set up an ambush. How long did you say it took them to change back into human form?"

"Leisurely, to save energy, it can take as long as ten minutes. Under duress, no more than two or three minutes. Think she or he's intending on stealing our SUV?" Lee asked.

"So far we're being played for suckers. We need to use our assets to turn the tables on them. How much time do we have, Lee?"

"Three hours, plus or minus, before sunrise. I'll have to get out of the light then but the sun won't fry a skinwalker. All it'll do is force them back into human form. They have the time advantage."

"So let's split up. We can come at them from two separate directions," Diane whispered.

"Okay. You take the rifle and get on the high ground to the west. That'll give you a little more distance from them, assuming they come at us from the east. Stake out the area around the SUV. I'll stay on the road and hopefully keep their attention on me. Use the night scope, and watch out in case one of them crossed the road again."

Lee watched Diane sprint off. She was in good shape

and light on her feet, but no vampire. He hoped she wouldn't take any chances. A mortal confronting skinwalkers hunting at night was at a clear disadvantage, and the night scope would only compensate so much.

Watching and listening, he proceeded slowly. After topping a low hill, he saw their SUV parked in the road where he'd left it. Though he couldn't see Diane, he knew she was around, watching, probably from behind one of the clumps of rabbit brush, or inside the arroyo looking out with the night scope.

As he got closer Lee saw a dark shape beneath the SUV. It was a crouched black jaguar. At night and hidden in the deep shadows under the car, it would have been virtually invisible to mortal eyes.

The big predator turned its head, looking quickly behind itself, then to both sides. Having spotted him, Lee reasoned, it was searching for some sign of Diane. Suddenly he heard an engine starting up. Lee did a half turn and realized a vehicle was coming up from behind him on the opposite slope of the hill, its lights out. It must have been a signal, because out of the corner of his eye he saw the jaguar explode from beneath the SUV, leaping toward him in long, graceful strides.

Lee ducked, and as he brought his shotgun up, a shot rang out from his left. The animal jerked slightly in midflight but kept coming. Lee fired as the cat reached him, but the shotgun was knocked from his grip by an extended paw.

The black panther hit the ground, blood running down its side from just behind the shoulder, pivoted drunkenly, then growled and attacked again, fangs bared. Lee was drawing his handgun when suddenly the panther swerved away.

Almost simultaneously the old pickup roared over the

hill—actually off the ground a foot or more owing to the speed it had gathered. As it bounced to the ground only thirty feet away, Lee stood. Timing his next move carefully, he leaped straight up as the pickup reached him, and cleared the cab by at least a foot as it passed beneath.

Landing lightly, considering his eight-foot leap into the air, Lee turned to locate the panther, only vaguely aware that the pickup had swerved to avoid hitting the SUV. The panther came in from uphill, low this time, targeting his legs.

Lee stood his ground and lowered his pistol. A rifle shot came from somewhere behind and to his right and the panther shook in midstride. Lee fired a shot into the middle of the creature's back. It crashed into him just below his knees, knocking him over and onto its back as it passed beneath him. Lee rolled off the animal and hit the ground, losing his pistol as his elbow struck the ground.

Scrambling to his knees, he grabbed his backup .45 from his jacket pocket and looked behind him. The pickup had collided with a big clump of brush but continued on into a low, wide, sand-filled arroyo, tipping over onto the driver's side and coming to rest against the far bank of the wash.

Lee saw the black cat motionless in the road, and he knew the skinwalker was dead. While the pickup was enveloped in a settling cloud of dust, Lee went to get his shotgun, automatically pointing the barrel down to clear it of any debris that might have entered the bore. Hearing movement to his left, he turned his head and saw Diane jogging up, rifle in hand.

"Something—a wolf maybe—jumped out of the passenger window and I lost sight of it," Diane muttered, breathing hard. She stopped and looked at the wrecked pickup, sweeping the area with the large, monocular night scope. Lee turned completely around, his back to hers while he checked back up the road and to the west.

"Are you okay, Lee? I've never seen a stunt like that outside a movie theater. Like a Hollywood ninja."

"I suppose all it takes is the right motivation." He continued to scan the area for more skinwalkers, but couldn't see any creatures at all, human or animal.

"Nice shot on the black cat. Did you know she was under there?"

Diane shrugged. "I saw something under the SUV, but I couldn't tell what it was until it made a move. My first shot was either high or missed completely, but on her second pass she came in slow enough for me to get a good hit."

"So much for the skinwalker who killed Agent Thomas," Lee said.

"Burt can rest in peace now," she said, her voice a bit unsteady. "He deserved a better end, but I've evened the scales for him just a little." Sorrow was laced through her words, but she pushed those feelings away. "Let's see who's in the pickup."

"Okay. Cover my back, and I'll cover yours." Lee walked closer to the cab of the truck then moved toward the windshield so he could take a look inside. Diane followed, watching behind them.

"It's the old woman. She's still alive and trying to shapeshift so she can heal herself," Lee said, keeping a firm grip on his shotgun.

They stared in amazement as the bloodied face of the woman, resting against the driver's door of the cab, slowly lengthened along the nose, forming a muzzle. Dark hair began to sprout from her face, her eyes began to lighten and change shape, and her ears began to taper as they lengthened.

The shape-shifter howled, throwing her head back as

it cried out in pain, trying to stand up. The creature weaved back and forth drunkenly, then slumped back. The animal features receded quickly, and blood flowed from the woman's nose. Her eyes closed, and she slowly sank down onto a heap like a discarded rag doll.

"I think she's dead."

"Then let's track down the other one," Lee whispered. "It was a wolf, right?"

Diane nodded, keeping her back to the wreck as she looked out into the dark. The brush made it difficult to see more than fifty feet.

"It's out there somewhere, hiding." Lee stood beside her, watching for signs of movement. His night vision was complete, but the colors were still faded toward the gray. A wolf or panther could also see quite well at night, he knew, but skinwalkers in animal form had one tactical advantage over the animals they mimicked. They thought like humans, and recognized the danger of guns and other human weapons.

"Think it'll come to us? I hate the idea of moving through Ambush Central half blind. This night scope is so limited." Diane had been using the device again, but now placed it back into her pocket.

"You need to stay in the open so it'll have to expose itself at the last minute before it reaches you," Lee said, moving away from the overturned vehicle onto the road. "Take the shotgun, for close-range firepower."

"No, you'll need that if you're closer to the brush. I prefer my pistol at close range. I'm more familiar with it. I'll sling the rifle over my shoulder. You keep the shotgun." Diane walked out into the middle of the road, looking up the hill as she adjusted the sling, placing the rifle on her shoulder.

He reached into his pocket for a shotgun shell, intending

on topping off his weapon, then suddenly realized this was an ideal time for a wolf that thought like a human to strike.

Lee turned his head just as a massive ball of fur and muscle shot out from behind the wreck. "Diane!" he shouted, bringing the shotgun up—too high.

The growling beast ducked beneath the roar of the flaming barrel and struck directly at his midsection with open jaws. It felt like he'd been jammed in the gut with a log, one with raking fangs. Lee gasped for breath as he doubled over the animal, somehow managing to grab one of the creature's back legs as the shotgun flew away in the opposite direction.

Vampire and skinwalker tumbled to the ground, twisting and turning in a deadly wrestling match. Something snapped at Lee's midsection, and the wolf's grip on his gut eased. The animal had bitten off his belt buckle, not his skin.

He rolled, trying to get free from the creature long enough to grab his pistol. Somewhere close by Diane was yelling, but the words were jumbled as he tried to concentrate on reaching his pistol. A fingertip on the leather told him the pistol had fallen out. Then Lee felt sudden, excruciating pain in his left forearm. The beast had clamped down on his arm with its powerful jaws.

Trying to block out the sudden, warm wetness on his sleeve, Lee doubled up, bringing a knee sharply into the beast's middle. The wolf grunted, but shook its head, digging further into Lee's arm, ripping up muscle and tendons.

An explosion went off close by, kicking up dirt, and he heard Diane curse. She'd obviously missed a shot to the creature's head.

The wolf snapped at Diane's leg, yanking her to the ground as it snagged cloth—and maybe flesh. Lee took advantage of the sudden release in pressure and slid his fingers down into his boot, finding the handle of his commando dagger.

Diane fired another shot, and the wolf yelped, letting go of her leg. Blood spurting from a foreleg, the animal turned back toward Lee, rage in its yellow eyes.

Lee sprawled backward, spreading his arms and legs apart. He was the perfect victim, and the wolf fell for it.

As the creature went for his throat, Lee brought his dagger up in a blur, braced against his upper chest. The animal was impaled at the throat, the dagger going in to the hilt from its own weight and momentum.

Somehow the wolf, obviously a female, pushed off his body and threw herself back, sitting on her haunches, swatting with her paws at the dagger as blood literally spurted out in rhythmic streams. Diane shot the beast twice in the side of the head and she fell slowly over, twitching just a few times before all movement stopped.

"Diane?"

"Lee?"

"You first," Lee insisted. "What about your leg!"

"Just my jeans. The bitch jerked me around, that's all. But your stomach—your arm."

Lee lay there, looking down at his midsection. He'd been raked with the canines, but the wounds were shallow. The large Western belt buckle had shielded him. "Good time to be a nightwalker."

"Stay down, Lee. Your forearm looks like crap."

"Hurts like crap too, but it's healing already. Just keep an eye out for another one of those wolves. I'll be fine in fifteen minutes."

He sat still, not moving his arm, and the pain began to numb, then go away completely. If the damage had torn apart his heart, or vital areas of his brain, it would have been the end. But tonight he'd been lucky—so far.

Finally, Lee stood. His arm felt fine, and he was ready for action. Bending over, he pulled his dagger from the dead skinwalker's throat and wiped the blood off on her fur.

Jamming the blade back into the boot sheath, he took his pistol back from Diane, who'd retrieved it, and the shotgun while she kept watch. Finally he picked up his silver belt buckle and wiped off the blood and saliva with his handkerchief. "Guess I'm going to need a new belt."

"Let's check the pickup again, and that jaguar too. After our last surprise, I don't want anything else to come out of the dark again for a while," Diane said, her voice still a bit shaky. "Close call, partner."

"You got that right." Lee checked his shotgun, cleared debris from the action, then moved with Diane over to the wrecked truck.

"She still looks dead to me. Should I check her pulse?" Diane asked, shining her flashlight on the body. The old woman's eyes were open, but they'd lost their shine.

"Don't bother. Let's just get away from this wreck. Smell the gasoline?" Lee's sense of smell was exceptional, and the scent was nearly overwhelming at the moment.

"Time to call the tribal police?" Diane asked, her eyes always searching the darkness beside the road.

"Yeah." Lee turned completely around as he took in the area around them once more before moving toward the SUV. "Clarence Atso is still unaccounted for, so we need to make sure that neither he nor the other members of the pack are still around. Keep an eye out while I use the radio. Then we'll go check on the house again."

Moments later Lee returned to where Diane was standing and, following her gaze, looked over at the dead jaguar.

"Death is such a waste," she said, her voice heavy. "She

killed Agent Thomas, I killed her, and it all amounts to one big zero." She paused, then biting off the words, added, "It felt good to kill her, I won't deny that, but now I feel nothing—nada."

Diane took a deep breath, then let it out again. "I wonder how we should explain what happened tonight?" she asked, looking back at the wrecked pickup.

"We questioned the woman, then encountered the cat when we returned to our vehicle. We believe she must have let it loose. When it attacked we were forced to shoot it. The woman tried to run me down, but had the accident. The wolf, who'd been riding in the truck, attacked and we killed it. I think that fits the superficial evidence and is basically true. I'll just have to change shirts before anyone else sees me wearing all this dried blood and wonders why I'm not injured. That's why I never leave home without a spare change of clothes in my vehicle."

"That solves a couple of problems. But the Navajo cops are going to be pissed off when they find out we came here without checking in with them first," Diane said.

"What can they do about it without making themselves look bad? We came at night, knowing that's when the jaguar might be allowed to roam. We successfully hunted down an animal who killed an FBI agent—what was in essence this woman's trained assassin. The cat tracks lead right up to her door, so the evidence supports our story."

"But you're right," Lee continued. "The local police won't forget. They weren't able to find the animal, and we were. Next time we'll have a hard time getting their cooperation if we need it. The public, on the other hand, will be thrilled that another dangerous neighbor is gone, but they won't talk about tonight. It's not safe to get too curious about skinwalkers. Traditionalists teach that talking about something like this means calling it to you."

"Do you suppose the crime-scene team will be finished before daybreak?" She looked at her watch. It was nearly 2 A.M.

"If not, I've got extra sunblock," he said, "and will apply it before anyone arrives. But, for now, let me change clothes. Then we'll check out the house before the troops arrive."

Less than five minutes later they drove up in front of the small house. The Lab puppy was in the front room, barking. Lee left the engine running with the headlights aimed directly into the front window. Anyone inside would have a hard time spotting them in the glare.

Lee watched the front until Diane had enough time to get around back, then ran up to the door. Crouching low, he reached up and tried the knob. It was unlocked, so he swung the door back and peered inside. The puppy ran up to the threshold, barking; then his tail started wagging furiously and he rolled over onto his back.

"Ferocious, aren't you?" Lee muttered.

The room was empty except for a worn sofa, two fabric chairs, and a small TV on a shelf made of cinder blocks and boards. A gas heater stood in the center of the room, vented via a metal chimney.

"Bedroom looks empty," Diane called out from behind the house.

"I'm going in, keep watch." Lee stepped past the dog and slipped inside, hugging the wall as he watched the doorway in the opposite direction. It led into the kitchen. He crossed over, knowing Diane was covering the bedroom, and peered into the kitchen. A small refrigerator was humming beside a gas stove, and in the center was a cheap dinette set with four chairs. Shelves made of cinder blocks and one-by-tens held groceries, dishes, and cooking utensils. There were no closets or cabinets.

"Kitchen is clear!" Lee crossed back into the living room,

still watching the other doorway. The floor was all vinyl tile and didn't appear to have any trapdoors or access below, so he'd ruled out a basement or root cellar. The ceiling was unpainted Sheetrock, taped and textured only. The only attic access was via a few small vents or from outside, perhaps.

Two minutes later they were searching the bedroom for anything that would indicate how many people lived in the house. They found women's clothing, coats, and shoes in three different sizes and also portions of a man's wardrobe. If anyone else had lived there in the past, their possessions had been removed. A lot of extra bedding was present, along with a folding cot and the sofa bed. This suggested that at one time several people had lived here, but other than that there was little to learn from their cursory examination.

Diane picked up the dog, who came eagerly, licking her hand, and they drove back to the site where the skinwalkers had died.

"We had a bit of luck tonight, partner," Lee said as he pulled up and parked fifty yards from the overturned pickup.

"Against an enemy like this what we need most is good intelligence, and sharp instincts," she said. "How many skinwalkers besides Clarence Atso are still out there?" She waved her hand around in a wide arc.

"Angela, for one." Lee had encountered the attractive young Navajo woman not long ago, but she'd eluded them. Angela had been from another pack living near Fort Wingate and was now the only survivor of that group. But he didn't like to think about Angela. The skinwalker reminded him of another woman he'd once loved—one who'd been as good as Angela was evil.

Lee noticed Diane watching him closely and added, "All it takes is one Navajo skinwalker to begin another pack. One nonlethal bite from someone infected with this disease and it's passed on. At least this affliction seems to be limited to Navajos only, but there are more Navajos now than ever before. The Navajo Nation itself is the size of West Virginia, so Clarence, and Angela, have plenty of places to hide."

"Vampires, werecats . . . what' s next, partner?"

"This is New Mexico, so maybe aliens from Roswell?"

"Forget I asked, Lee," she said, and reached over to pet the puppy, who was now between them on the seat. "Don't worry, pup, we'll find you a good home."

"Here comes the crime-scene team," Lee said, looking into the darkness ahead. "Get ready for tough questions from some angry-as-hell local cops."

# CHAPTER 2

The local sergeant was a prick, and as pissed off as Lee had expected. But after a while, the tribal officers wanted them gone just as badly as they wanted to leave, so that had lessened the headaches all the way around.

Lee and Diane finally set out for Albuquerque and managed to grab a few hours' sleep before starting all over again. A few minutes before 10 A.M. they drove up the ramp to the underground parking lot beneath the downtown Albuquerque FBI building. It was a previously scheduled meeting, a debriefing related to their earlier work.

After passing through the security gate, Lee parked his black and white patrol unit in the secure garage of the modern stone, concrete, and glass structure. Three minutes later, after going through a second security checkpoint, they reached the quiet, tastefully decorated office of Acting Special Agent in Charge Vernon Logan.

The SAC's secretary, whose ID badge identified her as Irene Herrera, motioned them to the small waiting area beyond her desk, then quietly informed Diane's supervisor of their arrival.

Lee felt calmer than he should have. True, they both knew what tack to take if any questions concerning what had happened last night came up. They'd been off-duty, supposedly, so there was the possibility they were going to be disciplined, or at least given a good reaming out.

Logan opened the door almost immediately. "Agent Lopez—Officer Hawk. Come in and join us."

Leonard Hawk was Lee's current alias. Only Diane and a Navajo medicine man knew who—and what—Lee really was.

SAC Logan, a broad-shouldered, pale blond and blue-eyed man in his late thirties, motioned them into the cluttered office, which contained several cardboard boxes stacked against one wall.

Rising from his seat, which took a while owing to his six-foot-six ex-Lobo basketballer's frame, was Lee's supervisor, Lieutenant Richmond. He, like Lee, wore a New Mexico state police charcoal gray uniform with medium gray accents. Like the SAC, Richmond had light blue eyes, but his red hair and freckled face had earned Michael Richmond the nickname "Mikey" when playing for UNM.

"Lee, Agent Lopez." Richmond shook both their hands. "I'd like to commend you two once again on your success in taking down those German terrorists."

"Yes, you two did a great job. I'm in complete agreement with the lieutenant here," Logan said, then added, "Some new intelligence on Muller has come to light. I thought you'd want to know that it's likely Muller was trying to buy freedom for a relative of his who was condemned to death for trying to kill an Iraqi general."

"CIA know about that?" Lee asked.

"The agency didn't know about Muller or any assassination plot. They're not happy that we uncovered it first."

Lee nodded. "Yeah, well, maybe they should pull their heads out of their . . . assets, once in a while."

"And on that note, there's an issue you need to clarify

for us now. The tribal police chief called with a major beef about your operation last night on the Navajo Nation. According to him, his department didn't even know you were in their jurisdiction until you'd bagged two animals and their keeper."

"They were pissed as hell, according to the brass up in Santa Fe," Richmond added, his Little Texas accent showing. "SAC Logan and I want an explanation—and it better be a damned good one. Why did you choose to make this move on your own initiative, Officer Hawk?"

Lee exhaled softly, counting how many times in the past fifty years he'd danced to this tune. The first time he'd been a state police officer, it hadn't been necessary. But Lee'd had many other identities and careers since he'd become a nightwalker, in 1945. Whenever his behavior or lifestyle began to prompt questions, he'd simply moved on, reinventing himself. However, Lee enjoyed being a police officer again after so many years, and he'd learned to cover himself expertly. Explanations, as far as he was concerned, were an exercise in creativity wrapped around the known facts. "After Blackhorse's death in Las Cruces, the Navajo PD stopped watching his house. We—Agent Lopez and I—figured that made the residence an ideal place for someone to hide that black jaguar. Since Blackhorse's home was in the middle of nowhere, and those cats stalk their prey at night—a time when most Navajos prefer to remain indoors—no one was likely to spot the creature when it was taken out and allowed to hunt."

"Officer Hawk needed backup and I volunteered. News of an FBI agent on Navajo land travels at lightning speed, so the whole thing had to go down quick and neat. When we saw that someone was living at Blackhorse's old place, we headed back to our vehicle. We were about to contact the Navajo police via radio when we were ambushed."

"That dog you found, a black Lab. It's not dangerous like the wolves, right?" Logan asked.

"No, it's a regular, run-of-the-mill puppy. I left it with a Navajo officer who promised to give it to the Bureau agent covering the Four Corners," Diane said.

Lee had known that finding that particular dog a home on the Rez would be all but impossible. No one there would have wanted anything to do with an animal that had belonged to a suspected skinwalker.

Logan's telephone rang, and he looked down at it with a scowl. It rang again, and he picked it up. "What, Irene?" Logan listened for a moment, then looked over at Lee. "Okay, fifteen minutes." Logan hung up and looked at them. "We'll have to cut this meeting short. The call was from state police headquarters in Santa Fe. Two undercover officers, one a state policeman and the other a Navajo officer, have been found dead east of Shiprock on the Navajo Nation."

"How did they die?" Diane asked.

"Multiple gunshot wounds, according to officers on the scene," Logan replied.

"Could it be connected to the Navajo cult that came after Officer Hawk and Agent Lopez?" Richmond asked.

"Might be, or perhaps the shootings are linked to last night's incident, which is why the call came here. The state police helicopter is on its way now, Officer Hawk. You're on this too, Agent Lopez."

Diane stood. "The Sunport?"

Logan shook his head. "No. We need to move fast. The helicopter is going to meet you in the west parking lot of University Arena."

They slipped out, walked quickly down the hall, and were in his patrol unit three minutes later.

Diane sniffed the air in the car and, with a grimace, rolled down the window. "I know we could be outside for a while, depending on where the bodies were found, but do you think you might have overdone that sunblock, partner?"

"Is it that strong? I've gotten used to it after all these years. I wish they made an unscented kind." Lee looked at his hands as they gripped the steering wheel. His fingertips were especially vulnerable, so at crime scenes he really appreciated the latex gloves.

Lee made a hard right with the traffic light in their favor, then pulled into the parking lot surrounding the Pit, the local name for University Arena. The helicopter was already setting down onto the asphalt, maneuvering carefully away from the nearby light poles.

The pilot waved, motioning them around to the door on the passenger side. As they climbed in, he yelled his name as a way of introducing himself.

Diane chose one of the back seats and Lee followed her in, taking the seat beside her.

"Where exactly are we going?" Lee yelled to the pilot, who was also a New Mexico state police officer, one of three or four who flew the department's fixed-wing aircraft and helicopters.

"West of Shiprock, and north of Highway 64, on the mesa above the river. Supposed to be several vehicles onsite. That's all I've been told." The pilot turned his head slightly in their direction, then looked forward again, watching the path of his ascent.

Once they were past the small San Mateo Range, steep mesas, deep arroyos, and canyons carved by wind and the infrequent rains spread out below them. The few green areas were scattered forests at higher altitudes or the floodplain bosque astride the San Juan River Valley. The rough, dry, relatively inhospitable region was the home of the Navajo people, fossil fuel in abundance, and a small number of hardy farmers and small-business owners.

In a little more than an hour the stomach-churning ride ended with a quick descent and one last jolt as the helicopter touched down a hundred yards from where several patrol units were parked. The pilot shut down the engine, then turned to Lee as he was unfastening his seat belt. "I'm supposed to stay here with the helo and give you a ride back. If I have to leave before you're done, I'll let you know."

"Thanks." Lee climbed down out of the helicopter, enjoying the feel of the ground once again, even if it was dry, dusty, and possibly inhabited by the ghosts of the dead. A sip of calf's blood would go down easy right now and soothe his parched throat, but this was definitely the wrong setting.

He turned to help Diane down, but with a distracted smile, she refused his hand.

"I am woman, watch me roar?" he commented.

She brushed past him, taking the lead. "Roar, hell. I bite."

"Me too," he smiled, quickly catching up as they approached a group of officers inside the yellow crime-scene tape. It was bright outside, and Lee glanced at his wristwatch, calculating he had at least one safe hour before risk of major sunburn. It was close to noon now.

A young Hispanic man who reminded Lee vaguely of the Cuban actor Andy Garcia broke away from the group and stepped up to meet them. His out-of-place gray suit and the expensive sunglasses, the same brand Lee was wearing out of necessity, shouted FBI to any police officer or deputy.

"Agent Lopez, Officer Hawk?" Seeing them nod, he continued. "Please examine the bodies and take a good look at the scene. See if you spot any connection at all to the cases you've been investigating."

Lee stepped under the tape and Diane followed. Almost in unison the other officers, three of them Navajo cops in khaki uniforms, turned to watch. Lee doubted that they'd speak to him or Diane unless absolutely necessary. These weren't the same officers as last night, but coming from a small department they probably knew all about it and would resent his and Diane's presence on the reservation again so soon. Local officers everywhere, Lee had observed, resented intrusions on their "turf."

As they walked over to the draped bodies, Diane nodded to the OMI man, a slim Anglo about forty years old with thinning hair and a sunburned forehead. Seeing the man's skin damage, Lee automatically adjusted his dark uniform cap.

"Officer, Special Agent." The Office of the Medical Investigators man, having met Lee and Diane last night as well, greeted them simply, then lifted back the first blanket. The body was that of a tall, slender Anglo man, obviously the state policeman. Lee recognized the plainclothes officer, though he'd never known his real name. As he studied the body he noted that the officer's shirt was covered with caked, dried blood from several gunshot wounds. Diane pointed to where the blood had run down the victim's side. There was none on the ground below that point.

"He bled out someplace else," she said, looking at the OMI man, who nodded, lifting the covering from the second body.

Lee looked at the body of the second, Navajo officer, noting that the body seemed relatively fresh. "This officer, like his companion, was shot with a shotgun and several times with a large-caliber handgun—also somewhere else," the OMI man said.

Diane caught the medical investigator's eye. "What was the time of death, approximately?"

"From the state of the bodies I'd say they were killed sometime last night. Twelve hours or less. We had a breeze just before dawn, and the bodies have some of that dust and plant debris on them. I'll have a better estimate later."

Lee didn't see any obvious indication that the two officers had encountered skinwalkers, at least in their animal form, but skinwalkers used guns when in human form if it served them. He found it interesting that both had been out of uniform when killed, an indication they were either off-duty or working undercover.

They searched the ground around the victims, and except for a few unmarked footprints that almost certainly belonged to either the officers on scene or the OMI man, there was nothing obvious. Whoever had dumped the bodies had rubbed out their tracks. Lee looked at Diane. "Are we finished here?"

"Looks like it." They walked back over to the yellow tape, where Agent Romero was standing alone. The remaining officers were watching and listening.

"Anything to suggest a connection between these killings and your respective cases?" Romero asked immediately.

"I didn't see anything that would suggest a link." Diane turned to Lee. "Did you?"

"All I can see is that these killings took place elsewhere and the bodies were dumped here. I might have more questions if the bodies had been found in the Grants area or near Fort Wingate, where the terrorists were based. Call us in again if you determine that the shootings took place in one of those areas."

He paused, then added, "As far as last night's incident, there are no points of similarity at all. These officers didn't die from an animal attack, and if it turns out they were killed after the lady died last night in the truck wreck, she obviously couldn't have been the shooter."

"Was there any physical evidence on or around the bodies that we should know about?" Diane asked.

"And how were the officers identified?" Lee added.

"Their pockets were empty and all jewelry such as rings and watches were taken. But the tribal officers here recognized their own man, and two of them had seen the state officer before," Romero said.

"Both of the deceased are out of uniform. What can you tell us about their current assignments? Were they working undercover on a case?" Diane asked.

"According to the police chief, they were working together, but I still don't know anything specific about the case. As soon as I get that information, I'll pass it on to you two—if I can," Romero said. "None of the officers here know anything, or if they do, they haven't shared it with me."

"Do you get the feeling this is an internal-affairs kind of investigation?" Lee asked, lowering his voice and turning his head so the other officers couldn't hear him clearly. "That cops were involved?"

"Not at all. The Navajo officer—I won't say his name for reasons you understand—usually investigated vehicle thefts, organized smuggling of contraband like liquor or drugs, property crimes, stuff like that. The state policeman worked on investigations related to smuggling, drug interdiction, and so on, and had done some interagency work before. Your people will know more," Romero said, looking at Lee, who simply nodded.

"Then I guess there's no reason to keep you here any longer," Romero said, giving them a return nod that looked impersonal and arrogant at the same time.

"We'd appreciate a briefing once you get more details," Diane said. "And on a more or less personal matter, did you get that black Lab puppy?"

Romero smiled. "Yes, and my children were thrilled. Worked out great for all concerned."

Lee and Diane said good-bye to Romero, then hurried

to the helicopter. Two minutes later, they were on their way back to Albuquerque.

Elka Pfeiffer gripped the armrests of seat C-1 tightly as the 737 bobbed up and down sharply for the third time in the past minute. The commercial aircraft was descending rapidly as it approached the western end of the Albuquerque runway.

Elka hated flying. Impacts at hundreds of miles per hour and explosions of aviation fuel took away the relative invulnerability she enjoyed as a vampire, and she'd never balanced the risks equally against the gains in time—sweating out each flight as if it would be her last. Vampires had plenty of time, and only decapitation, massive trauma to the heart, or being burned by sunlight or fuel could cut their lives short.

Yet despite the fact that they were hard to kill, death did find them on occasion. The knowledge stung now especially as she remembered her brother's death. Hans was gone forever. Although he'd adopted the name Wolfgang Muller later in his life, to her he'd always be Hans.

They'd shared many lifetimes, and the bond between them had always been strong. Now that he was dead there was a massive void in her life, one that would never be filled, but experience told her that, in time, she'd learn to go on. People—and vampires—usually found the will to survive, even after the death of a loved one. It was an ability that was practically encoded into both species.

Yet it was the way that he'd died that bothered her most. The instrument of his death hadn't been a plunging aircraft with a badly lubricated screw jack, or pilot error. It had been a young Navajo state police officer that her brother had, in a moment of desperation decades ago, made one of them.

But she hadn't come to New Mexico just to confront this Navajo policeman. Someone else was on her list and eliminating him was her first priority. Officer Nez and the woman who'd apparently helped him would die in due time, and then the hunt would be complete.

Elka smiled, grateful that this purposeful line of thought was distracting her from the roller-coaster flight that had troubled her stomach since Dallas. She loosened her death grip on the seat and looked into her travel portfolio. The folder with the tickets was sticking out for easy reach, and Elka checked her ticket to confirm the gate where her luggage would be delivered.

Her cover as a sales representative for luxury sedans was still intact and a valuable asset that could take her anywhere in the world—especially Europe and the Middle East. Her job provided her with a good living, especially with the freelance work she and the others in her family did on the side. Or had done. Now with her husband, brother, and the Plummers dead, only she and Bridget were left. Yet, even if the Navajo had already turned the FBI woman he worked with, Bridget and she would win the fight. They had experience on their side and, most important of all, they knew what was about to happen—the Americans did not.

# CHAPTER 3

A week had gone by since he'd left Albuquerque, and Lee was now back on patrol in south-central New Mexico. No word had come down from federal, tribal, or state agencies since the bodies of the two officers had been discovered on Navajo land. And although they continued their search, neither he nor Diane had been able to find a trace of Clarence Atso or Angela. Now both he and Agent Lopez had resumed their normal duties, and the search for the skinwalkers was more or less on hold.

His long night patrol had just ended, but Lee was still careful not to get complacent just because he'd arrived at home. He glanced up at the top of the doorjamb, noting that the match was still in place, wedged between door and trim. That was the warning mechanism any competent professional would have detected before sneaking into his apartment. That list, in his experience, included trained law-enforcement officers, intelligence officers, and vampires who'd managed to survive more than a few years. And maybe a skinwalker with black-bag experience, he added as he checked for the white thread, the backup indicator that only those with superior training would seek out. It was also in place.

Lee unlocked the door, opened it an inch, and saw the

paper match on the floor beneath the jamb. He'd placed that there to catch the most dangerous intruder, the paranoid genius. When they opened the door and saw it—he'd crimped it first between the door and jamb—they'd hopefully think it had been knocked out of place. If it wasn't on the floor, but wedged between the door when he returned along with the other indicators, he'd know he was dealing with genuine trouble.

Clarence Atso was just another skinwalker, not nearly as dangerous as Angela. But it wasn't because she was tougher. Angela knew who and what he was, and would be stalking him sooner or later. Angela—the skinwalker with the face he'd never forget—had survived the battle with him and Diane as well as one with three full vampires out for her blood.

Angela wasn't just lucky, she was dangerous on every conceivable level. First, she knew he was a nightwalker. That was bad enough. But what made her deadly to him was that Angela physically resembled his late wife, Annie. They looked so much alike that he was nearly certain that he'd hesitate at the wrong time one of these days and end up dead. Annie had been killed decades ago by skinwalkers who'd invaded his home, but in some ways it seemed like only yesterday. They'd come for him, but found Annie at home instead, alone and unprotected. She hadn't stood a chance.

The resemblance between Annie and Angela was so striking that Lee prayed he'd meet her in animal form next time. He still hadn't been able to figure out if Angela had been a relative of Annie's or just the twin everyone was said to have out there in the world.

Stepping into his apartment, Lee shut the door and paused, listening. He could hear the whirring of the electric alarm clock in the bedroom, the sound of the refrigerator, and the creak of the building's frame as if the place had already begun to sense the coming dawn.

Glancing around, he noted that his laptop was still on the dark maple computer desk, closed up but with the green light showing it was fully charged. The desk chair hadn't been moved, judging from the lack of imprints in the thin blue carpeting, and the inexpensive vinyl sofa and matching chair against the opposite wall were as he'd left them.

Turning his head, he saw that the kitchen area and dining table looked undisturbed as well. The bedroom door was ajar at the same angle as usual, and, around the corner, the open bathroom door revealed nothing unusual within. The apartment, virtually identical to the old one that had been damaged during a recent confrontation, was simple, utilitarian, and free of uninvited guests. The daddy longlegs spider in the corner against the ceiling didn't count.

It was dark outside, beyond the full-length curtains across the room, and it was nearly black inside as well to any normal human.

Lee removed his uniform cap and sunglasses, then turned on the lights to avoid undue suspicion concerning his true nature.

Tonight's patrol had been almost routine, and it was a relief after what he'd been through lately. Last night he'd spent his tour of duty pulling a half-dozen people over for speeding, then responding to a rollover on the Interstate involving three drunken teenagers in their daddy's SUV. It had taken two hours to extricate the upside-down kids, but it had ended unusually well.

Happily, he'd been able to tell the terrified parents that their dumbass kids had been uninjured despite being loaded to the gills with beer, because they'd actually been wearing their seat belts.

Stopping by the fridge, he grabbed the quart bottle of what appeared to be tomato juice, and poured himself a glass. It was only cow's blood, but it would have to do. The desire for human blood never went away, but this substitute kept it at bay.

It also became a constant reminder of what he was—and what he was not. He looked mortal, but he was different. For as long as he continued to exist, he'd be an outsider. He was part of both the human world and the dark world of the vampire, yet the truth was that he belonged in neither. Among them, but never one of them . . . He drained the last of the cow's blood, rinsed out the glass, and walked to the bedroom.

Flipping on the overhead light, he walked to the bed and removed his black leather boots and his commando knife and sheath from his left leg. Finally he removed his Sam Browne belt, the .45 Smith and Wesson duty weapon, and the rest of his gear, placing everything atop the generic-looking dresser.

With his small backup .45 in his uniform trouser pocket, Lee walked back into the kitchen and poured himself another glass of blood. He didn't like it chilled, but that was one of the many compromises he'd learned to make. He was forever bound to this world—searching for peace in a place where no peace existed.

He took a deep swallow, set the glass down, and pushed those thoughts aside. They did no good. Instead, he embraced his loneliness, welcoming it like the old friend it was, and letting that fill the emptiness inside him.

Lee sat back in his chair and read the E-mail message again.

No ID yet on possible witness from Fort Wingate area.
APD officers have been given copies of your sketch.
Any luck from your end?—DL

So Diane hadn't had any luck searching for Angela through the Albuquerque Police Department and FBI. In his many years Lee had developed some skill as an artist, and he'd made a sketch of the Navajo woman, which had included the light streak in her black hair, for other law-enforcement agencies. When Lee had seen her last she'd been in the form of a cougar—with a knife wound under her eye that Diane had inflicted while defending herself. But Lee was the only law-enforcement officer who had seen Angela in human form up close.

Sketching her had been easy, but looking at the finished image had been one of the most difficult things he'd done in years. Even Diane had noticed and asked him about his reaction. Once he'd reminded her of the old photo she'd seen of him and Annie, she'd understood and never mentioned it again.

Lee stared at the screen, then down at his ring finger, aware of the absence of his wedding band. After Annie had been killed by the skinwalkers, he'd hunted them down one by one and destroyed them. He'd worn the ring on his finger throughout as a reminder of his mission—blood retribution.

But his rage and the need for vengeance had nearly destroyed him. That evil had come upon him slowly and silently. Darkness had filled him, making him stronger. In his rage, nothing had touched him. But, in the end, he'd had to make a choice. To give in to hatred and let that drive him or to hold to a vestige of the man he'd once been and fight to even out the score for the ones who, like his Annie, couldn't fight back. He'd chosen the latter.

His vain attempt back then to live life as a mortal had

cost Annie her life. He'd never repeat that mistake again. Even now, more than forty years later, Lee sometimes reached down to feel the empty space where the narrow gold band had once been. Guilt was a bitch, particularly when accompanied by grief.

Lee typed an answer to Diane's question, admitting that he'd had no luck picking up Angela's trail either. The real problem was that the woman was being given low priority by law-enforcement people all over the state because they didn't realize what she really was.

Leaving his computer on, firewall safely in place, Lee went to fix himself a quick meal. Afterward, he'd check his E-mail once more, then go to bed.

It was midafternoon, judging by Lee's internal clock, when the phone rang, waking him up from a dreamless sleep. He grabbed the phone, nearly pulling the base off the nightstand. The cord, though inconvenient, was preferable to the cordless models that could be monitored all too easily. "Yeah?"

"Officer Hawk?" Lee recognized the voice as belonging to Jan Swenson, day-shift dispatcher at the local state police office.

"Yes, Jan. What's going on?" Lee sat up, trying to keep the cord from tangling.

"Lieutenant Richmond wants to see you in his office at four today, Officer Hawk," Jan announced.

"I'm on duty tonight. Any idea what this is about, Jan?" The dispatchers knew everything that went on in the local office, and were usually the people there during the evening and graveyard shifts.

"No, not really," Jan replied without inflection. "Patrolman Wiley is covering your shift, though, and the lieutenant said to come in wearing street clothes."

"Okay, Jan. I'll be there. Bye." Lee hung up. If Jan

didn't know, it was something out of the ordinary. Someone taking over his shift, coupled with the order to come in wearing civilian clothes, meant that Lieutenant Richmond had some definite plans for his time.

Lee climbed out of bed, took his .45 out from under the pillow, then threw the blanket back over the sheets. Weapon in hand, he took a quick look around the apartment, then headed for the shower.

An hour later Lee arrived at the state police office, which was located in a small strip mall in what was called downtown Las Cruces, not far from the courthouse and the Cruces police station. The office was locked, but Jan, a rail-thin blonde with a small bump in her nose that gave her character, looked up from the front desk and recognized him in spite of his baseball cap and dark sunglasses before he could ring the buzzer. Jan pushed the button under the counter, disengaging the lock.

"Good afternoon, Jan." Lee smiled as he stepped out of the dangerous radiation others referred to as sunlight.

"Haven't seen you in a while, Patrolman Hawk." Jan beamed him a wide smile.

Lee took off his sunglasses and placed them in his shirt pocket. "What can I say? I work nights, you work days." He glanced up at the clock on the wall. It was 3:55 P.M., so Lieutenant Richmond wasn't going to grumble about his being late.

"Life is conspiring against us, Lee." Jan scrunched up her nose, teasing as she always did. She gathered up her keys from the desk. With Jan out front, the evening dispatcher must have already arrived.

Lee was still trying to think of a response when he saw movement out of the corner of his eye. Behind the back wall, the top half consisting of bullet resistant glass, stood Lieutenant Richmond.

"We've got to stop meeting like this, Jan," Lee said, realizing how lame it sounded after he'd said it.

"One of these days you're not going to be in such a hurry," Jan replied. "But for now, you'd better not keep him waiting."

"See you later," Lee said, then turned and stepped into the inner office.

You've proven that you have the skills and instincts needed for this assignment, Lee. And, fortunately, there hasn't been any press coverage of you that includes your photograph, so you're not likely to be recognized, unless it's by someone you've issued a citation to. But let me put this another way—I'm tagging you for the job 'cause there's no one else I can send," Richmond said.

Lee had an almost photographic memory, one of the useful side effects of being a nightwalker. The image of the two dead officers at the crime scene he and Diane had been flown to examine outside Shiprock almost ten days ago was vivid, especially their multiple wounds from more than one weapon.

"So let's see if I got this right. These officers were attempting to infiltrate a smuggling operation. Considering the Navajo connection, and the fact that the trail seems to begin somewhere in Mexico, the motives that come to mind are peyote, pot, or illegal aliens—the kind who come across the border, not arrive in spaceships. The politically correct term keeps changing, so I can't remember what to call them anymore."

He paused, but Richmond didn't comment. "Come on. There's gotta be more to it than that."

"The smuggling involves the illegal importation of Mexican turquoise and other gemstones used in making

Southwest jewelry. Probably silver as well. We believe the stuff's being smuggled to Albuquerque, then distributed to jewelry makers in the middle Rio Grande and Four Corners area," Richmond replied. "The smuggling cuts into the legitimate wholesale markets and the volume of traffic means that big money's involved."

"And in order to protect their profits, whoever's behind it is willing to risk the heat brought on by killing two police officers," Lee said thoughtfully. "They must be pulling in some serious cash. What else do you have on this investigation that'll help me out?"

Richmond handed Lee a file. "We've gotten nowhere since the two officers were killed—which is the main reason we need a new strategy. The Navajo officer was posing as a jewelry maker, assembling beadwork and stringing, mounting stones and whatever else it is they do. He'd made a living at that before joining the tribal police. Our own man, Sergeant Archuleta, had been posing as a jewelry dealer, and made contact with a silversmith in Gallup who'd promised to introduce Archuleta to his supplier—a company calling itself Silver Eagle. But Archuleta was unable to file a report of that meeting before his body was discovered."

"What about the Gallup contact?" Lee skimmed the report, looking for details.

"He can't be found, and nobody seems to know anyone by the name Archuleta gave. It might have been an alias," Richmond said. "The Navajo officer was going with Archuleta to meet the Silver Eagle rep and examine some quality Mexican turquoise. We know that much from his reports."

Lee noted something in the folder. "A lot of the independent suppliers and silversmiths deal in cash. I see that these officers had around three thousand bucks between them and the money was missing when their bodies were found. How do we know that these officers weren't just robbery victims who were set up?" Lee asked.

"We don't, but the case they were working on makes it highly probable that there's a tie between the Silver Eagle and their deaths. The Silver Eagle operation seems to be very well organized—but they're not listed anywhere in state or local records. Officially, Silver Eagle doesn't exist. We've had officers all across the state working on this, but we haven't had any luck intercepting jewelry-making contraband," Richmond said. "And, of course, until we know how the goods are being smuggled in from Mexico, we won't be able to break up the operation."

"How did the smuggling operation get uncovered in the first place?" Lee asked.

"Some of the wholesalers found out that while their sales were dropping, shops and vendors were actually buying more and more jewelry from the silversmiths, and most of the new pieces sold contained turquoise that didn't come from mines in the U.S."

"How could they tell?"

"Stones vary in color and half a dozen other ways depending on their origins," he answered, then continued. "Eventually a few of the silversmiths began talking up the great deals they'd been getting on Mexican and South American turquoise and silver, but refused to reveal their source," Richmond answered. "We did a little more digging, and Silver Eagle was the name that kept cropping up."

"So what's the plan? We find out how to infiltrate the Silver Eagle, then work our way backwards to the smugglers? I could go undercover as a silversmith. I've picked up on a few skills over the years," Lee said.

He'd learned silversmithing, one of many occupations he'd had after becoming a nightwalker, back in the late sixties when he'd been living on the Arizona side of the Navajo

Nation near Teec Nos Pos. But he'd never paid much attention to where the turquoise came from as long as he could get matching stones. He'd called himself Lawrence Johnson then, Lee recalled.

"That kind of knowledge will be useful to you. Here's the plan. We'll give you a partner from a federal agency so we can cut across state lines—preferably someone with wholesale and retail sales experience. We'll set the two of you up as a new wholesale supplier and have you start undercutting the Silver Eagle operation right away. You'll be the salesman, contacting the silversmiths, most of whom are independent contractors working out of their own homes and shops. Once Silver Eagle starts losing business, you should get their attention. They'll probably make a move to either buy you out or close you down. At that point, you sell out your partner and get inside the Silver Eagle operation. We want names, details of the smuggling operation, and we need to know who killed our undercover people."

"Are the Mexican authorities part of the investigation or are they working with the smugglers? They must have some idea where the stones are coming from. I know a lot of the turquoise mines are small family operations."

Richmond shrugged. "The possibility of corruption is there. That's why no agencies in Mexico have been contacted."

"Could someone in our department or the Navajo police have tipped Silver Eagle off about our undercover officers?"

"Anything is possible. That's why we're keeping a tight lid on this. We're using resources with deep pockets that can't be tracked back to either PD."

"Sounds like the FBI. Who am I working with?"

"Agent Diane Lopez. It's your lucky day."

# CHAPTER 4

Lee left his police cruiser at the office, driving away in a faded silver SUV fresh off the Las Cruces PD impound lot. He stopped by his apartment for extra clothes, backup weapons, and extra sunblock, then got onto the closest on-ramp for I-25 and headed north. The drive would take three and a half hours, give or take.

The thought of working with Diane again was both a blessing and a curse. She was an excellent investigator, smart, reliable, good in a fight, and totally trustworthy—something he couldn't say about anyone else in this world.

Although he still felt guilty thinking about any other woman besides Annie in a romantic way, he couldn't deny that he cared about Diane—far more than he should. He just wasn't ready to get emotionally involved with anyone who'd grow old right before his eyes, someone vulnerable to threats that he could shake off or avoid, whether that came from disease, injury, or the forces of evil that stalked him relentlessly. He'd done that once already, with disastrous results. He wouldn't make that mistake again.

Lee was scheduled to meet Diane at her Albuquerque office. As he was coming into the city from the west, down Nine Mile Hill, his cell phone rang. He grabbed the receiver on its second ring.

"Lee, it's Diane," came the familiar voice. "If we're going to be working undercover, I don't want to risk us being seen together around the Bureau office. It should be safe and all that, but you never know. Come to my new apartment instead. It's north of Academy." After discovering that he hadn't received the card she'd sent him before he left Las Cruces, she gave him the directions.

Diane never stayed in one place long. It was a precaution Lee also took routinely. Although inconvenient, it beat the hell out of waking up dead some morning.

When Lee arrived at the apartment complex, close to I-25 on the north side of the city, he parked in a visitor's slot beneath a large carport. The facility had outdoor lights, shielded so that they wouldn't glare into residential windows.

An old woman in a housecoat was walking a small white terrier down one of the sidewalks, but other than that the grounds were vacant. It was too late for day workers to be coming home from the day shift, and probably a little early for others to be coming back from dinner or dates. Noting the numbers on the apartment walls, he quickly found Diane's place. A dark shape beside one of the curtains on the second floor moved out of view, confirming to him that someone was at home and had seen him arrive.

He climbed up a gentle flight of stairs and knocked twice.

"Hi. Saw you pull up." Diane opened the door, stepping back behind the door to let him in. She was wearing knit slacks, a white V-neck sweater, and sensible shoes. He also noticed that she had her duty weapon at her waist. With a strand of light brown hair over her big, beautiful eyes, she reminded him of Jennifer Lopez, only much more dangerous.

A fast glance took in her living room and dining area.

Diane's apartment was dimly lit except over the small, round wooden kitchen table, where there were papers and books scattered about. The TV/VCR combo was tuned to a twenty-four-hour news channel with the latest updates scrolling across the bottom of the screen. Six cardboard boxes full of miscellaneous books were stacked beside a half-constructed particle-board shelf unit. A small sofa with a trunk in front of it, an end table with a lamp, and an overstuffed chair made up the rest of the furnishings.

"Glad we're working together again—officially. Sounds like this one's a high-risk op," she said, inviting him to take a seat on the sofa.

"Did you volunteer, or were you drafted like me?" he asked.

"This is Logan's first time out as an SAC and he wants the assignment to become permanent. Getting me out of the office where there's a chance I'd be meeting some of the Washington suits is all part of his game plan."

"He can hear your footsteps?"

"More like my fingernails clawing at that glass ceiling," she said with a wry smile. "But let's get down to business. Too damn many of our people have been killed in the past few months and I'm beginning to get really pissed off about this trend." Diane cleared away some of the papers on her table, then sat down across from him.

"Shall we get down to it then?" Lee said. "Our first step has to be setting up our business and getting the attention of the Navajo silversmiths."

"Here are some business cards and our letterheads." She reached over to the counter and handed them to him. "I had some experience working in a jewelry shop in Old Town when I was going to UNM and I've been boning up on the wholesale jewelry-supply operation. Logan mentioned that you had some silversmithing experience?"

"Just one of several careers I followed in the years after my 'death.' The work allowed me to blend in among the *Dineh,* the Navajo people, during a more stable phase of my life." His voice must have betrayed him, because Diane picked up on it immediately.

"Back when you were married?" she asked.

Lee nodded. "It allowed me to work at home, indoors and out of the sun."

Diane allowed the silence to stretch for a few moments, then continued. "Part of our cover is that we've been holding other jobs until recently when we decided to go into the business together. We're newbies. That'll cut us some slack if we screw up."

"I learned silversmithing when I was a teen, then ran off and enlisted. After that, I got a job as a security guard. How's that?"

"I had a retail job in California, then moved back. We met at a bar in Albuquerque, hit it off, and decided to pool my money and your knowledge of jewelry making. You're going to be the buyer, right?" Diane asked.

Lee nodded. For the next few hours they went back and forth, discussing their cover backgrounds. Finally, around one in the morning, Lee reached for his jacket. "I'll find a motel down by the freeway. I'll give you a call after I check in so you'll know where to reach me."

"Take my couch. It'll be safer than having housekeeping open the door before you've put on the morning sunblock. Besides, we need to keep an eye on each other. Look what happened to the last two guys who had this assignment."

"Good point."

"Tomorrow we'll hit the floor running. We'll go to our new office and twenty-four hours after that, we'll open for business. Then the fun will start and we can get busy making new enemies. Just what I live for."

"Coffee, glazed doughnuts, badge, and a gun. What more is there?" he nodded, sizing up the couch.

Two days later, Lee delivered a free "sample" of their wholesale jewelry supplies to a potential customer. The Navajo silversmith, a longtime Albuquerque resident in his mid-forties, had been anxious and urged Lee to leave quickly before his current supplier arrived. The silversmith didn't want any trouble if the two accidentally met at his house. Lee had agreed, but the news had given him the opportunity he was looking for—the chance to check out the competition.

Lee knew he was on the right track. The silversmith, after polishing off three bottles of beer during Lee's visit, had let the name Silver Eagle slip. Lee walked briskly to his vehicle, carrying a small cardboard box with samples of their inventory. This was a poor neighborhood in northwest Albuquerque, east of the railroad tracks and west of I-25, and rap music was blaring from a Chevy low rider cruising by. A westerly breeze seemed to blow the notes right at him and the subwoofer made the windows on his car rattle. Four teenaged boys looked in his direction, possibly because of the box he was carrying, but continued on their way.

Lee got inside and set the box on the seat beside him. He'd park a block or two away and stake out the silversmith's house. It was already after sunset and for ordinary people it would soon be too dark to see very well. A nondescript green Chevy with the headlights already on passed by on his left, slowing as if to stop as Lee pulled away from the curb. Lee automatically checked out the driver.

The young Navajo man at the wheel looked over quickly in his direction at the same time, and their eyes met for a split second. Lee, familiar with the aggressive attitude among young men, and sometimes women too, that linked more than casual eye contact with "mad-dogging" and a threat, looked away without expression and continued on.

In his rearview mirror he could see that the Navajo man was still watching him. He remembered the silver watchband on the man's left hand, and his gut told him that the driver was the Silver Eagle supplier. He'd seen Lee parked beside the silversmith's house and had probably spotted the cardboard box he'd been carrying. Either that or he was feeling particularly curious and hostile. In an era where drivers tended to pull guns on each other over minor traffic incidents, it paid to remain alert.

Lee began looking for a place to turn around, then glanced back and noticed that the green Chevy was making a U-turn in the street. Lee made a right turn at the next intersection, intending on circling the block to see if the Chevy would follow. It did, with the headlamps now extinguished. There weren't any other cars moving on the street at the moment and the man following him obviously didn't want to stand out.

Lee turned on his own vehicle lights, deciding to continue out of the neighborhood while allowing the man to keep up. He knew he could lose the tail, but he had more to gain now by finding out who the man in the car behind him was and who he was working for—hopefully Silver Eagle.

At this point he knew only one thing for sure. If the Navajo man in the Chevy was part of the group who'd killed the cops, he wasn't the head man—not if he was out making deliveries.

Swinging out onto Second Street, which had plenty of traffic from the commuter crowd, Lee noticed that the green Chevy continued to follow. The man had his headlights on to blend into traffic.

It was cooling off now and Lee rolled up his window. He continued north on Second, using the opportunity to call Diane on his cell phone. She was in their hole-in-the-wall office downtown, an ancient brick building that had once contained a jewelry store. The next building over was a bail bondsman's office that saw a lot of business.

Her number was on speed dial. "Hi, it's me," Lee said as soon as she answered. "Our contact was in a hurry to get rid of me. His supplier was due to make a delivery and he was worried I might run into him and hurt his source."

"You staked out the place, I hope?" Diane was all business over the phone, a quality of hers he respected.

"I was just pulling away from his house when I picked up a tail. I think it's the supplier and it looks like he's worried about what I've been doing visiting his client. He's played a few amateur games so far and I'm leading him north out of the city. I'll end up on Highway 313."

"There aren't many houses between there and Bernalillo, especially when you get on Sandia Pueblo land. Think he'll try and pull you over or make a move to check you out?" Diane sounded eager now. "This isn't quite what we had in mind, but it could still be a way of making contact with the Silver Eagle people."

"I hope so. I'm trying to pace myself so he doesn't have to run any lights. It could screw up my tactics if he gets T-boned." Lee checked his mirror again. The Chevy was still about an eighth of a mile back.

"Want me to head your direction?" Diane asked. "Nothing is going on here, and I'm about to lock up."

"Yeah. Come up Second from downtown. If anything happens, I'll let you know."

They both said good-bye and ended the call. Lee was at the north end of Second now, where that street and Fourth became Highway 313. The Chevy had slowed considerably to avoid closing the gap between them, so Lee turned right off Second Street onto the highway, then moved over to the left-hand lane and slowed. The right-hand lane led east to I-25, and Lee didn't want to lose his tail at this junction.

Fortunately, it didn't happen. Lee drove down the old highway, the former northern route into Albuquerque before the creation of the freeway, as locals called I-25 and I-40 throughout the metro area. A quarter mile back, on the nearly deserted road, came the green Chevy. The man had picked up speed to narrow the gap.

After they had gone another mile, the driver in the Chevy, now less than fifty yards back, turned on his emergency flashers and began flipping his high beams on and off. Lee hit the speed dial on the cell phone, and when Diane answered he said, "We just passed mile marker five and he's signaling for me to pull over. Talk to you later."

"I'm less than fifteen minutes away. Be careful."

"Always." Lee disconnected the call, touched the brakes, and slowed to a stop on the narrow gravel shoulder of the road. The Chevy pulled up about thirty feet behind Lee's vehicle and stopped, the engine running and the headlights shining brightly so he couldn't make out the driver in the glare. Leaving his own vehicle running, Lee stepped out of his SUV and moved just a few steps toward the road, far enough from the glare to see the driver.

The man noticed what he'd done and quickly opened his own door, exiting but keeping the door between them. Lee could see the driver's left hand on the window frame, but his right hand was out of view.

"Good evening—sir. Did you know your taillights are blinking on and off? You must have a short in the electrical system," the young Navajo man said, a trace of nervousness in his voice.

"Really?" Lee stepped closer, noting that the man was

wearing jeans with a long-sleeved wool shirt and Western boots. His long, greasy hair was not regulation in any law-enforcement agency Lee knew about. He glanced at his taillights. "They're back on now. You a pueblo cop or something?"

The man hesitated for a moment, reaching down for something with his right hand. If it was a gun, Lee was pretty confident he could draw and fire his own weapon first.

"No," the man continued, his eyes narrowing slightly. "I'm actually a state patrolman working undercover." He stepped out from behind the door and displayed a state police gold shield in a leather case.

Lee's eyes were good enough, even at twenty feet, to note from the badge number that it belonged to the dead state policeman, Sergeant Archuleta. Was this man his killer, or just a Silver Eagle member too stupid to realize what a damning trophy that was? "You must have ESP, Officer. I saw you east of Edith a while ago in a residential neighborhood, and you followed me from there before I ever turned on my lights. Yet you knew I was going to have a problem with my taillights." Lee stepped closer, and the man slipped his hand around toward his back pocket. Lee saw him sniffing the air, like an animal, and suddenly he knew what had attracted the man's attention!

Lee moved quickly, closing the ten feet between them in a heartbeat, slamming the man in the sternum with the heel of his palm. The man grunted and fell backward, landing hard on the gravel while the handgun he'd been reaching for skidded across the ground.

"What are you?" The young Navajo man writhed in pain, clutching his chest. In spite of his injury, he was still curious about Lee's vampire scent. It seemed to attract skinwalkers like bees to honey and that made it one huge disadvantage for Lee when hunting the shape-shifters.

If the wind was right, they could always smell his unique blood and single him out for attention. From the moment they'd caught his scent a bloodlust seemed to take over. It was especially so with those who'd been turned recently and had less control over their newly acquired predatory instincts.

Lee picked up the 150-pound skinwalker by the front of his shirt and spun him around face-forward against the door of the Chevy.

"Never mind. It doesn't matter. I know what *you* are. And now I'm about to find out who as well." Lee controlled the man with a pinch hold on the nerves in the back of his hand, then used his free hand to retrieve the skinwalker's wallet and search his pockets. Along with the badge, there was a roll of cash held together with a rubber band, a pocket knife, three quarters, and a rubber comb.

Still gripping the man with the pinch clamp, which required little pressure to bring about incapacitating pain, Lee flipped open the wallet, which contained a New Mexico driver's license for Jacob Tsosie, who had a southeast Albuquerque address. The photo matched the man.

Tsosie squirmed, making a real effort to break free. Lee swung him around and punched him with a lightning jab, holding back enough so he wouldn't break the guy's jaw. Tsosie's head rocked back as he passed out. Lee let him slump to the ground, then patted down the inert figure, checking for extra weapons and finding none.

Reaching inside the Chevy, Lee turned off the headlights and ignition and pulled out the keys. On the split ring were the ignition and trunk keys, plus a house key and another smaller silver key that Lee knew opened a cheap padlock, storage cabinet, or lockbox.

He brought the unconscious skinwalker around to the

trunk, unlocked it, and checked inside. Nothing in the compartment held his attention, so he quickly tossed out the jack, the jack handle, and a screwdriver, then stuffed the skinwalker inside so he wouldn't have to watch him. If Tsosie woke up and decided to change into animal form, the wolf, mountain lion, or whatever would still have to break out of the trunk to do any damage.

Taking a quick glance down the road in both directions, Lee reached back into the Chevy and turned on the emergency flashers. No sense in having some drunk ram into the car while he was working.

Lee checked on the passenger-side floorboard of the Chevy, noting a cardboard box with the silversmith's name and address scrawled upon it in black marker. More important, perhaps, was the name Silver Eagle, today's date, and a figure of 215 dollars listed as Total.

The labeling was a good touch. It added legitimacy to the delivery and was less likely to attract the attention of law enforcement if the man was pulled over by a traffic cop or seen by someone other than a customer.

The box probably contained the turquoise stones, silver castings, and other Southwest jewelry makers' supplies. He would have a look inside in a few minutes to confirm it. On the passenger seat was a bag that had the scent of roast-beef sandwiches, if the fast-food label wasn't enough already to reveal the contents.

With no need for a flashlight, Lee quickly discovered a cell phone under the driver's seat and picked it up by the aerial before dropping it into an evidence pouch, but nothing else was inside the vehicle except for a few candy wrappers in the back. With the exception of the murdered state policeman's badge, there didn't seem to be any incriminating evidence inside the vehicle or on his person.

But finding out he was dealing with a skinwalker and knowing that they usually ran in packs added a whole new dimension to the Silver Eagle organization.

He reached into his pocket for his cell phone, then noticed headlights coming in his direction at high speed. This was either Diane, or trouble.

# CHAPTER 5

Lee walked behind the Chevy to give himself some cover. As the car got closer he recognized Diane at the wheel. She pulled up behind Tsosie's vehicle, turned off her car lights, then stepped out of the vehicle. "Where's the driver?"

Lee stepped back around into view between the Chevy and his own SUV. "He's taking a nap in the trunk. I found out why he was so interested in following me."

"*You* in particular?" Diane's eyebrows went up as she came over to join him. "Don't tell me he's a skinwalker."

"If you insist. But if he isn't, I'll be really surprised. Our windows were down and I think he caught my scent earlier. When one of his kind smells a vampire, instinct usually takes over."

Lee brought out the state police badge he'd taken from the Navajo witch, holding the leather case by the edges. "He actually flashed this, hoping to impress me."

Diane took it from him, also by the edges, and held it in the headlight beams so she could see it clearly. "This belonged to the murdered state cop, all right. I suppose I should put it in an evidence pouch. But if you're sure he's a skinwalker, we're going to have to kill him."

"I don't see another choice. If he goes to jail there are

lots of ways he could escape using his special abilities." Lee paused for a moment. "And I can't afford to have anyone else roaming around who knows I'm a nightwalker—especially a creature who preys on my people."

"Do you think he's just working for the Silver Eagle dealers and kept in the dark about where they get their merchandise, or is he one of them? And if the latter is true, are we talking about a gang—sorry—pack of skinwalkers who have their own criminal organization?"

Lee thought about it for a while. "It would be real easy for animals such as wolves or mountain lions to wear a simple pack and smuggle contraband across the border. With their physical abilities, they could escape detection easily."

"If that's the case, then we're in real trouble. How are you going to be able to infiltrate a group like that? One sniff and your cover's blown."

"We'll have to come up with another plan. But, in the meantime, let's see what Jacob Tsosie can tell us."

Headlights appeared in the distance, and Lee gestured, calling her attention to them. "Probably just a passerby. Let's pretend to be working on a tire."

"I'll step over to my car and grab a flashlight."

Lee walked around to the back of the Chevy and picked up the lug wrench he'd removed from the trunk earlier. He listened, but no noise was apparent from inside. Tsosie was either still out or playing possum.

Moving around to the left rear tire, Lee pretended to be tightening a lug nut as the pickup drove by. Someone in the vehicle gave a wolf whistle, obviously seeing Diane coming back in his direction. She was wearing slacks and a nice sweater, and he understood the reaction.

"Asshole," Diane mumbled as she came up beside him, aiming the flashlight at the tire to complete the deception.

"Men can be such animals," she said, a smile lighting up her eyes as she looked at him.

Lee watched the truck continue down the road. Their luck was holding. "Speaking of animals, we're going to have to decide how to deal with our prisoner. Why don't you head back to the apartment? I'll handle this."

"You trying to protect me? No need to get macho. I know what has to be done. We're in this together, remember, partner?" Diane looked down the road in both directions, then pulled out her handgun. "But we should let him change into animal form first. It'll not only confirm what he is, it'll really save on the paperwork."

"Killing him outright won't get us the information we need. Let's lock him in the walk-in safe at the office for a bit."

"Why wait? Let's see if we can get some answers now. Do you suppose that he's still out cold? What did you use, a sleeper hold?" Diane reached into the Chevy and brought out the keys. There was no trunk release in this model sedan.

"Let me open the trunk. If he makes a move, I'm quicker than you are."

She tossed him the keys. "Go for it."

"Stand clear and have the flashlight beam ready to shine in his eyes."

Diane took a position to the right of the trunk. If he jumped out and made a run for the underbrush, he'd have to make it past her.

Lee stood to the left of center, brought out his .45 because of the better hitting power at this range, then held it ready with his left hand as he reached down with his right hand and slowly inserted the key into the lock.

As soon as the lock clicked, the door flew up with a thump and a black panther erupted from the trunk in an explosion of fur and muscle, knocking Lee onto his back.

Lee let go of his pistol and grabbed the animal by the neck, trying to keep the fangs away from his throat. Diane shot the creature in the side and it howled in pain, jerking back and loosening Lee's grip.

The creature leaped toward the underbrush just as Diane fired again. Dirt kicked up on the ground where the creature had been an instant before.

Diane fired rapidly, trying to track the panther with her flashlight and pistol as it blended into the darkness of the willows, Russian olives, and other vegetation across the low fence that separated the right-of-way from pueblo land.

Lee sat up, drew his Beretta, and squeezed off two quick rounds as the changeling leaped the fence. The animal landed in a heap on the other side.

"It didn't sound like a solid hit. Keep him in your sights and I'll take a closer look." Lee took three steps and leaped over the four-foot-high wire fence in stride, as if he were running the hurdles.

"Damn, you make it look so easy," Diane said as she walked toward the fence line, her flashlight and sights on the magnificent monster sprawled in a heap a dozen feet beyond.

Lee watched as Tsosie's fingers lengthened, his muzzle shrank back into a human face, and the long black fur receded into brown skin. The bloody groove on the man's skull where one of their bullets had grazed him receded, then disappeared, leaving only a pale welt. A jagged puncture in his shoulder was also disappearing rapidly.

"I've only seen a skinwalker heal during shape-shifting once before. It happens when they're unconscious but not gravely wounded," he said to Diane without taking his eyes off Tsosie.

"I guess this was what the old woman was trying to do

when she died, except going in the opposite direction," Diane said as she stood beside the fence, watching.

Lee nodded. Once the skinwalker looked completely human again, Lee handcuffed his hands behind his back.

"Want me to get his clothes out of the trunk?" Diane offered.

"Good idea. It might be difficult to explain why he's naked if someone pulls up alongside my car on the way back to the office." Noticing that Tsosie had turned his head slightly to listen, Lee held his finger to his lips to indicate they needed to be careful what they said.

A half hour later, Lee was driving south down Fourth Street, Tsosie beside him in the passenger seat. Lee's prisoner was tied and handcuffed in place so he couldn't move unless the seat went with him. Diane, who was following closely in her own car, had agreed that the trunk wasn't a good idea anymore because they wouldn't know if he tried to shape-shift again. Tsosie's car was scheduled to be picked up and stored in the county's impound lot, but the silver supplies inside the box were locked in Diane's car for safekeeping.

The man hadn't spoken a word since he regained consciousness, though Lee had noticed that Tsosie was watching him carefully. No skinwalker had ever lived this long beside him and Lee wondered what sensory information was being gathered by the changeling. It wouldn't make any difference, however, unless Tsosie managed to escape, and Lee knew that wouldn't happen.

"What kind of Navajo are you? You don't smell like any other human I've met," Tsosie muttered, not looking at him.

"I'm the one who's going to ask the questions," Lee snapped.

"You and the woman cops? You sound like them with all your questions and whispering back and forth. So take me to jail already. Without my lawyer I'm not saying another word." Tsosie sat up as straight as he could, considering his restraints, and was even starting to sound a little arrogant.

Lee waited for a full five minutes before answering. "If you want to live, you'll answer my questions. It's that simple."

"You're a cop. You can't touch me."

"Wrong, I'm a businessman willing to do whatever it takes to make a whole lot of money. On the way to your new home you'd better think about what's left of *your* future. It's completely in your hands now. No, I take that back. Your future is in *my* hands." Lee didn't bother raising his voice or using any particular emphasis. A matter-of-fact tone often worked best under these circumstances.

Tsosie slumped down a little and sat silently, watching the landscape change from rural to the old Alameda neighborhood, then become more and more urban as they proceeded toward the downtown area several miles farther south. When they passed Roma Avenue, then Marquette, Tsosie sat up and looked at him. "Hey, you missed the turn. The jail's back there."

"You're the one who mentioned jail—not me. I'm heading for a butcher shop with a nice, cold meat locker." Remembering the packing plant just east of Fourth Street downtown had practically inspired him. "If you can't tell me what I need to know before we get there, tomorrow morning when you're frozen solid, you're going to be the other white meat. Maybe sausage."

He checked the rearview mirror, looking for Diane, making sure she was having no problems following him. Once they got to the packing plant, she put together what he was doing and followed his lead. She was quick on the uptake.

Turning left at the next light, Lee drove east. At the far end of the next block was the packing plant. The name of the establishment was painted across the second story in letters at least five feet high. "You're running out of time. You really want to become a hot dog?"

Lee turned right at the end of the block, then drove down the street until he reached the alley. A minute later, he stopped in the employee parking area. A loading dock stood beside them.

"Last chance. You won't be able to change into an animal after you become, what, a hundred pounds of weenies?" Lee looked over at Tsosie.

"You're bluffing," Tsosie blurted. His tone was still defiant but his eyes now showed traces of fear. As Diane pulled up next to the SUV, the skinwalker glanced over at her.

"Don't expect any help from her. She's the one who shot you. Compared to her, I'm the nice one." Lee opened the door and climbed out.

He walked around the SUV and met Diane. "He didn't have anything to say. Too bad."

"For him," she said, staring at Tsosie with cold eyes.

"Well, at least we won't have to worry about anyone finding the body. Let's get this over with." Lee opened the door to unfasten the ropes holding their prisoner to the seat.

"What do you want?" Tsosie said, a desperate keen in his voice.

"We're entrepreneurs," Lee smiled. "You're selling quality turquoise to silversmiths and jobbers around the state at prices we can't hope to match. So we want to even the playing field, if you understand what I'm saying. Where are you getting the stones? Mexico?"

"If I tell you anything without approval from my boss, I'm dead."

"Ah, so he's a skinwalker too?" Lee watched his eyes and knew from Tsosie's failure to react that it was probably true.

Lee continued. "So, Mr. Tsosie. Do you want to be dead now for sure, or take your chances on later?" Diane reached into her pocket and brought out Tsosie's pistol.

"Not here, not in *my* car," Lee said, shaking his head. "There'll be blood all over the seats. No brains from the looks of it, though."

"Flash-freeze him first?" Diane shrugged, lowering the weapon. Tsosie hadn't taken his eyes off it.

"Just like last time," Lee lied. "No bullets, no noise, and no mess *we'll* have to clean up."

"Okay, untie him and let's get it over with. It's getting late, and I want to go through the stuff you found in his car," she said.

Lee reached down to unfasten the ropes that had his legs tied to the seat. "No! Wait! Mexico. We get the stones from Mexico."

"Not enough." Lee began to untie the first knot.

"We call our company Silver Eagle. The stones are cheap because we get them directly from several small mines in Mexico. I don't know exactly who the sellers are because all I do is deliver the stones and silver directly to the silversmiths. No taxes, no duties, no government involvement on either side. That's why we can undercut all the local suppliers." Tsosie sat up now, and was looking back and forth at them in desperation while he spoke.

"I saw the name on the box in your car and checked on the way over here. There's no Silver Eagle company in this area, at least with a telephone number." Diane motioned for Lee to keep working on the knots.

"Our customers know how to contact us, and they don't ask questions as long as we provide quality merchandise at rock-bottom prices. We only deal in cash, and all they're given is a telephone number." Tsosie looked down at Lee, who'd stopped for a second. "We ship our supplies out of a front business, an auto-repair shop in the North Valley on Fourth Street."

Lee stood. "How do we make contact with Silver Eagle?"

"You don't, not directly. We work through referrals, one silversmith tells another, and so on. We got started by tracking down potential clients—watching people come and go at the competition's business outlets." Tsosie sounded as if he were having trouble finding his voice, and his breathing was ragged. "You're going to need my help or you'll never get in the door."

Lee recalled from the files that some of the legitimate wholesalers had believed that their customer lists had been compromised—stolen, probably.

He glanced over at Diane. "Sound like the truth to you?"

She shrugged. "Let's check out the place before we start trusting Mr. Tsosie. We can always kill him later. Meanwhile, he can stay in our shop."

The office space they had rented had once contained a jewelry store, and within fifteen minutes their prisoner was locked inside the large closet-sized safe. A small vent much too small for a creature with his mass to escape through would keep Tsosie from suffocating. The only things in the safe now besides their prisoner were the wooden shelves, a plastic jug of water, and a security camera in the ceiling so they could watch Tsosie from a monitor.

Lee placed the last of three boxes containing their "inventory" beneath the desk in the back office. The front room, which faced the street, contained only a glass display case—empty at night—a high counter, a few chairs, and a few paintings and posters of Southwest jewelry on the walls.

Diane was sitting in the chair normally facing their computer, which contained their business software and access to the Internet. Across the small room was the reinforced metal safe door, and beside it on a shelf, the black and white monitor. She could see Tsosie inside the safe, sitting on the concrete floor and looking around for a way out. The monitor switched images every few seconds, giving them a view of the exit door from a second camera outside in the alley.

"Now let's get a good look at what Tsosie was delivering to his customer." Diane had unpacked the plastic bags Tsosie had in his car and was looking at the turquoise, which had already been sorted according to size and color.

She pointed to one of the bags. "These are really high quality stones here. Spiderweb matrix, and judging on the number, destined for a squash blossom. Take a look."

Lee opened the bag and dropped three of the blue-green oval stones into his hand. He whistled low. "Very good-looking and rare these days. Outclasses most of what you see even in the best shops. If this is what the Silver Eagle has gotten their hands on it's no wonder they're doing so well with area silversmiths."

He replaced the stones, sealed the bag, then looked at the rest of Tsosie's stash, which included some excellent red coral and quality silver castings along with the essential silver stock in various sizes. Finally he put everything back into the cardboard box.

"Let's see what his cell phone can tell us." Diane picked up the bag containing the small receiver, then turned it on without having to take it out of the plastic. Quickly she scrolled through the menu, reading the stored information to Lee, who wrote down the numbers from incoming calls along with those stored numbers. "We can have the Bureau check out these numbers and give us names and addresses. The one I find most interesting is the stored number listed as 'SE.' Silver Eagle, you think?"

"Sounds reasonable. If your people can get a list of

incoming and outgoing calls, we might be able to tell if that's the order number for Silver Eagle. I found out from the silversmith I spoke with before encountering Tsosie that orders were placed over the phone. I didn't get the number from him, but we can certainly find out if it corresponds to that auto-repair place," Lee said. "The address will be easy to confirm with the reverse phone book."

Diane got on her cell phone and made the call to the Bureau number she'd been given for the operation. After asking for the information she needed, she hung up. "Someone will be getting back to us tomorrow morning, but we do have an address to go with that 'SE' number—Frank's Automotive in the North Valley. Now what? We can check out the address tonight, I suppose, but I don't think we can trust Tsosie to introduce us. As soon as he's among friends he'll turn on us."

"Yeah, that's true enough."

"And they have no reason to share their inventory. Then, there's the problem with your scent," Diane added. "I have a feeling, based upon Tsosie's reaction, that any skinwalkers we come across will be much more interested in you and what you are than conducting business."

"We're going to have to keep Tsosie on ice for a while, then, until we come up with a plan that works. And we're going to have to solve the problem of my scent. Going undercover among a pack of skinwalkers, or just one more, will be impossible once they can detect what I am."

"What about John Buck, the *hataalii*? Do you think that as a medicine man he knows a way to counter your scent, or at least suppress it for a while?" Diane asked.

"He's moved, so we'll have to track him down first. The feds sealed off the area after the plutonium was discovered near his home, and it may be years before they'll let him return."

"I have his address and new phone number," Diane said.

Lee's eyebrows rose.

"The DOE bought him a nice house that happened to be on the market that was adjacent to tribal land near To'hajiilee. They even provided a truck and paid his relatives to help him move. Part of the settlement includes appropriate building materials and help in constructing a new medicine hogan."

"And you know all this because . . . ?"

"The feds were so anxious to quiet things down and minimize talk about the radioactive material recovered that they did a walk-through on all the paperwork, funding approval, and so forth. Damnedest fast track I've ever seen in government. As the federal employee most connected to the events, I spoke back and forth on the phone to John a few times, then asked for and got all the details. A report is trickling down to you via the Bureau. The state police chief is probably getting his copy right now."

Lee smiled.

"Hey, I *was* going to tell you. We just had all these other things on our minds recently," Diane said.

"So our medicine man is what, a half hour away?" Lee knew that To'hajiilee, formerly called the Cañoncito Navajo Indian Reservation, was about twenty-five miles west of Albuquerque.

"I've never been there, but that sounds about right. Why don't you call and see if John's at home. He can give us directions." She brought out her cell phone, punched in a few numbers, then handed him the phone.

The initials JB were listed beside a number. Lee made the call, and ten minutes later they were on I-40 headed west.

# CHAPTER 6

"If it wasn't for the trees, I wouldn't have come to live here, even with the *Dineh*, our people, as neighbors," John Buck said to Lee and Diane. "Or maybe I'm getting soft. This house even has a hot tub and what they call a sauna."

They were standing out on the porch, the veranda of his large adobe-style home, gazing toward the Sandia Mountains to the east. The faint glow of lights all along the Rio Grande Valley, at the base of the mountains, was visible from the gentle slope of the long hill where the house had been constructed.

The previous owner, a retired executive from California, had planted probably a hundred or more evergreens, mostly piñon pines, around the house, with a belt of Russian olives around the outside of the miniature forest in a great circle. Well designed in a purposeful but seemingly random layout, the trees served as an excellent windbreak for the house, which stood alone on the basically treeless west mesa extending from the rim of the river valley below.

"Your dog getting used to all this luxury?" Diane waved toward the mutt lying on the carved wooden bench against the wall. The dog was watching her and Lee curiously. She took a sip of coffee from the glass mug her host had handed her as he showed off his modern kitchen. It was almost as big as his old house just by itself.

John nodded, sipping from his Redskins mug. To Lee, John hadn't changed since the first time he'd met the middle-aged Navajo medicine man. John's long hair, plaid flannel shirt, blue jeans, and worn cowboy boots identified him as a traditionalist. The presence of a deerskin medicine pouch at his belt and the blue headband he wore told other Navajos he was a *hataalii,* a healer to the People.

"I need your help, old friend," Lee finally said. "I've uncovered some criminal activity that's going to put me right in the middle of a pack of shape-shifters." He avoided the word "skinwalkers," because it was believed that saying the word out loud would draw them to you.

"And you want to keep them from knowing you're a nightwalker? We discussed that once briefly, don't you remember? Back then I told you that I didn't know of any way to hide your unique scent from them."

"But now you do?" Diane pressed, hearing the minute change in his tone.

"Maybe, maybe not." The healer glanced over at Diane with a hint of a smile, then took a quick look at his dog. The animal was lying on his side, half asleep.

Lee waited patiently, sipping the last of his coffee.

"Hunters sometimes spray their clothing with a chemical taken from the scent glands of their prey. That allows them to get closer to their target. If we could collect, say, the scent of a shape-shifter, you might be able to mask who you are."

Lee and Diane exchanged glances. He knew where they could get some skinwalker sweat right now.

"I assume this isn't a problem at the moment?" John commented, seeing their reaction. "But wait. There's another complication," he added, his gaze resting on his dog. "Consider a dog and its master."

"I think I know where you're headed," Lee said. "Dogs use scent to identify their owners, but they also rely on visual confirmation. If I wore your scent I might confuse your dog, but not fool him. He knows what you look like."

"So, basically, if Lee was trying to pass himself off as an animal the rest of the pack knew, it would only work if the pack couldn't see or hear him," Diane said. "That's not much help."

"In the past, I've tried masking the scent with aftershave and that was a dismal failure. But what if I wore the scent of another Navajo—a man the pack didn't know?" Lee asked. "Would that successfully mask the scent of my nightwalker blood?"

"It might work, but that's providing you don't stick around too long. Once you started sweating, it would alter the scent. But I'm only guessing here," John said.

"Do you want to give it a try?" Diane looked at Lee.

"Yeah. I do. Sounds like it might work," Lee said.

"Then let's get started. You can use my sweat," John said.

"Are you sure? If they realize I'm a nightwalker, but all they can detect is your scent, they'll search for *you* thinking you're the nightwalker," Lee said.

"That could only happen if some of the pack with that scent memory survive," John said. "You don't plan to let that happen, do you?"

"No," Lee said honestly.

"Then I'll risk it. I've seen your hunting skills. But it may not work anyway, so don't get your hopes up too high."

"How are we going to make you sweat?" Diane asked with a tiny smile. "Make you do your taxes? Or maybe we should force you to install a new modem in an old computer."

Lee looked at the *hataalii*. "I think the Navajo way might be better. Do you agree?"

John nodded. "That sauna *might* work as well as a sweat lodge. I haven't tried it out yet, but the woman who originally showed me the house said it worked great. The California guy who built the house used it once a day, she said."

A few hours later, at nearly 2 A.M., Lee and Diane were back in Albuquerque in the alley beside their business office. The streets were relatively empty at this hour. A passing police car had given them the once-over as they'd left the Interstate a few minutes earlier, then driven off in the direction of the main police station.

"I'm going to spray myself with some Buckscent before we check on our prisoner," Lee said. "I'll stay in the front office out of sight, so you'll need to watch him carefully and see if he gives you any indication that he can still smell me." Lee brought out the spray bottle that had come from John Buck's new laundry-room cabinet. If it worked, John promised to send some via FedEx every other day.

Diane crinkled her nose. "Just when I think I've heard and seen everything, you manage to come up with something really gross and off-the-wall."

"I've tried just about everything else, including women's perfume and skunk descenter enzymes. But it never occurred to me that smelling like some other guy—gross as it seems—might do the trick."

Lee unbuttoned his shirt, then sprayed his chest and armpits. Lastly, he squirted more liquid onto his hands and patted his face as with aftershave.

Diane shook her head. "I like John, but having his scent in a bottle? No thanks." Diane took the Buckscent from him and placed it back in Lee's vehicle, then locked up the car. "Let's go," she said. Turning off the alarm with a special key, she unlocked the door.

"Careful," Lee whispered.

Diane pulled out her pistol as she stepped into the front office and Lee slipped in behind her, turning on the lights. He didn't hear any sounds from the other room.

Giving Diane a nod, he stepped out of sight. Diane opened the inner door, pistol ready, turned on those lights, and walked over and checked the monitor. Tsosie appeared to be sleeping on the floor.

Diane stepped over to the heavy safe door and, hearing the click of the locking mechanism, Lee stepped back out of sight, his own pistol ready.

As Diane opened the door Tsosie stood blinking against the brightness of the room lights and instinctively took a step closer to the door. He stopped in midstep as he noticed the barrel of Diane's pistol pointed at his chest.

He stood still for a moment, sniffed the air, then smiled. "Who's the new guy? Another Navajo? Didn't think I'd know he's in the front room?"

"He's going to be your zookeeper for a while. If my partner and I manage to hook up with your Silver Eagle acquaintances, you may still get out of this alive. If something goes wrong, you'll disappear. Got that?"

Tsosie looked at her strangely. "Why are you letting me out, if you don't want me to come with you?" He glanced at the pistol, then stared back at Diane, trying to read her expression.

"You've been locked up for hours, so I'm going to give you a minute or two to use the bathroom. I'm not being nice, either. I just hate having to stand guard over someone while they clean up their own mess. But don't try anything, or your life will end right now."

She motioned toward the door to the tiny room, which had a small sink and a toilet. The only opening was for an air duct in the ceiling. But he'd have to remove the vent cover first, and even then his shoulders would be too wide to squeeze through.

"Maybe when this is all over, we'll end up working together," Tsosie said with a shrug while he walked to the bathroom. As he went past the darkness of the front office, he sniffed the air, but Lee was out of sight completely.

Tsosie stepped into the bathroom and started to close the door, but Diane interrupted him.

"Don't close that door completely, Tsosie, and remember that bullets will cut through that door and the walls here like paper. You have three minutes."

Lee stepped into the doorway of the inner office. He hated playing games with the man, knowing that he'd eventually have to kill him anyway. Skinwalkers had an incurable affliction, according to everything he'd seen or heard from medicine men, and anyone who preyed on innocents had to be stopped—permanently. Lee braced himself for action. If their prisoner was going to make a move, it would be now.

Diane glanced over at Lee, then looked back toward the bathroom. "You have two minutes left."

Tsosie cursed, then shut the door. "I'm taking my time. Go ahead and shoot if it makes you happy. You're never going to get into Silver Eagle without my help anyway."

Lee stepped into the room. Listening at the bathroom door, he waited, his pistol ready. Soon there was a loud metallic scrape and the thud of something hitting the floor.

"He's at the vent!" Diane yelled.

"Damn." Lee stepped back and kicked the door, splintering it in half lengthwise. The vent cover was on the floor, and on the ceiling was a rectangular hole where the duct began.

"He shape-shifted!" Diane yelled, her weapon aimed up toward the ceiling of the bathroom. "He's gone up through the duct somehow."

"Step back, but cover me!" Lee jammed his pistol into his pocket and crashed through the remnants of the door as if it were cardboard. Spinning around, he reached toward the only blind spot in the room, where the big black panther was crouched. Lee grabbed the animal around the middle as it tried to slip past him.

"Gotcha, fur ball!" Lee hung on tightly as the animal leaped through the doorway. The room shook as they collapsed in a heap in the center of the office floor.

Lee threw out his left arm to protect his throat from the razor-sharp fangs of the cat as he groped for his handgun. The cat, which was already twisting around as they rolled across the floor together, sank his teeth into Lee's right biceps.

Lee groaned and instinctively grabbed the animal's throat. He was vaguely aware of Diane shouting for him to get clear; a breath later, the room exploded from two earth-shattering blasts. The panther shuddered, then slowly relaxed and slumped to the floor. Lee pulled his arm free, blood flowing freely around the deep punctures and dripping down onto the dead animal, then scooted away from the body, still on his back on the floor.

Lee saw Diane holster her handgun and reach for a hand towel, so he held out his arm. "Who the hell do you think you are, Siegfried and Roy and Hulk Hogan all rolled into one?" she demanded. "What were you going to do, pin his shoulders to the floor and count to three?"

Diane, who was trying to stop the bleeding, didn't look up from her work. Lee noticed that her hands were shaking but he didn't know if it was from concern or anger.

"I was hoping to keep him alive just a little longer in case his story about Silver Eagle's North Valley location was a crock. The numbers match an address, but that doesn't mean the place is dirty or the one we want to hook up with." Lee reached out and put his free hand on her shoulder. "It'll stop bleeding in a minute."

"The cat could have ripped out your throat instead." Diane increased the pressure she was putting on the towel covering the wounds.

"That's what he was going for. Fortunately, I managed to get my arm in the way." Lee smiled grimly. "We seem to be getting better at this, aren't we? Good thing you're such a damn good shot." He moved his injured arm. "I think it has stopped bleeding now, but I'll leave the towel around it a few minutes longer."

"I didn't think a skinwalker could shape-shift that fast. How did you know he was trying to set us up?" Diane stepped back out of the small room, but kept an eye on the panther's body.

Lee reached over with his good arm and shut the window, then joined her in the small office. "Even if he could have fit through the vent, we'd have heard him scratching and clawing his way up that metal duct, to answer your second question first. And his transition was particularly fast, all right. He must have started to shift as soon as he closed the door, but had enough of his voice left when he called out to you."

"You think I made a mistake giving him a moment alone like that?" Diane sat down on the office chair, took out her pistol, and replaced the magazine with one completely full.

"Except for Angela, I've never kept a skinwalker alive like this before, so I'm not going to second-guess you. It seemed like a reasonable thing to do at the time." Lee confirmed that the panther was dead, then unwrapped his bandage. The arm was bloody but the wounds were closing up now. He placed the plastic-bag-lined wastebasket back upright—it had been overturned earlier—and dropped the ruined towel into it.

"So, you think he knew I was still here, or was he pretending not to smell me before?" Lee asked.

"He thought someone else was here, I'm pretty sure of it. He probably wouldn't have tried to escape if he'd known you were in the other room. He'd already seen how quick and strong you are."

"Well, for him, it's over. Let's wait awhile in case the gunfire attracted attention, then get rid of the body." Lee looked down at his wristwatch. It was nearly three in the morning.

# CHAPTER 7

The sun was just peering over the Sandia Mountains as Lee drove south through the ever-increasing traffic heading toward Albuquerque. He had buried the carcass of the shape-shifter in the county landfill, selecting a place where the big bulldozers were going to work today. Diane had stayed at the office to erase the surveillance video and clean up the mess.

Lee drove past the Fourth Street address Tsosie had given them. One quick glance told him the basics. There was an auto-repair business called Frank's Automotive at the site and, although there was a CLOSED sign in the window, a hot-looking Ford Mustang and a older-model pickup were parked outside to the right of the entrance. Two other vehicles with yellow cards on their windshields were parked in front of the bay doors on the left or southern side of the entrance.

Lee committed to memory the license-plate numbers for the Mustang and the pickup, assuming the other vehicles belonged to customers. He noted that the posted garage hours were 8 to 6, so the place would be opening shortly. When it did, he'd be there posing as a new customer. After that, he'd play it by ear.

Buckscent was about to get its first—and possibly its

last—trial. If any of the employees were skinwalkers, he'd know in a matter of seconds. The fact that it was daytime would prevent any of them from shape-shifting, so he'd only have to worry about an attack from humans, possibly armed. It was a risky proposition, but he'd been through worse.

Bridget Anderson woke up with a start. She lay atop her bed in the semidarkness of her new apartment, her heart beating rapidly. When the vehicle horn sounded again in the parking lot below and she realized what had woken her up, she relaxed. There was a pistol within arm's reach. Stealing it had been a piece of cake.

She'd been a good thief—until the day Elka had caught her breaking into her hotel room and had given her a choice: Either die, or live forever as a member of her family. Now, with her new abilities, she was no longer a good thief—she was an exceptional one.

The family Elka had drafted her into had turned out to be a group of vampires who made their living by selling special services to the highest bidder. Mercenaries who packed a punch. But for someone like her, who'd survived on the streets since she'd fled her fourth foster home, it seemed good to be wanted, to belong. And the work paid very, very well.

But now the stakes were much higher. Bridget was being paid to take a life, and help Elka take another. It was a bad idea, and Bridget wanted out. She felt no loyalty to Elka or to the ones who'd died. She'd been with them only six months—less time than she'd spent in some of the crappy foster homes she'd endured until finally running away. She had no intention of taking orders from Elka for the rest of her days—particularly ones that included murder.

Bridget took a quick look around the apartment just to

verify once again that she was alone, then closed her eyes. Tonight, she'd have a long drive ahead of her.

Lee walked into the small office of Frank's Automotive and looked through the open doorway leading into the garage bays. One of the vehicles he'd seen outside earlier was on the rack getting a brake job, from what he could tell, and the other was beside it, the hood up. A radio was on somewhere in the back, tuned to a local news and talk radio station. To him that seemed a little odd, since he'd expected music. But to each his own.

A dark-haired man in faded green overalls was working on the brakes and had his back to Lee, but the other mechanic working under the hood must have heard the bell above the door ring as Lee had entered.

"What can I do you for, pal?" the skinny Anglo called out, peering around the hood. His voice was a little strange-sounding, probably because of the wad of chewing tobacco stuffed in his cheek. A dribble of nicotine leaked out of the corner of his mouth.

"My engine dies on me nearly every time I put the thing in reverse. Annoying as hell," Lee replied. The man doing the brake job turned curiously, gave him the once-over, then turned back to his job. Lee decided the man was Hispanic, not Indian, and probably no skinwalker, but he'd applied the Buckscent liberally just before arriving, which, with luck, would eliminate any threat of detection. Lee had already ruled out the Anglo as a potential skinwalker.

A reinforced metal door with a deadbolt indicated that there was another room behind the garage bays, probably a storeroom. The presence of a tiny window of reflective, obviously one-way glass in the door got Lee's interest immediately. It seemed out of place and reminded him of back-room gambling establishments he'd raided as part of a strike team. His next step would be to find out if Silver Eagle was operating out of that room, or at least using it to store their merchandise.

"I can take a look now, buddy, and give you a quick estimate of the problem. Unless it's something very simple, though, you're going to have to leave the car. There are a few repair jobs ahead of yours," the Anglo said, walking toward him. Lee could see a name tag—BRUCE.

"I understand. Want me to start it up?" Lee asked, heading toward the entrance. He passed a small counter and saw a sheet containing self-adhesive stickers, the kind used to indicate dates and mileage between oil changes. Tsosie had had an identical sticker on the inside of his door. Of course it would have been natural for Tsosie to have his car work done here, that is if Tsosie hadn't lied to them in the first place. He'd get the license-plate numbers of the vehicles in the shop, just in case he'd been telling the truth, and have them run as well.

"You wanna pop the hood?" Bruce followed Lee outside, and within a minute, while Lee was writing down the vehicle tag numbers of the other cars, had identified the low idle setting as the problem. The guy was honest, at least this time, because Lee had created the problem himself less than a half hour earlier on the way over.

"I can set this pretty well by ear right now, or hook up the electronics later today and charge you thirty-five dollars' labor for setting the idle to factory specs," the mechanic said, pulling a screwdriver from his shirt pocket. Lee was standing by the fender, staring at the engine, which was still running, though it sounded like it might die any second.

"Just fix things so the engine won't die every time I put it into reverse. If you can do it right now without all the computer crap, that will be good enough for me. Twenty bucks okay?" Lee asked, reaching into his wallet and bringing out a bill.

"Sure enough." Bruce took the twenty and put it into his pocket. "I'll work my magic, you test it out until you're satisfied, then you can be on your way."

The guy adjusted the fuel screw with a quarter turn, listened to the engine for ten or fifteen seconds, then gave it another eighth. "Okay, see if you can put it into reverse now."

Lee had only turned the fuel screw a quarter turn in the opposite direction, so he knew it would be more than enough to work. He put the vehicle into reverse, backed up ten feet, then put on the brakes and let it run for a while. Pulling forward, he went through the same motions again, successfully.

He pulled back into the parking slot and gave the mechanic a thumbs-up. "Thanks. Seems to work fine now."

Bruce nodded. "Come on back if you have any more problems, buddy." He turned and walked back into the garage bay.

Lee drove away, turned off Fourth two blocks down, then came down the alley that ran behind the businesses lining the busy street. He slowed as he passed Frank's Automotive. There were no back entrances and the outline of the storage area was obvious. It took up a space about half the size of the garage bays he'd seen inside. In the recess beside the storage area were three more vehicles. None had yellow work orders under their windshield wipers, so he assumed they belonged to shop employees—or smugglers. He'd seen only the two mechanics, so it could mean there were three or more others behind that storeroom door.

Or maybe these cars were there for a completely innocent reason. He'd have to come back later and see if any of the vehicles belonged to delivery people. His guess was that the automobile-repair operation was legitimate, a cover for whatever was taking place behind that locked door. Lee drove up the alley for another block, stopped long enough to write down the tag numbers for the three vehicles parked out back, then continued onto Fourth Street. He planned to orbit the neighborhood while he consulted with his partner.

"Got a look inside the garage," Lee told Diane, and filled her in.

"I've got some news for you too. The cell phone numbers you had our people run last night are for area silversmiths, probably Tsosie's clients. The number we got for SE on the cell matches the address for Frank's and is unlisted, which makes sense. The legal steps for a wiretap have already been approved, but the Bureau is waiting for the go-ahead from us before monitoring calls to and from the Frank's Automotive unlisted number. I suppose you want to stake out the place now?" Diane asked.

"It's probably a good idea. We'll see what kind of activities take place later today and especially tonight. If we see any confirmation that the place does serve as a distribution center for Silver Eagle, as Tsosie suggested, we can go ahead with the plan."

"If you weren't a nightwalker going into a crowd of possible skinwalkers, it would sound like another boring stakeout. You're really putting your life on the line, Lee. What if that Buckscent isn't as effective as we hope, or wears off just at the wrong time?"

"Hey, remember the commercial? Never let them see you sweat? I'm covered—literally. And I plan on refreshing myself before I go back in there."

"Very funny. I'd really like you to wear a wire so I can at least hear if you get into trouble."

"Can't do it. If they decide to talk about what they're

really doing and let me in on the operation, they're going to frisk me first. We still don't know how the two undercover operatives were blown. These guys are pretty wary of outsiders."

"If they're all Navajos, and shape-shifters, that would be natural, wouldn't it? Anyone not part of the pack?" Diane speculated.

"Exactly. But you know, all this could end up being nothing, or maybe just a bit of illegal gambling in somebody's back room."

"Then all you have to do is play poker and try not to lose too much money."

"Hopefully this won't be a total waste of time. I'll find a place to stash my vehicle close by the garage but out of their sight and you meet me there. You closing shop now?" Lee continued circling the neighborhood, trying to find a parking place where his vehicle would be within a quick run on foot in case they needed to split up later.

"Yeah, I'm locking up now. I'll be in the area within twenty minutes, maybe less."

Lee found a residential street a block east of Fourth and parked in front of a house listed for sale. The white stucco home was obviously empty, so he didn't have to worry about a curious homeowner. After meeting Diane, they found a good location for their stakeout near a fast-food place just south of Frank's Automotive. From there, they could see the front of the business and the alley on both sides of the building.

"The SUV in front of the garage apparently belongs to a customer, and the other vehicles haven't moved since my first drive-by this morning," Lee said.

A few customers came and went from the garage, and a courier from an auto-parts store delivered a battery. Finally noon came. The mechanic named Bruce crossed the street in the pickup and bought seven drinks and an equal number of bags of fast food. Lee ducked down to avoid being seen but Bruce didn't come near the car.

"All that food for two guys? He had to make two trips just to load them up. Maybe we'll finally get a look at whoever's in the storeroom," Diane said when Bruce went back to Frank's. "Can you make out that storeroom door from here? It's almost too dark to see even with my binoculars. I wish I'd brought my night scope."

"You did. Me. But that door hasn't opened an inch since we got here. Let's see if somebody comes out now that Bruce has returned with lunch," Lee answered.

Bruce brought out the bags and set them on the counter beside a stack of shop manuals, and the other mechanic, the brake guy, came over and took a bag and a drink for himself.

Bruce grabbed the other drinks, which were in a cardboard carrier, and brought them over to the door. There was a pause, and then the door opened halfway. "I can see inside now. There's a guy there who looks Indian, maybe Navajo, with long hair. He's taking the drinks and handing them to someone else. All I can see are his arms," Lee said.

"Wish I had vampire eyes," Diane mumbled.

"No, you don't. Then you couldn't get out of the car without being fried."

"Well, there's that. See anything else?"

"The guy just inside is lifting his arm. I see some cardboard boxes on metal shelves, but that's it. Wait, I can see some writing on a box. It says 'findings.'"

"Bingo. Do you know why they call jeweler's clamps, wire, swivels, and things like that 'findings'?" Diane asked absently, leaning toward Lee, still trying to see inside the storeroom.

"Not a clue. Is it worth looking up?"

"Nah. What else do you see?"

Lee watched as the Indian man at the door took four of the bags from Bruce. He still blocked the door with his body, and the mechanic made no effort to look inside. Maybe he'd learned it was healthier not to know too much.

"I see another two boxes. One says 'beads,' and the other ends in 'ay.' Inlay," he corrected as he got a better view. Then the door closed.

"Well, now we know that Tsosie was right about somebody storing jewelry-making supplies in there."

An hour later, the storeroom door opened and a man came out with a cardboard box identical to the one they'd found in Tsosie's car. "This isn't the same guy that was at the door earlier, is it?" Diane asked.

"No. We already know there are at least two in there, and the number of lunches suggests five. This guy looks Navajo to me. Hair color, shape of face, body type."

"He's heading to the back," Diane observed as the man disappeared around the corner. A minute later he drove out from behind the rear of the building in one of the cars they'd seen earlier, turned right onto Fourth, and headed west.

"One down and maybe four to go. Still want to hold off running the plates?" Diane added.

Lee nodded. "Every computer stroke entered on the government systems is recorded and saved in this age of paranoia. It could come back to haunt us. And not only would we be flagging whoever runs the check, we'd have to put hard data like that into our reports. If these people are skinwalkers too, I'd rather they disappear than end up in jail."

"I understand. But if we got some useful information like where they lived, we might be able to take them on one at a time. I'm not looking forward to tackling a six-pack of wolves, cougars, panthers, or whatever," Diane said. "And, speaking of reports, we're going to have to make another one tomorrow morning, especially after giving the Bureau all those telephone numbers and asking for the wiretap."

"But for now . . ." Lee motioned with pursed lips across the street. "Here come two more Indians out of the storeroom, both with boxes."

They watched as the two drove away in different directions with their apparent deliveries. Hours went by, punctuated by the work of the mechanics in the bays. A few minutes before five, the brake mechanic put his tools away, swept up his area, then closed his bay door and drove away.

Bruce continued working for another half hour, then drove off. The garage was closed now. A low-wattage light glowed inside and another outside the office door.

"Drop me by my car, then pick a new position to watch the front," Lee said. "I'll park in the employee spaces, then go through the office and see if I can get the attention of whoever's still in the storeroom. I think offering them what Tsosie failed to deliver will be the ticket. If you hear shooting, call the cavalry and come in with guns blazing."

"And if you don't get any response?" Diane started the engine, then pulled out onto the street as soon as traffic allowed.

"We'll have to track one of the delivery guys during daylight so he can't pull any shape-shifting stunts," Lee said as he brought out his spray bottle of Buckscent.

"Make sure you use a lot of that. But if we're wrong about this stuff working . . ."

"You'll hear gunshots, hopefully mine." Lee looked down the street and pointed. "My car's over there."

Five minutes later, Lee pulled up in front of Frank's Automotive. The two cars out front hadn't moved an inch that he could tell.

He looked around casually for Diane, then located her car in the parking lot of a pizza place. The sun was about to set. Skinwalkers were only minutes away from being able to transform into animal form. If he was going to infiltrate Silver Eagle, he'd have to do it now, while they were still human. As animals, Navajo witches tended to be surly and unreasonable.

A quick glance confirmed that no police vehicles were within view and that the sidewalks were empty of pedestrians. It took Lee less than half a minute to pick the lock on the office door. There was no alarm.

Lee took a quick look around, not knowing if whoever was inside the storeroom was watching. But there was a faint glow around the rim of the glass where the one-way-view stick-on film hadn't covered. Either the light had been left on or somebody was definitely at home.

Lee turned on the overhead light at that end of the garage, grabbed a rubber mallet from a tool rack, then walked over to the door to the storeroom. Standing where he could be seen from inside, he held up the box of silversmith's supplies with one hand and hammered on the door twice. "Knock, knock. A man named Jacob Tsosie said to come here and return this turquoise and silver. You want to unlock the door and let me in?"

Lee's hearing was exceptional. Though it had been nothing more than the whisper of a breath, he turned around. A Navajo man with hair down to his waist in old warrior style, whom Lee recognized as one of the delivery men, was advancing toward him with a long shank screwdriver, holding the blade out like a dagger.

"Whoa, Long-hair." Lee dodged, avoiding the man's forward lunge. But now he had his back to the door. With a quick flick of his wrist, he threw the rubber mallet at his attacker, striking him in the chest with the rubber head.

The man grunted and staggered back a step, obviously surprised and suddenly short of breath. Lee took advantage of the pause to set down the cardboard box, but his respite was short-lived. The man growled angrily and swiped at Lee this time with the tip of the screwdriver, missing his stomach by a mile as Lee slipped sideways along the wall, then moved out into the garage floor where he'd have more room to maneuver.

"Hold on," Lee suggested, holding up his hand. "I didn't come here to fight."

"You chicken shit!" Long-hair said, smiling wickedly and baring his teeth like a wolf. He faked a backhanded swipe with the screwdriver, then lunged at Lee's extended hand.

Lee slipped inside the attack, grabbing Long-hair's wrist and clamping down hard. Anchoring his feet, Lee swung the man completely around, slamming him into the wall and at the same time grabbing the screwdriver.

Startled by Lee's speed and strength, the man froze for a second. As the man kicked out, Lee stepped close, raising him off the floor by the throat. Lee jammed the screwdriver through Long-hair's arm just above the elbow, impaling him to the wall a foot off the ground.

Long-hair screamed, slapping out with his free arm at Lee, but the effort must have been excruciating with him dangling from the wall, gushing blood like a leaky hose. He cursed in pain, grabbing frantically for the screwdriver with his free hand.

Lee punched him sharply in the solar plexus, then yanked the screwdriver free from the wall and the man's arm. Long-hair collapsed to the floor like a sack of potatoes, out cold.

Lee jammed the screwdriver an inch deep into the wooden workbench, then turned and brushed himself off before walking to the door and knocking once more. "You'll need a wet mop to clean up the mess out here, and a body bag if you don't hurry," he said. "I'm here to do business, but if you want to take me on too, I can use the workout."

Although he could detect angry voices speaking in what sounded like Navajo, he had no idea what was being said. Thirty seconds went by; then he heard a sound at his feet. A piece of paper slid out from under the door.

"Who are you and what do you want?" was the message written in black marker.

Lee set the box down. "My name is Lee Nelson. I just opened a Southwest jewelry supply business selling turquoise and other stones, castings, findings, and silver stock, and other supplies. The same type of merchandise Mr. Tsosie delivered for your outfit."

Lee reached into his pocket and brought out one of his bogus business cards, then slid it under the door. "If you have a phone, call the number and you'll get our answering machine. I have a woman partner named Diane Santiago."

There was a pause, and then another piece of paper appeared from the gap beneath the door. "Take what's in the box and hold it in front of the glass," the note said this time.

Lee reached inside and brought out two of the plastic bags containing three matched sets of spiderweb turquoise obviously intended for squash-blossom necklaces. He held them in front of the glass for about ten seconds, then put them back in the box. Inside were some silver castings intended to be part of a concha belt, probably. They looked somewhat unique, so he held them up in their plastic-bag containers.

"Are you a cop?" a man's voice called from down close to the floor inside.

"After just beating the shit out of your pal and sticking him to the wall? Pull your head out of your butt. I'm exactly who the card says I am. Check for new listings by calling four-one-one. I see a telephone wire leading into there." Lee pointed to the wire above the door, wondering if anyone was looking. Then he took a quick glance back at Long-hair, who was still alive, apparently. Blood continued to enlarge the pool on the concrete floor.

"You want to save your pal or not?"

"You carrying a weapon?" the man called out from inside.

Lee opened his jacket and showed his handgun in the civilian holster, assuming somebody was watching through the glass. "Of course I am. I sell jewelry supplies and do a lot of cash business. I bet you're packing too, if you carry quality merchandise like Tsosie brought to me. Now can we quit passing notes and whispering under the door like a class of third graders and finally do some business?"

Lee knew that as long as he heard voices, the speaker hadn't shape-shifted. Of course there was someone else in there, and that person could be a two-hundred-pound panther by now.

There was a metallic click, then another, then the door opened a few inches. "I'm coming out," a distinctly feminine and somewhat familiar voice called out softly. "Would you please step back?"

Lee's eyes narrowed as he tried to remember where he'd heard that voice before; then suddenly he recalled a clear, cold night and the scent of piñon. Just as the memory passed from speculation to reality, a beautiful young Navajo woman with a small, light streak in her waist-length ebony hair stepped out from the storeroom. The all-too-familiar face smiled sweetly. "Mr. Nelson, is it? We're not traditionalists here either, so we don't mind using our names. Just call me Angela."

# CHAPTER 8

Bridget drove around the Las Cruces apartment complex slowly, casing the grounds for security cameras, nosy old men or women looking out their windows, or dogs that might bark at just the wrong moment. She hadn't seen State Police Officer Leo Hawk's unit parked anywhere, but then again she hadn't expected it. The sun had set, and according to messages sent to Elka prior to the loss of her brother, the Navajo cop worked the night shift like any self-respecting vampire. If that had changed in the recent past, she'd soon find out.

She noted an old, seedy-looking van with a New Mexico license plate indicating it was from San Juan County parked in a visitor's parking slot beside the building she was going to enter. The driver was inside, reading a newspaper. It was a common way to hide your face while keeping watch.

The person could be just waiting for someone to come home from work, or possibly staking out the place, like she was. She'd known some burglars who'd liked hitting an apartment or home just after a couple had left to go out to dinner or a movie.

But her career as a burglar was about to end. By the time she left New Mexico she'd be a very wealthy woman and she'd never have to worry about work again—no matter how long she lived.

She looked like a teenager, though she was barely twenty-one, and couldn't even get into a bar without being carded. But she'd grown up inside well beyond her years, and had the real-life experience one could get only from years living on the streets.

Since that terrifying night when she'd been turned into a vampire, one of the things that continued to amaze Bridget was that nothing about her own personality had changed. Well, except for the fact that she was now paranoid about getting a really deep tan. All the movies and the books she'd read depicted vampires as nasty, supernatural creatures with evil hearts. But not her. Of course she was a thief, but she'd been one before when she was so-called normal. The only difference was that now, as a vampire, she could carry out that profession with capabilities so enhanced she was almost unstoppable.

Once it was quiet at the residential complex, Bridget would go check out Officer Hawk's apartment. Elka's orders had been clear. Four or five quick shots into his face with the silenced .380 autoloader, removal of his head with the meat cleaver she'd bought at the local Wal-Mart, and Patrolman Hawk's immortality would come to an abrupt end.

The problem was that she'd never really killed anyone. She'd lied to Elka about that. The closest she'd come was when she'd turned fourteen—the last night she spent at home. Her stepfather had sneaked into her room after midnight. She'd screamed for her mother to come and help, but soon it became clear she was on her own. Bridget had fought him off with a kitchen knife, left him with a few souvenirs, then locked the door. The next morning she'd stolen money from her mother's purse and run away.

Once or twice since becoming a vampire she'd

considered going back and ripping off one or more of her stepfather's body parts. But that wouldn't have solved the real problem—the reason she'd never return home again. Her mother had been in the house that night and had heard her scream for help, yet she'd done nothing about it.

But all that was history. After they finished with Elka's retribution, she'd be on her own. Elka had agreed to let her go when the job was done. And five million bucks would make sure she could get as far away from Elka as she wanted.

Killing Officer Hawk was worth three million. Helping Elka get the ex-CIA man responsible for the destruction of Elka's vampire family was worth an additional two million. After that was all over, she'd be rich and, more important, free.

Lee tried not to let recognition show in his expression. They'd met before, and though Angela had caught the scent of his vampire blood, he'd allowed her to escape. He'd hoped to use her and her skinwalker pack to help him track down the vampires he'd been after. It had been a good plan that had worked—except for one little glitch. Angela was still alive and a very real threat to him now.

The young Navajo woman still mesmerized him. She looked so much like Annie, his late—and only—wife. But this woman was a predator with a black heart. His hand moved imperceptibly toward the grip of his pistol as he tried to think of what to do next.

"Mr. Nelson, you're staring at me. Shame on you." She smiled again, her whole face lighting up. Angela was acting, of course, but the results were almost convincing. His gaze drifted down slowly to her tight satin blouse and formfitting jeans. If she was carrying a weapon at all, it was either at her back or neck. It couldn't be beneath her blouse; everything there was natural. Her shoes were slip-on, the kind women called pumps, so he could rule out a boot knife.

The real issue right now was exactly when and how she'd expose him as a police officer—or worse, a vampire. "I'm sorry, Miss . . . Angela. I was expecting another tough Navajo, built like a cement truck. Maybe a little tougher than the guy over there bleeding to death."

She glanced at Long-hair's inert body indifferently, then walked slowly around him, subtly trying to hold his attention as a man came out of the storeroom. Her Navajo companion fit the built-like-a-truck description. He was in his late forties, and had long stringy hair that nearly reached his waist. His face was streaked with light-colored scars that must have come from an encounter with a barbed-wire fence or a major knife fight.

Lee knew that the nonfatal bite of a skinwalker was what turned Navajos into shape-shifters, but whoever had bit him in the first place must have paid a terrible price. The man carried a sawed-off shotgun in his hand the way anyone else would hold a pistol. Lee decided he'd be equally dangerous when taking animal form and couldn't help but wonder if the guy was big enough to become a bear.

Big bear guy grabbed Long-hair by his good arm and dragged him into the back room, leaving the unconscious man there on the floor, out of sight. Then the big guy came back out.

"They call me Stump," the man said, introducing himself. "Jacob Tsosie was supposed to make a delivery the other day, but never showed up at the silversmith's shop. How did you meet him, and what are you doing with his delivery?" Stump's voice was higher in pitch than Angela's, but Lee kept a straight face. A smile could be fatal, and he was already living on borrowed time.

"Like I said, this guy calling himself Jacob Tsosie came

into my shop, told me that he had to leave town in a hurry, but wanted me to take this merchandise to the people he worked with. Silver Eagle, it says on the box. He offered to pay me fifty bucks and even said that my business and yours might be compatible. He told me where you were, and suggested I come and let you see what was in the box. But he warned me that you'd probably be pretty squirrely at first. Guess that was an understatement."

"Is that it, Nelson?" Stump's voice went down a pitch, but Lee could see his grip tightening on the shotgun.

"No. He didn't say where he was going, but he did mention that if I tried to screw with you guys I'd get eaten alive. Then he laughed and drove off in his Chevy."

Out of the corner of his eyes, Lee could see Angela running her tongue along her lower lip. She was toying with him, letting him worry about what she'd do next. At least the Buckscent seemed to be working. He'd never been around a skinwalker before that had showed this kind of restraint when confronted with his scent, much less two at a time.

"That's why I'm trying to be up front with you now. If your people have a source that can provide the quality of the turquoise and other supplies Tsosie was carrying, I definitely want to do business with you and Silver Eagle. Is that going to be possible?"

"Our business isn't like yours, Nelson," Stump said without expression.

"After meeting your welcoming committee, I gathered that. But I'd really like to deal with a source who can deliver turquoise and silver of this quality. I'll keep my clients and you can keep yours. And, of course, we'll make it worth your while." Lee was going with the plan now.

"And your partner? Is this her decision as well?"

"You bet. How do you think we got the cash to start up our business? A bank loan?" Lee countered.

Stump thought about it for a moment. "I work with other people and we're going to have to talk about this first." He motioned to Angela to pick up the cardboard box.

Lee nodded. "Okay. You have our number. Just leave a message when you decide."

"But like Tsosie said—don't screw with us." Stump brought the shotgun up and wagged it in the air to make the point. "I'm a little more difficult to deal with than that other fool."

"I'll bet," Lee said, seeing that the meeting had ended.

"Good night, Mr. Nelson," Angela said sweetly, flirting with her eyes. She opened the storeroom door enough to slip inside with Tsosie's box, picking her way around the blood trail so she wouldn't slip and fall.

Stump stood and watched as Lee walked over to the office door. He nodded to Stump, who responded with a movement of his eyebrows. When Lee stepped outside and felt the cool air against his skin, he suddenly realized he'd started to sweat. His exit couldn't have been better timed.

He kept an eye on the garage as he stepped into his car, noting that Stump had walked over to the office door. As he pulled out of the parking lot, Lee knew he was still being watched.

Diane and he had agreed to meet at a designated coffee shop a half hour after he left the garage, so Lee went through the motions he'd learned to shake off anyone who might be following him, then drove directly to their meeting site.

Diane was already inside, sipping coffee, when he stepped into the all-night establishment.

Diane was trying to read his expression as he sat down in the chair across from her, but before he could speak a waitress moved toward their table with a carafe of coffee.

Lee allowed the woman to pour his coffee. "You want

cream with that, darlin'?" the waitress asked, beaming a tired smile.

"None for me, ma'am. Just keep the coffee coming."

After the waitress had left, Lee finally met Diane's gaze again. "Well?" she whispered.

Lee took a long look outside before turning back to her.

"Think you were followed?" she asked quickly.

He shook his head. "I doubt they had the skill or the time to set anything up. I just wanted to make sure." He looked back at her. "I've got some good news and some really bad news. Which do you want to hear first?"

"Just tell me what happened from beginning to end and I'll judge for myself."

Lee nodded, then gave Diane a quick summary before getting down to details. The news about the fight with Long-hair had her shaking her head, but when he got around to Angela, Diane's jaw dropped despite her cool, professional attitude.

"I don't see how you can risk meeting with any of them again, even if the man you nearly killed has already shape-shifted and healed himself. Angela's going to be the problem. The fact that she didn't give you up just makes me wonder what she has in mind. But for sure she's got an angle—count on it."

"My guess is that Angela wants me to herself. She's hoping for immortality and relative immunity from death and I'm her ticket."

"Okay, suppose I buy that for a moment. That means you can trust Angela to protect you from the others. But who's going to protect you from her? You'd really have to watch your back around that girl," Diane said, pushing her coffee cup aside and leaning forward for emphasis.

"Yeah, but one thing that might work to our advantage is that she's only been in that pack for a short time. And I got the idea she's a very small part of their organization. I think she's allied herself with them only as a stopgap."

"You'll still have to walk on eggshells, Lee. I don't like it."

"We've got to move forward on this, Diane. Can you think of any other way to get inside and learn who's responsible for the deaths of Sergeant Archuleta and Officer Whitehorse?"

"We could raid the place tomorrow with a couple of SWAT teams and pick up their delivery men individually. It would close down their operation."

"And what would we have then? It would be hard—if not impossible—to prove that the stuff in that storeroom was obtained illegally. The risk of a SWAT operation isn't justified when all we may end up getting them for is failure to get a business permit or for delinquent gross receipts taxes."

"Yeah, you're right. And everyone who had the common sense to give up peacefully would be back on the street before morning. Do you think they carry the stuff across the border while they are in wolf form?" Diane yawned despite the coffee and checked her watch.

"Hell, I think the guy called Stump could carry it all by himself. He dragged Long-hair around with no effort at all. Imagine a two-hundred-and-fifty-pound wolf." He smiled grimly. "Let's see what they do next and take it from there. For now, shall we call it a night?"

Diane nodded, glancing out into the parking lot for the tenth time in the last hour. Lee caught the attention of the waitress, pointed to some bills he'd set on the table, then walked outside with Diane.

Watchful for any form of attack, he moved away from her, giving them both enough space to maneuver and pull their weapons if necessary. Moments later Diane put her car into motion and Lee followed in his own.

# CHAPTER 9

Diane went right to bed when they returned to her apartment, but Lee stayed up, going over the day's events and making notes for his next report for Lieutenant Richmond. Nightwalkers didn't need much sleep.

The next morning, Lee retrieved their office messages. There were a few business-related calls from new clients but nothing from Silver Eagle.

They'd gone to work behind the counter and were showing some matched turquoise stones to a walk-in customer when the entry bell rang. Lee looked up and saw Stump standing there in a long topcoat and headband. His arms were crossed in front of his chest and the sight reminded Lee of one of those "professional" wrestlers promoted on television. He could just see Stump's face and name on a black T-shirt.

"Oh, my," Diane muttered. The long-haired Anglo customer in front of her, a silversmith in his mid-fifties and reminiscent of a sixties hippie except for the designer jeans and polo shirt, turned his head and just stared.

Lee smiled, but thought of the shotgun that might be under the coat. His right hand went down to rest on the grip of his handgun. "May I help you, sir?"

"Yeah. Where's the bus depot?"

"From here, go south to Silver, then east. It's between First and Second. You can't miss it."

"Okay." Stump looked at Diane, the slack-jawed customer, then back to Lee. Then he turned and left.

Their customer looked back at the turquoise. His hand was shaking slightly as he picked up one of the small plastic bags, and he laughed nervously. "Street people were a little less intimidating in my time."

"And in my time as well," Lee joked.

Diane smiled, but the customer just looked at Lee strangely. Five minutes later he left with sixteen carefully matched turquoise stones intended for a squash blossom securely in his pocket.

"That guy in the trench coat had to be Stump," Diane said, putting the remaining stones back below the counter again.

"Yeah and, for a moment, he sure had me wondering, but I guess all he wanted to do was see if our business card was for real."

"So you think we're going to hear from them?" She reached down and checked her own weapon, tucked away in a small holster at her waist.

"Maybe not in that way," he replied, and she looked up and saw he'd seen what she'd just done. "But beware of strange Navajos in long coats, they may be concealing a sawed-off shotgun, or worse."

"What could be worse? A flamethrower?"

The afternoon passed slowly, and just as they were locking up for the day, the telephone rang. Diane picked it up. "Turquoise Sky, this is Diane Santiago." She turned and nodded at Lee. "Yes, we hoped you'd be interested in discussing a business arrangement. Yes, that will be fine. Nine tonight will work for us. Who should we ask for? The Nelson party. Of course the dinner will be on us. See you then."

She hung up, then raised her hand and high-fived Lee. "Yes! We're meeting with 'their people' tonight at Cabezon's for a business dinner. The bad news is they booked a table under your name."

"Stump could break our budget. Anything else?"

"Here's the playback." Diane replayed the conversation, which was automatically recorded on their system.

"I don't recognize the voice of the man. That wasn't Stump. You heard his voice, he sounds like an eight-year-old Michael Jackson," Lee said.

"Tell *him* that."

"No thanks. Shall we go home and get ready for our dinner with the bad guys?" Lee locked the front door.

"You think we'll actually be able to set up some kind of deal, or can I expect something out of the Godfather?" Diane asked.

"I remember the restaurant shooting in the book. That the one you mean?" Lee added some sunblock to his hands from a small squeeze bottle he kept in his pocket.

"Right. I rented it on video a few years ago. Wanted to see what you old folks enjoyed," she said with a teasing grin. "But I was just kidding about the shootout. That would be bad for their business as well as ours."

They'd already worked up a plan to E-mail in their required reports—encrypted, of course. Since operations like these demanded that an undercover team change the original plan as often as the situation required, staying in touch in this manner was a necessity.

Once they'd sent in reports detailing the day's events—minus the skinwalker aspects—Lee and Diane prepared to meet with the Silver Eagle smugglers.

Five minutes before the set time, Lee and Diane drove

up in his vehicle. Both were wearing dressy leather jackets, which helped conceal their weapons, but since most restaurants in the area couldn't care less about ties, Lee hadn't bothered with one.

Lee noticed that Diane looked especially nice tonight and wondered if she was expecting Angela to attend the meeting and was making sure she didn't look like anyone's consolation prize. Diane didn't know it yet, but she had nothing to worry about. They were both beautiful women, but Diane had a lot more class. If he hadn't known she'd grown up in a middle-class family from the North Valley, he'd have thought she was old money.

The restaurant was on a side street, with half of the tables outside in a courtyard patio area under a big tree. Their "guests" had already arrived and been given a large round table in a corner of the patio with a high wall to their backs. A large outdoor heater kept the chill out of the air and was noticeable immediately as they stepped closer to the table.

Lee touched Diane's hand lightly, then switched sides with her as they approached so he could sit farthest from the heater. Although he'd sprayed himself just minutes ago with Buckscent, he didn't want to perspire on his own and alert their dinner companions. He hated smelling sweaty in public but, fortunately, according to Diane, he wasn't quite at the locker-room level.

Lee nodded to Stump, who was wearing a long leather coat, white shirt, and black slacks. Tonight, his hair was tied in a ponytail. He didn't look much like a street person anymore, though he was obviously security, not the brains.

Beside him was a striking Navajo woman in her early fifties, perhaps, with long silvery black hair topped with a beautiful coral and silver barrette. As he drew closer he noted the intense, shiny black eyes that stared back at him.

Beside this matriarchal figure was a tall, slender Navajo man who could have been her son. He had a narrow face for a Navajo, with delicate features and squinty eyes. He was wearing a beige Western-cut suit with a powder blue tie. A slight bulge beneath his arm suggested either a very fat wallet or a handgun.

"Good evening," Lee said smoothly, introducing himself and Diane. The woman introduced herself simply as Marie, and the young man at her side, who had already checked out Diane twice before they reached the table, went by the name of Raymus. A waiter appeared, taking their orders for drinks. Lee and Diane had coffee, but the others ordered bottles of the finest wines on the list. Lee wondered if the state police or the FBI would be picking up the tab. He'd choose the deeper pockets of the Bureau, of course.

Diane began immediately. Details of their original plan had been altered after their encounter with Tsosie, but they were still on track. "My partner has already told you that we'd like to do business with whoever is providing you with those magnificent stones. We'd also be open to making a deal directly with you. You could buy extra inventory from your supplier and then sell the merchandise to us for, say, ten percent less than your regular wholesale price. In turn, we won't attempt to contact your current customers or try to undercut your prices."

"Why should we sell to you when we can market our merchandise directly to our own clients for ten percent more?" Raymus grumbled. Marie glanced at the young man. Something in her eyes got his attention. He shut up immediately and became totally absorbed in the menu.

"What do *we* have to gain by doing business with you?" Marie asked softly. Her voice was compelling, and even Stump switched from his constant survey of the restaurant's guests to look at her.

Lee kept his voice low, firm, and unemotional. "Think of us as your new biggest customer. We'll take as much of your inventory as you can deliver, pay you your costs plus a percentage to be agreed upon, then kick back an additional percentage of our profits when we sell them to other jobbers, wholesalers, and silversmiths throughout the Southwest. The increased volume will easily make up the difference in your selling price to us."

Nobody spoke as their dinners were ordered. Then, while Raymus was pouring more wine for Marie, Diane reinforced what Lee had said. "We have connections with virtually every big supplier in the West. Basically, you can keep your customers and sell them what you want. We'll double or triple your sales without any work on your part. All we need is the stuff you provide."

Diane reached into her purse, slowly because she was aware that she had Stump's undivided attention. She brought out a folded sheet of paper—a typed list of the jewelry supplies they were interested in obtaining, along with estimates on the number of stones and supplies they could sell. The list had been constructed to insure a high demand for merchandise they knew or suspected had been smuggled in from Mexico, such as the turquoise with the spiderweb matrix.

"We'll have to see if our sources can handle the increased traffic—if we come to an agreement," Marie said after examining the list for less than a minute. She waited a while longer before adding, "We'll send word to you."

The rest of the dinner was almost cordial, though the simple exchanges were mainly about the food. Stump ate quickly, his eyes moving about constantly. He was obviously serving as Marie's bodyguard. Raymus fawned over the older woman. Whatever his function in their organization, he was also Marie's boy toy. She was definitely in charge—the alpha bitch of the pack. There was no question in his mind that they were all skinwalkers. Navajo witches never associated with other Navajos for long. The risk of being discovered was too great, especially at night, when their animal instincts became harder to control.

Lee hadn't mentioned Angela's absence, but he really hadn't expected her to be present for a business meeting. She'd only been with Silver Eagle a short time and undoubtedly was below Stump in the pecking order.

Once dinner was over, and with no other business to conduct, Lee sent for the bill. As he complimented Marie on the craftsmanship of a Zia-style bracelet composed of dozens of hand-set teardrop-shaped turquoise, she reached out and held his hand with an unexpectedly strong grip.

"No discussion of what is legal or illegal has taken place here tonight, and that was wise of you, Hosteen Nelson," she said, using the Navajo term for "mister." "But if all of a sudden we start having problems of any kind with the police, I will hold *you* personally responsible. I promise that you and your beautiful señorita will pay with your lives, and that your deaths will be neither quick nor peaceful. We deal with those who become our enemies in ways you can't imagine."

Lee, having seen the work of skinwalkers too many times already, imagined the worst quite well.

Marie released his hand and stood, revealing that she was quite tall for a Navajo, probably six-one or -two. She looked very fit for someone her age, and there was no doubt in Lee's mind that when shape-shifted, she'd be a formidable predator.

Marie turned to Diane, her voice still low enough not to be heard by other guests, but clear and cold. "Maybe I should have given the warning to you instead. There's a lot more to you than your soft voice. Watch over your partner and yourself by never letting me regret this meeting."

The three skinwalkers left without another word.

When they had disappeared outside the gate of the restaurant's courtyard, Diane turned to Lee. "Guess who's not getting a thank-you note and fruit basket?"

# CHAPTER 10

Ten minutes later, they were on I-25 heading south. They'd exit farther south to the west, then get back on again and head north, exiting east. With Diane keeping watch, any potential tail would be lost. Her apartment had to stay secure.

Finally they were off the freeway and on their way to her apartment. "I don't know how skinwalker packs operate. Is that Raymus character her lover, her assistant, or her son?" Diane asked, still watching for familiar vehicles behind them.

"Maybe all three, as unpleasant as that may sound. But my gut tells me to watch out for him if it ever comes to a showdown. Stump is the obvious threat, but I believe Raymus was playing mind games with us pretending to be a lackey. He's not their leader, but I'd put him at the top of the list of suspects when it comes to cold-blooded cop-killing."

"Really? I'd have put him in the pussy-whipped category the way she cowed him with just a look. What makes you so sure he was putting on an act?" Diane asked.

"Did you notice his hands when he was pouring the wine?"

"No, but I guess I would have expected to see manicured nails and a gold watch."

"Just the opposite. No watch or rings and his knuckles were scarred and callused. He's been in a lot of fights, and probably won most of them. His face looks like nobody has ever laid a hand on him," Lee said.

"I did notice he was wearing a shoulder holster but, to tell you the truth, I was more concerned about the big guy, Stump. Do you think you could take him on?"

"Yeah, but it would be bloody."

Diane said nothing for several moments, then finally broke the silence. "We're liable to get chewed out via E-mail for not taking the wineglasses so our guys could lift prints. Knowing the real identities of that group would have been an asset. But I agree with you. If we're going to have to take them out eventually, it would be better not to give the Bureau and your department more info that might just complicate matters in the long run."

Lee turned north onto the side street where the apartment complex was located. "Let's use this excuse: We suspected that there might be another member or two of the group watching us after they left to see if we started acting like cops."

"You think they might have really done that?"

"Another Indian man and woman arrived after we did, and were still there when we left. They had a clear view of us the whole time. I don't think they were Navajo, but they could have been, I suppose." Lee turned left at the entrance to the apartment complex.

"I know who you mean. The good-looking guy who never took off his hat, and the woman in the velvet jumpsuit with the expensive gold necklace. Either she didn't like him very much, or they'd just had an argument. Or, like you say, maybe they were there by arrangement."

Together, Diane leading the way by two steps, they climbed up the stairs to the apartment.

Bridget looked around to make sure she was alone in the hall, then quickly examined the mailboxes. It was a quiet building, and only a few of the apartments she'd passed had on their television sets or music, but what noise was there would be enough to mask her movements.

Secure in the knowledge that her keen hearing would pick up the sound of approaching footsteps, Bridget picked the lock of his mailbox and took out what appeared to be a personal card. A little intel on the guy she was targeting might help her now. She then hurried down the hall and worked the lock on the door to his apartment. Her hands started shaking, but concentrating on the payoff helped her fight the sudden attack of nerves.

Twenty seconds later the mechanism snapped open. Bridget stepped back and took one last look at the door. Something was stuck between the door and the jamb at the top, probably a paper match. Hawk had undoubtedly put it there to let him know if anyone, like a snoopy landlord, had come in while he was gone. It was an old trick, one she'd used herself on occasion.

Using a spot on the ceiling as a marker and future reference point, Bridget opened the door. "Anybody home?" she called out as she stepped inside the darkened apartment with her plastic bucket of cleaning supplies. Below the rags and containers were the meat cleaver and pistol. She was wearing puke green scrub pants and a blouse with big pockets. They were the same color and pattern she'd seen earlier that day while watching a cleaning lady scrubbing out a newly vacated apartment.

She propped the door open with her cleaning bucket,

then took a quick look around to insure that the place was really empty. Lastly, Bridget picked the match up from the hall carpet, set it back in its place and closed the door, taking the bucket with her.

It was darker inside than out this time of night, but that was no problem. She put on thin latex gloves, took her pistol out from beneath the cleansers, attached the makeshift silencer, then stuck the weapon into her pocket, just in case the man arrived unexpectedly.

Bridget looked around the apartment and found that there was a thin layer of dust over everything. Either he wasn't very domestic or he hadn't been here for a few days. A look in his fridge revealed no fresh meats or produce inside, which was unfortunate, because she was hungry. Contrary to common lore, vampires ate a lot because of their high metabolism. She smelled the milk in the carton; it was going bad. In the freezer was a plastic jar of what looked like tomato juice. She unscrewed the lid and sniffed. It was calf's blood. Maybe she'd take it with her for quick energy later. Moving a frozen dessert, she discovered a box in a plastic wrapper. It contained .45-caliber rounds.

Bridget wished she could use a .45 against the Navajo vampire, but their earlier tests had shown that the improvised silencers wouldn't work nearly as well on a caliber above .380 or for any round that went supersonic. At least Elka had trained her with target practice in the dark. Bridget knew she could hit any head-sized target at twenty feet with nearly one hundred percent certainty.

Hoping to take the edge off her growing anxiety at the thought of actually killing someone, she looked through his desk, but there were no photos or private papers stashed inside, just a box labeled TAXES containing receipts and rental agreements.

She'd learned from Elka that smart vampires didn't

keep many things that could be used against them or that couldn't be left behind if they had to disappear in a hurry.

According to Elka, Hawk—whose real name had been Lee Nez—had been a vampire since 1945. He was the same age as Bridget's grandparents. Bridget wondered what he looked like—all she had was a description sent to Elka by Hans before he'd been killed. The Navajo cop who'd taken out three members of Elka's family was obviously either lucky or very adept at staying alive.

Remembering the card that had been in his mailbox, she opened it up and found a brief handwritten note with an address and little else. It was signed "Diane."

Instinct told her that this was critical information. If Nez failed to show up here, she was sure she'd be able to track him down through FBI agent Diane Lopez's new address. Lopez would become an optional target then.

An hour had passed. Bridget found herself fidgeting and pacing, taking out her pistol every five minutes and checking to make sure the safety was off and a bullet was in the chamber. The latex gloves were getting sweaty now, so she pulled them off, dropping them into the bucket.

Suddenly there was a faint scraping sound just outside in the hall, and Bridget's heart stopped. She'd forgotten to lock the door! Hawk would know someone was waiting for him.

A man who looked Native American slipped into the room just as Bridget turned toward the entrance. The beam of a flashlight blinded her for a few seconds as the door snapped shut.

"Hey, who are you? Ah, you must be the entertainment." The flashlight beam lowered to her breasts. "Nice body!"

Bridget saw that Nez was holding a large pocketknife in his hand, the blade pointed toward her. He was so close she barely needed to aim. Quickly she raised the .380 and shot the cop just to the right of his nose. The pistol jerked in her hand four more times as she continued to fire. Hawk's face erupted into a mess of blood, but he managed a step forward before sagging onto the carpet with a heavy thump. When he hit the floor, the knife fell from his hand and slid across the carpet, coming to rest by her foot.

Bridget's heart started beating again, so loud she could hear it thumping against the wall of her chest. In a panic, afraid he'd somehow get right back up, she slipped the pistol down into the mop bucket and reached for the cleaver, cutting her fingertip in the process.

"Aw, hell." Bridget licked the blood off her finger, then walked quickly over to the body. She took a step sideways to get into better position, then crouched down, raising the cleaver up as she took aim at the exposed neck. Hawk was facedown, blood oozing out onto the carpet.

Bridget took a deep breath and, shaking life a leaf, swung the heavy blade. There was a sickening crunch and hollow thud as a warm spray of blood flew up into her face. The cleaver wedged itself into the wooden subflooring and Bridget had to yank the bloody tool loose with a twisting motion.

"Shit, shit, shit," Bridget whispered, resisting the impulse to wipe away the blood. Her hand was soaked, dripping everywhere now. Standing up slowly, she looked at the ruined head, severed completely, sitting there four inches from the neck. The body was twitching slightly, probably from some nerve or muscle spasm. Suddenly she was aware of the foul taste in her mouth.

Bridget ran into the bathroom, barely making it to the toilet bowl on her knees before she threw up. Undigested food came up in torrents that stung her throat. She could barely catch her breath when another spasm shook her. It felt as if her insides were being pulled from her body, dissolving in the acidic bile. After a few minutes in agony, her stomach was completely empty. Feeling shaky and cold, she grabbed a towel, wiped her face, then rinsed out her mouth and washed her hands.

Her stomach still hurt as she walked back into the living room, and stood for a second staring down at the body. Something was wrong. A big prybar and screwdriver were tucked in his belt—and those were burglar tools. "You're supposed to be a highway patrolman. Why aren't you in uniform?" she mumbled. "And where are your pistol, handcuffs, and radio?"

Bridget took a deep breath, stepped back, then remembered her latex gloves. Putting them back on again, she reached into the dead man's hip pocket and took out his wallet. Instead of a police badge or ID card, there was a New Mexico driver's license belonging to a twenty-three-year-old man named Clarence Atso from Rattlesnake, wherever the hell that was. The photo on the ID was a reasonable likeness of the way Clarence Atso used to look before his face had become a mass of bloody tissue riddled with holes.

"Oh, you unlucky shit. You must be the guy from the van. What the hell are *you* doing in Hawk's apartment?" Bridget thought for a moment, then walked around the body and locked the door. She had to wipe away any fingerprints she might have left behind, change clothes, then get as far away as possible before Officer Hawk returned. There was no way she was going to be able to surprise him now—at least not the way she'd intended.

Elka Pfeiffer sat in the restaurant of Los Alamos's Anasazi Inn, finishing her rainbow trout, eggplant, and fresh tomatoes. The fare was at least palatable, which was in stark contrast to the Southwest breakfast she'd had this morning. Someone had stuffed diced potatoes, scrambled eggs, bacon, and green chile into a rolled-up flat piece of fried bread called a tortilla, then melted cheese all over the gooey log. The waitress had said it was their specialty, but the entire meal had been just too hot and spicy for her stomach. At least they had bottled water and decent coffee here, and the fried bread was light and flaky, reminding her of beignets.

Just then Paul Rogers walked in with another man, probably a low-level bureaucrat from the local labs, judging from the cheap suit and security badge hanging from the lanyard around his neck. Rogers's companion didn't appear to be carrying a handgun, though Rogers, the CIA case officer who'd "hired" her family months earlier, was known to wear a pistol at the small of his back, inside his jacket. Hans had seen it once and told the family it was a small revolver, probably a .38.

Elka realized he was still packing when she noticed him fidget and grimace slightly when he sat down at the table across the room. Rogers was a heavy man with a big ass, probably nurtured by the habit of getting some fool to do his dirty work for him while he sat behind a desk, nice and safe. That explained why he was still alive. A quick draw would have been impossible for a man who'd have to extract his pistol from his butt blubber first.

Elka had traced him to New Mexico after Rogers "retired" just a month ago—if CIA employees ever really retired. He had supposedly been hired as a security consultant at the labs and was living at the inn until work on his new home was completed. All this she'd learned from a listening device she'd placed in his rented car just yesterday.

She planned to put one in his room as well, but the room had one of those electronic locks and she hadn't been able to get hold of a passcard yet.

She had plans for Rogers—big, dramatic plans that would be seen live around the world. While Bridget was taking care of the Navajo cop, either later tonight or before dawn tomorrow, she'd be here in Los Alamos studying the man's activities and schedules. Then she'd know when and where to make the critical move.

Lee and Diane were working across the table from each other on updated E-mail reports to their supervisors when Diane looked up from her laptop. She'd changed into a comfortable sleeveless T-shirt and slacks, but he still wore his dressy slacks and shirt, minus the jacket now. "You going to speculate in your report why Angela wasn't at the meeting tonight?"

"No. I'm also leaving out the fact that I recognized her."

"How do you think Angela will affect the outcome of what we're trying to do?" Diane asked. "This whole thing gives me the serious creeps."

"It should. She's a wild card. The other skinwalkers probably don't trust her very much either, especially after she flirted with me so openly the other night." Lee smiled at the memory; then, realizing that Diane was watching him, he became serious again.

"So, is Angela really such a hottie?"

"Yeah, and she's not the least bit shy about using her looks to get what she wants."

"Be careful. You said she resembles your late wife, and that makes you vulnerable. If she attacks and you hesitate at a critical time . . ."

"I'd thought about that," he admitted, "but I think that when the time comes I'll do the right thing without holding back."

"Maybe the ultimate choice will be mine and not yours," Diane said quietly.

"Could be," Lee answered, glancing back down at his computer screen and starting to type again.

Diane was in the kitchen when her cell phone rang. She picked it up from the kitchen counter and looked at the caller ID. "It's SAC Logan."

Diane listened for about ten seconds, then ended the call.

"Must be important." Lee saved his file and looked up. "We weren't going to communicate directly unless it was absolutely necessary."

"It's crucial, according to him. He wants to meet tomorrow morning at six just inside the Truman gate at Kirtland Air Force Base." She stood and stretched, then smiled when she realized he was watching her.

"Did the SAC give you any indication what it's all about?" Lee closed the top of his computer and placed it beside him on the sofa.

"One thing. Logan mentioned that he'd just learned something that could pull us back to our last case."

"And that could mean more . . ."

"Vampires," she finished, looking around until she spotted her pistol and holster by the coffeepot.

Lee nodded, then automatically looked toward the window, his hand reaching down to touch the butt of his pistol, which had never left his side.

# CHAPTER 11

The Truman Street gate was one of the entrances on the north side of Kirtland Air Force Base. Here, base security screened civilian employees and military personnel before allowing them through.

They'd been extra careful en route, checking for a tail, but the fact that they were going into a secure area made the meeting much less dangerous than in public.

When Diane drove up in her car, a uniformed airman with a sidearm motioned her to stop. After a quick look at her Bureau ID and Lee's state police badge, the airman glanced at a man in a long coat who was standing inside the doorway of the guardhouse to their right. It was Logan, who nodded back. "Pull into the parking area, ma'am, sir," the airman barked, then stepped back to focus his attention on the next vehicle in line.

A few minutes later, Logan, Diane, and Lee were seated on chairs inside one of the small rooms of the guardhouse, a holding and interview area containing little more than an overhead light, a wooden desk, and a fourth wooden folding chair leaning against a wall. Nods and one- or two-word greetings had been sufficient to this point.

Without preamble, Logan began. "We've been monitoring traffic to your business Web site and have had some hits with the links concerning your credentials and phony backgrounds—your legends. Somebody, probably your contacts, have checked up on you. I've already looked over the report from the meeting you had last night with the suspects. You think they'll let you do business with them?" he asked, glancing at his watch.

"We've got a chance, sir." Diane shrugged. "There's a fourth chair. Are we waiting for someone?"

"He's coming now, I think," Lee said, hearing a car door slam somewhere close by. "My lieutenant?"

Just then Richmond knocked on the door, entering at the same time. He was wearing his charcoal gray state police uniform and had to duck to avoid knocking off his cap.

"Sorry I'm a few minutes late. Long haul from Cruces and there was a rollover accident south of T or C. I stopped to help the locals for a little bit," Richmond said with a slight southeastern New Mexico accent reminiscent of West Texas.

Logan looked up at the red-haired officer with raised eyebrows. "T or C?"

"Truth or Consequences, New Mexico. Used to be called Hot Springs until that TV show got them to change their name," Lee explained.

"Before my time." Diane shrugged, catching Lee's eye to make sure he got the joke, which only he would appreciate.

"Whatever. Okay, people, I've got some other intel you definitely have to hear. I received some reports from an agency that was curiously silent and seemingly uninformed during the entire German-terrorist episode last month. Now we finally know why they've been holding out on us."

"Not the U.S. Air Force?" Richmond asked.

"No. I picked this site for security only." Logan shook his head. "I'm talking about the Agency—the CIA."

Lee nodded. "Those rumors about Muller and his people being part of some mercenary group or terrorists must have some substance to them. The CIA knew about it but stonewalled. Am I close?"

Logan looked at him curiously. "Real close. Muller's group was in reality being led by someone else—another German named Jochen Pfeiffer, or his wife Elka. We know the other couple, the Plummers, were married, and the CIA says they were basically a small family group—closemouthed, well trained, and obviously very loyal to each other. They did freelance work, mainly black-bag jobs and assassinations for the intelligence services of what the CIA calls 'friendly governments.'"

Diane nodded to Lee. She understood how effective a group of vampires could be, given their physical abilities and night vision.

"Well, something happened to finally motivate the CIA to come clean about what they know," Logan continued. "A CIA case officer operating out of a Middle Eastern country managed to acquire Pfeiffer's family as assets. The plan was to have them eliminate some of Iraq's best generals and increase tension among their military by making it look like an inside job. It was hoped that would make it possible to manipulate the Iraqi leadership into replacing the dead officers with politically reliable but less capable men, reducing the effectiveness of their military."

Lee was beginning to suspect a deeper connection, considering what they'd already heard, but he remained silent and Logan continued. "Jochen Pfeiffer was captured southwest of Baghdad when one of the Iraqis he'd recruited blew the operation. The CIA denied everything and pulled out their man, leaving Pfeiffer on his own. But they didn't count on Pfeiffer's wife, Elka, who may really be the brains behind their operation. Elka cut a deal with Iraq, offering to procure some weapons-grade plutonium and trade it for Jochen's release. Enter Fort Wingate, New Mexico."

"Wait a minute. That 'enriched uranium' in the cover story was really plutonium?" Richmond growled. "Did you know that?" Richmond looked at Lee, who shrugged.

"Sorry, it was on a need-to-know." Logan's apology was automatic. "If word ever got out about how dangerous that stash was, half the citizens of New Mexico would be up in arms. The original storage box was placed in a more up-to-date container on-site and moved along with some of the soil that had surrounded it to a storage facility near here." Logan motioned with his head in the general direction of the Manzano Mountains, at the eastern perimeter of the base. The area was known to be filled with deep bunkers that had been used to store nuclear weapons for decades.

"So Muller and the Plummers came to New Mexico, somehow having learned about the plutonium that had been missing since 1945," Diane added. "Any idea how they knew about it and where it lay hidden?" She could tell even without looking at Lee that he was also interested in the official story.

"Speculation abounds," Logan answered, "but the best answer is that the Germans had somebody on the inside way back during the days of the Manhattan Project. One of the few scientists still alive who was part of the project remembers their first batch of plutonium was lost in transit to Los Alamos. But that was so deeply covered up he never found out what happened."

"You still haven't told us why the CIA finally spilled the beans," Lee said.

"I'm coming to that. The CIA's 'asset,' Jochen Pfeiffer, was killed by the Iraqis when they failed to get the plutonium. After stonewalling about Muller and his cohorts, the CIA finally contacted the Bureau in Washington about a new problem that has cropped up as a result of their fiasco in Iraq. This problem leads straight to New Mexico."

Lee looked at Diane, who had a definite "oh shit" expression on her face. "You mentioned Elka Pfeiffer. Don't tell me she's managed to find her way to New Mexico and is looking for whoever is responsible for killing her people."

Logan cursed, and nearly stood, glaring at Lee. "How did you know that? Your sources always seem to be better than mine."

Lee nearly laughed. "My sources are between my ears. Muller was in contact with them, according to the NSA or whoever it is that bugs everyone's E-mail. Muller must have told her about us. After all, he carjacked Agent Lopez."

Diane nodded. "It all fits. But I have two questions. Do you think a mercenary would risk everything just for revenge, and secondly, did she come alone?"

"And how did she get into New Mexico, and when?" Richmond piped in.

Logan grumbled. "I'll tell you what we think we know. Elka Pfeiffer entered the country at Dallas, via Mexico City. Her name was flagged when she used her passport. An image was captured on camera and compared with a photo the CIA case officer managed to take of her when he was recruiting Jochen.

"That was when the CIA finally, as Officer Hawk put it, spilled the beans." Logan glanced from Lee to Diane, then to Richmond. "Except they moved just a few hours too late to pick up Elka Pfeiffer."

"The final destination for Elka Pfeiffer was Albuquerque, New Mexico?" Lee asked.

"Right. Her position as a Mercedes sales rep has allowed her to travel all over the world, including the Middle East. Mercedes sells a lot of vehicles in that part of the world," Logan added.

"Any idea where she is now?" Diane asked.

"We just don't know," Logan said. "But we have people looking for her." He handed them each a photograph. "Here's what she looked like in Dallas."

Lee quickly memorized the image. Elka looked a lot like Hans. "Was Elka related to the man we knew as Wolfgang Muller?"

"I see it too, Lee. Maybe his sister?" Diane looked at Logan.

"I'll ask the Agency and find out what they have on that." Logan took out a small notebook and wrote it down.

"I suppose you have special agents questioning airline employees, including the flight crew, and checking to see if she rented a car or took a cab or shuttle?" Diane asked. "Or maybe she had a Mercedes waiting for her from a local dealer?"

"All of that is in the works," Logan said.

"If she wanted to make it tougher, she might have stolen a vehicle right from the lot. People often keep their parking-lot tickets in the vehicle, and she could have found one in a few minutes. With the skills she probably has, getting into the car wouldn't be too hard," Lee said.

"I'll check the stolen vehicle reports," Richmond said.

"What else should we know?" Lee asked Logan.

Logan scowled and, after pausing to collect his thoughts, added, "The CIA case officer who recruited Pfeiffer and his group of mercenaries retired as soon as he returned to the States. He knew his career had ended, probably, once Jochen Pfeiffer was killed by the Iraqis."

Lee said nothing. He'd already known about Jochen, who'd apparently chosen to live out his life as a mortal instead of having his wife turn him. The fact that he'd been able to go out in the daytime, unrestricted by the limitations of sunblock, had served his family well.

"Who is the CIA man, and where is he now?" Diane asked.

"His name is Paul Rogers, and he's a security consultant at Los Alamos. We've contacted Rogers via a secure line and he now knows Elka Pfeiffer is in the area," Logan answered. "The Bureau offered to provide him with twenty-four-hour protection, but he declined, saying that the lab security around him should be enough."

"Confident bastard," Richmond muttered.

"That was my impression too, but we'd rather use our resources tracking down the German woman than babysitting ex-spooks," Logan said, then stood. "To add another complication to this situation, the President of the United States is coming to Albuquerque for a brief ceremony and photo op at the airport. The visit highlights funding for high-tech research, so lab honchos from around the state will be here. Security will be really tight, and because there's always a chance that Elka is targeting the President instead of Rogers, we've clued in the Secret Service. Naturally we have to commit most of our resources to protecting the President, though, more likely, Pfeiffer is gunning for Rogers or you two. Watch your backs."

"Always," Diane responded. "One more thing? Can you give us a number for Rogers, and maybe an address?"

Logan looked at his notebook and read them the information. All three, including Lieutenant Richmond, wrote it down.

"Okay, then let's get to it, people," Logan said, shaking hands with everyone, including Lee, who'd become used to the Anglo custom despite old Navajo taboos about touching strangers.

Five minutes later, Lee and Diane were on Girard Avenue heading west toward the valley. Within another ten minutes, they were inside a fast-food restaurant, ordering breakfast. Diane picked up the food while Lee stood back, keeping watch. They had decided against drive-up windows, where it would be too easy for ambush vehicles to trap them front and rear. Thickly coated with sunblock, even a full vampire might risk leaping out of a car or van for a hit.

The advantage they had, Lee knew, was that Elka Pfeiffer and anyone who might be working with her didn't know where they were and what they were doing. It was doubtful that Elka would even know for sure what they looked like, though she'd probably read a description given to her by Muller. All things considered, the biggest danger they were facing at the moment was from the Silver Eagle group, who knew where their office was located and what they looked like.

Intending to eat breakfast at their office, they drove on and approached from the rear of the building. Lee examined the back door and the locks. He'd placed a thin piece of clear plastic by the door hinge and that was still in place. The trace of dust he'd placed on the doorknob hadn't been disturbed with a handprint either. They had an internal zone alarm system which required an entry code to disarm, and that too was undisturbed.

"If anyone came in, it wasn't through this door," Lee announced.

Diane turned off the alarm by punching in a number code, and Lee entered first, flipping on the lights for Diane's benefit as he made a quick sweep of the place.

"Someone slipped a note under our door," Diane called from the front room. "Let me put on some gloves before I open it up."

"I'll bring in the food," Lee replied, then carried in the sacks containing the breakfast burritos, orange juice, and blueberry muffins. Diane joined him in the back office with the note, holding it gingerly by the edge as he was setting the food on the desk. He locked the back door while she stepped into the rest room and fished out a pair of latex gloves from a small box.

"Still smells like bleach in there," Diane grumbled as she reappeared, closing the new door Lee had installed.

"It was a good idea to spray the place down. The bleach will denature any DNA enough to disguise whatever blood might remain unseen," Lee said, looking at the folded piece of lined paper, identical to that used in spiral notebooks.

Diane unfolded the paper. It was a typed list of silversmithing and jewelry-making supplies with a price-per-unit given. At the top of the paper were the words "Write down how much of each you want to buy. The price includes your discount. Someone will come by today to pick up this paper and tell you when your order will be delivered."

"If we check for fingerprints the Silver Eagle people will know when they pick up the note," Diane pointed out, setting the paper on the counter, then removing her gloves.

Lee started to set out their breakfast. "Then forget the fingerprints. We'll make a copy of the note after we fill out the order. That's all we'll have."

"How long do you think it'll take us to deplete their current stock so they'll have to make another smuggling run?" Diane asked, turning to add water from the small sink to their office coffeemaker.

"Let's place the mother of all orders, heavy on the Mexican turquoise, and try to deplete their inventory right now. It'll take most of our capital, but if their greed exceeds their caution, we'll be able to pull it off," Lee said, handing her a package of coffee grounds from a box on a small shelf.

"That means we'll have to start staking out Frank's Automotive on a twenty-four-hour basis once they get the order.

But what if the skinwalkers who handle this end of the business aren't the ones who smuggle the goods in from Mexico?" she asked.

"We'll cover all the bases just in case. Marie or whoever leads the pack will still have to contact whoever she's dealing with in Mexico. Whether that's done by telephone, or, more likely, in person, someone will have to place the order. But my guess is the smugglers and the dealers are one and the same. I've never seen a pack of skinwalkers with more than a half-dozen people. Unlike real wolf packs, which may have as many as fifteen or sixteen animals, skinwalker packs that large are really too conspicuous. And except for an occasional outsider like Angela, they rarely take in someone from another pack. They're too territorial to cooperate with other skinwalkers. Experience tells me that we've seen all but one or two of the Silver Eagles," Lee answered.

"Okay, assuming you're right, we have Marie, Raymus, Stump, Angela, Long-hair, and the other two couriers we saw leave Frank's Automotive the other day. That would total seven now, with at least one of them a newbie—Angela. Sound about right?"

"Considering the fact that this pack is more or less urban, yes. They may or may not live in the same house, but they *will* live close to each other. Never in apartment complexes, though; too many strangers who might get curious."

"You've certainly done your homework on these creatures, haven't you?"

Lee nodded. "But I'm still learning. I just hope I haven't missed a detail that'll turn out to be my death sentence."

"From your lips to God's ears. Now why don't you refresh your Buckscent in case one of them just happens to drop by. Then we can eat breakfast. Afterward, I'll call my boss and arrange for the monitoring to begin on the Silver Eagle telephone. Agreed?"

Lee nodded. "And I'll get the order ready for them. You double-check it, then we'll wait for the pickup."

# CHAPTER 12

The barrel-chested Navajo man in his mid-twenties who came to pick up their order after lunch wasn't one they'd met, but both recognized him as one of the men they'd seen leaving Frank's Automotive with a cardboard box.

"*Yáat'ééh,* friend," Lee nodded. "How may we help you?"

The man didn't speak for a moment. Instead, he stood there checking out their layout and security. "No cameras?" the man asked, his eyes narrowing slightly as he looked at Lee, then Diane.

Diane shrugged. "We prefer guns."

Lee wordlessly placed his pistol down on the counter, his hand over it.

The Navajo man held his hands out, palms up. "Hey, it's cool. I'm just here to pick up your order."

Diane reached under the counter, brought out an envelope with their letterhead on it, and handed it to him.

"That's more like it." The man took the purchase order out of the business envelope, looked at it quickly, then smiled.

He placed the empty envelope in front of Diane, wrote a number on it with a felt-tip marker, then slid it slowly across to her. Their order went into his shirt pocket along with the marker. "This is all the paperwork we need. Don't worry, I'll remember this came from you two. Just have the cash ready when I make the delivery."

"When will that be?" Lee almost smiled. Finally it looked like they were about to get some real physical evidence on this investigation.

He shrugged. "Usually afternoon the next day, but this is a big list. I don't know if we have it all, so it might take two or three days. But have the money ready tomorrow anyway, just in case I'm wrong about that."

"Is that it?" Diane asked.

"Yeah. Call the number on the envelope *before* noon from now on when you need something. You kept a copy of our list, right?"

Diane nodded.

"Good. Keep it handy. We can sometimes get items that aren't on the list, but that usually takes longer." With a nod, he opened the door and left.

Lee looked at the telephone number on the envelope as he placed his pistol back into its holster. "No surprise there. That's the Frank's Automotive's number—the unlisted one we took from Tsosie's cell phone. The person monitoring the calls back at the Bureau will be able to speak Navajo, right?"

"Yeah, I requested that. The secretary in accounting is Navajo so she'll be called in to translate. We'll also get an E-mail with the text of every conversation. They'll be transcribed immediately. If anything comes through that the tech thinks is urgent, we'll get a call. Of course, tapes are being made and we'll get updates burned onto CDs once a day," Diane added. "We can pick it up on a PDA if we're in our vehicles, or get the text read over a tactical frequency on radio."

Lee shook his head slowly. "I remember wiretaps, listening in on party lines, black boxes, and lipreading. Eavesdropping has come a long ways in a short time."

"Speaking of short time, I'd better get going. If I see anything other than what look like normal deliveries, I'll call. You can take over for the night shift for obvious reasons." Diane grabbed her jacket.

"Be careful. Let me know if anything seems out of kilter or you think you've been made. Got a disguise, right?" Lee walked with her toward the door.

"Trust me. Just watch out for that Elka woman, and remember she may not be working alone." Diane unlocked the back door, looked around briefly, then left.

Lee walked over to lock the door and watched through the peephole until she drove away. Alone, he went back to check the laptop computer. Nothing had come in from the Bureau tech.

Elka was sitting in her car in the parking lot of the Anasazi Inn, watching Rogers's door while pretending to study a map of Santa Fe National Forest. Suddenly a large white Chevrolet Suburban pulled into the parking space beside his vehicle. Two security types with sidearms and matching blue jackets jumped out of the front at the same time two more exited from the backseat.

The curtain of his room parted slightly. Elka crouched down low, counting on the overcast skies to further block her from view. Two of the new arrivals, probably FBI or maybe even Secret Service, turned to keep watch while the other two, one of them an older-looking man, probably their leader, knocked on Rogers's door. All of a sudden security around the ex-CIA man was being beefed up and

Elka had a good idea why. The FBI or Homeland Security had picked up on her flight from Dallas to New Mexico and the CIA had made the connection between her and Paul Rogers.

It had been a calculated risk, but she simply hadn't had enough time or resources to come up with another identity. Jochen had been their forger. It was getting harder all the time to sneak in and out of a country, not like the good old days. The world had changed a lot since 1878.

Patience was a virtue and one false move now could gain too much attention. She'd checked out right before breakfast and was now disguised as a much older, tired brunette with a deep tan and thirty extra pounds, all in the wrong places. Her car, which she'd stolen late last night, had different plates.

She waited a full five minutes, then started her engine and drove slowly out of the parking lot. One of the guards outside Rogers's room gave her a brief glance, then turned his attention elsewhere.

Never complacent, Elka usually changed her look every time she switched locations and was grateful that the habit had protected her now. The FBI wouldn't be looking for a woman fitting her current description.

In a few hours she'd be in Albuquerque again. Still on their communications blackout, she wouldn't check her E-mail or meet with Bridget until tomorrow if the situation was still secure. Hopefully, by then, news of State Policeman Leo Hawk's death would be in the newspapers and on television, and they could get on with planning the next really big task.

There was a light tapping at the alley door and Lee walked over to investigate. It could be a street person, one of the other business tenants, or someone planning on killing him the moment the door opened. The steel door itself would slow down or stop anything smaller than a high-powered rifle projectile, but he'd learned to expect the unexpected.

There was a video camera aimed at the rear entrance as well as the front, and he changed the channel on the monitor to pick up the feed. They really should have had two monitors, but they'd run out of resources and time.

A young woman stood there, wearing a long, lightweight, dark-colored jacket and a scarf over her head. Her face was turned away from the camera, probably intentionally.

He brought out his Beretta, and, moving quietly, looked through the peephole. Now he could see her face—it was Angela.

The lens on the peephole had good viewing characteristics and he could see that no one else was within fifty feet. He sprayed some of the Buckscent onto his clothes, a new supply that had arrived just an hour ago via FedEx, then opened the door a foot, not stepping out but letting her see him and his pistol. "What are you doing here?"

"I'm risking my life coming here, so I don't have long. I'm alone and I wasn't followed, so come outside, away from the cameras, and talk to me a moment. The Chicano cop or whatever she is can watch your business."

It would probably be more dangerous not to talk to her, and he wasn't about to explain to her that their only inside camera monitored the walk-in safe. "I'm stepping out back a few minutes," he called to the empty shop. He didn't want her to know that Diane wasn't there.

Lee slipped on his cap and sunglasses and stepped outside into the bright light, hoping his sunscreen hadn't worn off his hands. His pistol went into the holster, but was within a second's reach.

"Let's get out of sight, Lee Nelson, or whatever your name really is." Angela looked up at him with her big brown eyes, showing more human fear than animal predator at the moment.

He pointed to the small recess where one slightly smaller building joined the next. There was a patch of shade that would protect him from direct light. The downside was that it would be impossible for him to see all the way to the end of the alley.

Angela grabbed him by the hand and pulled him with her into the shade. She wore a subtle perfume that reminded him of roses, and her lips were red and full. Standing this close to her, he found it difficult to remember how dangerous she was.

"You smell differently than before, but I know you. I remember your strength and your power. That night, before you let me escape, I was dizzy with the need to taste you. Your blood is . . . special. What kind of man are you?" Angela's husky voice trembled slightly.

"You know I'm a police officer. Why have you kept that from your new friends? Or have you?" Lee wasn't going to give out any information about his true nature. If she knew that he was, in fact, a vampire, she might know he could heal himself and had the potential to live a very long time.

"I don't owe them any loyalty. To them, I'm still a stray. I don't really trust them, and they don't trust me either." Angela reached out and held his arm, snuggling closer and pressing her thigh against his. "I don't want to share you with anyone else."

"You won't have to unless you betray me to the others." Lee smiled and put his arm around her waist. "But I'm going to have to bring them to justice, you know that. Can I count on your help?"

"Only if I get what *I* want in return." She reached over

and tickled him on his left side. He noted that she had the common sense not to touch him on the right, where his pistol was kept.

"Were you there when they killed the two cops?" Lee stepped back slightly, putting some space between them.

"No, they don't trust me with weapons yet," she said, keeping her hand on his forearm. "I'd only been with this pack a few days when that happened. They put me in the back room of the shop that night, getting orders ready for the customers. Jacob was with me. The others, including Marie, shot the Navajo cop, and the state policeman too. When they came back they bragged about which of them actually fired the shot that killed them. Even Marie," Angela whispered. She poked her head out and looked down the alley. "I'm making Jacob's deliveries now that he's gone. What really happened to him?"

"I made a deal with him and he told me how to hook up with Silver Eagle. I don't know where he is now," Lee said. Even if she could have seen through his sunglasses, he knew his lies wouldn't show in the size of his pupils. They hadn't for decades now.

She looked at him carefully and he wondered what she was thinking. Then she looked back down the alley again anxiously. "I've really got to go."

"Not yet." He took her hand. "How is the stuff brought in from Mexico?"

She smiled. "First promise me I'll get what I want from you." Angela reached up and teased his throat with her ruby red fingernails.

He honestly didn't know if she wanted to rip out his throat or jump his bones. Angela could tease better than any woman he'd ever met. "You tempt me, but I'll have to think about this. The one thing I can promise you is that I won't do anything to hurt you when the time comes—unless you harm the woman with me. Now, about the smuggling?" He took her hand and held it against his chest so she could feel his heart beating.

The gesture softened her eyes. "They travel as wolves from a house near the border and carry their clothes and the money in special packs. They're able to cross the fences at night, unseen, in that form. They travel very swiftly, but change back once they cross to Mexico so their suppliers won't know what they really are. Once they're alone again they change back to wolves and return. One night for the trip south, the next night back again. That's all I know."

"You've never gone with them?"

"Not yet. Stump told me how it goes down because I'm going to take Jacob's place next time." Angela pushed away from him gently and he let her go. "I have to leave now. If I can, I'll be back tomorrow or the next day."

"Let me know when they're planning to leave for Mexico," he said.

"How?"

"Do you ever answer the telephone there? In the room in the back?"

"Yes. I take the orders from the silversmiths now. Marie says they order more from a woman with a sexy voice." She held his gaze, a slow smile playing on her lips. "Does it work for you?" she asked, letting her gaze drift downward to his groin.

"See for yourself," he answered, feeling his body tighten. "Do you get orders every day?" he pressed, making sure they stayed on track.

She nodded. "Usually, but only in the mornings. The afternoon is for deliveries. We do a lot of business."

"You're going to get a lot of that from us. Diane or I will call every day to make some last-minute change in our order, or the next one coming up. Once you know when they plan to make a run, comment on the sexy voice of the caller—whichever one of us happens to be on the phone that day. Got that?"

"Yes. I'm going now." Angela turned and walked down the alley.

"Where do you live?" he called out softly.

"Next time," she said, looking back for a second but not breaking her quick stride. Angela turned the corner and was gone.

Lee sighed, then turned around and hurried back inside, locking the door behind him. The front door was set up with buzzer and automatic lock, so he didn't have to worry that someone had entered unannounced. A quick look on the laptop showed there still hadn't been any phone traffic at Silver Eagle. It was afternoon, however, and he didn't expect anything.

His cell phone started to vibrate and he flipped it open. "Hello."

"It's me," Diane said. "There was an extra delivery person who went out today. A good-looking young woman that matched the drawing you made. Angela, right?"

"Yes. She came by here."

There was a long pause. "Why?"

"She wanted me to know why she was keeping quiet about who we really are. It's just as we discussed. She wants me for herself—in just about every way imaginable."

There was another long silence. "I can imagine a lot, Lee. Did you make some kind of deal with her?"

"Not in so many words. She says she has no loyalty to the others, and gave me some information we can use. I think Angela's attraction to whatever she imagines I am is stronger than her allegiance to the new pack. She thinks she has a chance to get something from me and doesn't want to share. That'll keep her from working against us—for a while anyway."

"What did you promise her so far?" Diane asked.

"Not much, really. Just that I wouldn't harm her unless she turned against you or me."

"Is she starting to get to you?"

Lee wasn't sure, but he knew he had to say something positive to keep Diane from worrying. "I've handled her so far, but we'll never be able to trust Angela. Be careful."

It was dark when Lee arrived on foot carrying a bag of fast food. After circling the block, he'd approached from behind and slipped into the passenger seat of Diane's car.

"What's the situation?" he asked as he brought out a fresh cup of coffee for her and placed a bag between them on the seat. "I brought you dinner."

"Thanks." Diane took the cup, looking him up and down carefully.

"What? Angela didn't bite me or anything. Not even a hickey."

"Very funny. Now, about the situation—the mechanics are closing up the shop, and there has been no sign of any other activity." Diane sipped the coffee.

"Okay. Here's what I've got. There haven't been any calls at all on the phone being monitored. Based upon what we've been told about them taking orders during the morning, that would figure," Lee said. "Now, here's what else I learned from Angela." He gave her the relevant details about the smuggling operation.

"Did she think our order would be enough to exhaust their inventory and send them back on another smuggling run?"

Lee shrugged. "I really didn't have time to ask her, but I'm hopeful. I told her we're going to call that number every morning to make some small change in our order, and if they're planning another run, she's to let us know by commenting on the caller's sexy voice."

"Sounds like a tipoff signal a man would come up with," Diane grumbled. "What if I'm the one making the call?"

"Hey, that's between you and her," Lee replied, then smiled. "You *do* have a sexy voice."

"That's one compliment that's going to get you nowhere."

"Tell me something I don't know."

"What if they take off for Mexico in the afternoon without letting Angela know ahead of time?" Diane changed the subject back to the situation at hand.

"They could do that very easily. That's why we need to keep tabs on their movements. Angela said they don't trust her yet."

"It's easy to see why. If they'd been part of Angela's original pack, it would be different, though. Right?" she asked.

Lee nodded. "I've seen skinwalkers sacrifice themselves trying to protect each other. That blood bond is strong when pack members share a common 'parent.'"

"You know, this could all be an act, hoping to get you somewhere alone where you'd be relatively vulnerable. If the whole pack came at you at once . . ."

"What other choice did we have once she showed up as part of the Silver Eagle crowd?"

"I know, I just don't like it. If Angela thinks for even a moment that she can kill you, she will. Does she know you're a vampire, and what a vampire can do?"

"I doubt it. She's just acting on what her scent information tells her—that I'm strong and different. The odds of her having encountered a vampire before are pretty damn slim. Skinwalkers don't live very long, maybe ten years tops near as I can figure. I guess it comes from the stress of changing body forms in such a short period of time. Much more demanding than just healing a wound. Their high mortality rate also comes from their violent natures. But, for all I know, my blood would do more harm than good to a skinwalker, or make no difference at all."

"Let's do our best to make sure we don't find out. By the way, did Angela say where she lives, or where any of the others stay when away from their business?"

"That was my last question, but she was walking away at the time and just said 'Next time.' I'll follow either her or Marie when they finally leave. Chances are, they all sleep together."

"Together-together or in the same house?" Diane asked.

"Not *all* in the same bed—probably in two adjoining rooms or one big room like with one of these newer homes where the builders combine living rooms, dining rooms, and kitchens. Skinwalkers are den animals."

"Do you think they'll manage to ditch us on their way home? We can't afford to follow too closely."

Lee reached into his jacket pocket and brought out a small electronic device she recognized as a receiver for a global positioning device. "I put the sending unit of this underneath Marie's car. We don't have to follow them very close at all."

"Ah, that was you, then, passing by in the alley? You worked fast, and with the vehicle in the way, I never got a good look at you. How do you know it's Marie's car?"

"Well, it's the fanciest car, and I smelled her expensive perfume—the same scent she wore when we met her at Cabezon's. Angela wouldn't dare use the same perfume. Her car is probably the beat-up pickup, being the new skinwalker in the pack."

"Glad you're on my side."

"Me too," Lee mumbled, his mouth half full of roast beef and pickles.

"They're coming out now," Diane said, setting down her cup and picking up the night-vision scope she had brought with her. Lee kept chewing, but reached into his jacket pocket for his binoculars. He recognized the three delivery men, including Long-hair, who were already outside the front entrance to the garage. Angela followed, then Stump and Marie. Raymus came last, locked the door, and caught up with Marie. Stump opened the back door of the fancy car, and Marie got in, followed by Raymus. Angela got in the driver's side and Stump took the front passenger seat.

Diane set her night scope and food aside and started the engine. One of the other vehicles, a fast-looking Mustang, pulled out onto Fourth Street with all three delivery men inside. The sedan driven by Angela followed.

Lee looked down at the global positioning receiver. A green light was blinking and he turned on a small LED display, which revealed a map image of the area. "Working as planned. Give them a full minute before we follow."

"Right. You think they're going home, or someplace else?"

"They didn't stay long after the delivery guys returned, so maybe they're planning a run to Mexico right now. We don't know how they contact their suppliers at the other end, but I doubt they use a telephone. They may just show up," Lee said.

"With luck, they'll still have to go by home to get whatever gear they use when carrying the smuggled stones and silver."

Lee nodded. "If they split up, we're sticking with Marie's car."

. . .

The vehicles stopped in a wooded area of the bosque just south of Sandia Pueblo land, which began at the northern terminus of Fourth and Second streets. It looked like a dead end and was off their road map, so Lee and Diane decided to wait beside the highway farther south and see what happened next. Fifteen minutes later, both vehicles drove back south to the highway, then stopped at a gas station farther east on Tramway Road, halfway to I-25.

"Guess we're going on a trip or they would have gassed up on the way home instead. Shall we stop and gas up as well?" Diane looked down at the fuel gauge as they sat at the side of the road a half mile away.

"Might as well top it off. We'll get better mileage than that luxury sedan but I'd still like a good margin of error. We can also stock up on snack food and water."

"I'll give them a five-minute head start," she said, looking at her watch. "Let me know when they start moving again," she asked Lee.

"They're going now," Lee said shortly.

"What if they switched who's in which car at the station?" Diane asked.

"Why would they do that unless they knew they're being followed? Once we get out on I-25, and that looks like where they're headed," he said, looking at the small screen in his hand, "we can close up a bit and I'll have a look with the binoculars to confirm everyone is still where they were."

"I forgot they can't hide from you in the dark."

Within ten minutes, it was clear that the two groups of skinwalkers the pack comprised were driving south on the Interstate. If they were indeed going to Mexico, it would take over three hours just to reach the border, assuming they averaged over seventy miles an hour. Lee betted on four or more, having pretty much lived on New Mexico roads as a state patrolman.

During the trip south, Lee and Diane debated back and forth about tactics and strategy. If they were able to identify the Mexican suppliers and catch the members of the Silver Eagle in possession of smuggled goods, they could shut the business down. But unless they found forensic evidence—like the guns used to kill the police officers—they wouldn't have enough to put the members of that group in jail for more than a few years.

Angela was a skinwalker and totally undependable. Her testimony wouldn't mean much, either, since it was mostly hearsay. To put an end to the operation permanently, they had only one choice, and that was to manipulate events so that no one in the Silver Eagle group got out alive. They'd have to sacrifice their own integrity along with the lives of the creatures in the cars speeding toward Mexico.

# CHAPTER 13

Hours later, with Lee still behind the wheel, they continued to follow the two cars as they left I-25 before it became I-10 at the southeastern tip of Las Cruces. At this point they were only about thirty miles from the border with Mexico.

Past Cruces now and at a slower pace on two-lane highways and side roads, they proceeded through the tiny community of Vado, where they crossed over to the west side of the Rio Grande. Moving through a farming, ranching area dotted with fields, side roads, and an occasional stock tank along the former floodplain of the river, they approached the southernmost all–New Mexico community in the area, Santa Teresa. With traffic scarce in the area Lee was forced to remain farther back and they missed a few turns, having to backtrack twice rather than risk being spotted.

A few miles southeast from where they were now lay Texas and El Paso. South was the combination New Mexico–Texas community of Sunland Park, then the state of Chihuahua, Mexico. El Paso was the closest port of entry of any size, but Lee doubted Silver Eagle had anything legal in mind tonight.

His headlights off now–the road was basically deserted this time of night—Lee spotted the brake lights on the vehicle ahead and slowed, using the engine and gears rather than his own brakes, not wanting to give the skin-walkers any indication they were being followed. The vehicles ahead were either slowing for an animal in the road or about to turn. He slowed further and watched as both vehicles, which had closed up the distance between them after passing through Cruces, turned down a narrow dirt road. An old adobe hacienda with a newly constructed detached garage was located near an arroyo that drained east toward the river.

"Is this their destination?" Diane asked, then yawned as she reached for her night scope.

Lee pulled over and let the car coast to a stop before turning off the engine. "Probably. We're only five or six miles north of Mexico. There will be border-patrol vehicles roaming about, but there's enough cover for a pack of wolves if they're careful. There are a lot of stray dogs around border towns anyway, so the officers probably won't give them a second look unless they spot the packs Angela said they carry."

"I got a mailbox number on the last house, so if we have to call in backup they'll at least have a clue where we are. But let's stick to the plan we have for now."

First they traded places. Diane rose up off the seat, and he slid across underneath her. It was like kids playing on the sofa. As they brushed each other closely Lee enjoyed the physical contact.

Once he was on the passenger side, Lee emptied his pockets of nonessentials like his wallet, then picked up four granola bars and a water bottle, placing them into his now empty pockets. With the tracking device safely attached to Marie's car, they'd been able to stop for supplies a second time and catch up again later without losing them.

He also adjusted his tan baseball cap and his gloves, and once again checked to make sure he had plenty of sunblock. "I'm not going to use the Buckscent. If they manage to smell me or my trail, I'd rather them not connect the scent to my cover identity. That would blow the operation."

"Angela would recognize your scent, though, and wouldn't the rest of them be able to tell you're a nightwalker—like she did?"

"Skinwalkers detect that my scent is different than other humans', and are attracted by it, that's true. Whether it would sidetrack their operation and cause them to come looking for me, that's another matter. I just don't know. Tsosie did follow me instead of delivering the supplies to his customer."

"If they can't control it . . ."

"I'll have to take the risk. Using the Buckscent would guarantee they'd all know who was following them. Angela was able to restrain herself when she could smell the real me, and Marie seems even more in control. I think their alpha bitch will motivate them to finish the job, even if it means biting their butts to keep them in line. I'll carry my cell phone, just in case I can link up with you and need some extra firepower, but I'll keep it shut off to save battery power until it's needed."

"I'll keep a sharp eye on things here in case someone stays behind. If not, I'll take a look inside the house."

Lee watched the house while munching on one of the extra granola bars. Marie's car had been parked in the garage. The driver of the Mustang had parked next to the garage, being careful not to block it. Then he'd closed the garage door and gone into the house to join the others. No light had been on inside before, but one was on now, though he couldn't see through the curtains.

"What if they wait until tomorrow night to cross the border?"

"Then we back off a bit more and wait. They didn't come down here to bale alfalfa."

A half hour passed, and then the light went out inside. "It's one-thirty." Diane yawned for the second time in five minutes. "They'll still have four to five hours as wolves before daylight, right?"

"That's plenty of time for them to make it into Mexico from here. Let's just watch and wait."

Less than five minutes later Marie opened the front door, looked around for about thirty seconds, then stepped out. She held the door open as five large wolves came out quickly, followed by a slower but even larger one. "That big male has got to be Stump," Diane whispered, her eye glued to the single-lens night scope.

"They're wearing some kind of fabric saddlebags. They look pretty well designed and won't slow the animal down that much or inhibit movement. The smallest wolf must be Angela," Lee added. Lee knew that Diane wouldn't be at all surprised to see that Angela was a wolf instead of the cougar she'd been when they'd last met in battle. By now Diane knew only too well that skinwalkers could shift into a variety of animal forms.

He placed the binoculars into a jacket pocket, buttoned the flap, then checked his gear one more time. His sunglasses were inside his shirt pocket in a hard-sided case.

"They must have their clothes inside those backpacks. They'll be changing back to human form and getting dressed before they meet their Mexican contacts. Dome light out?" Diane asked without taking her eyes off the animals clustered around Marie. The older woman was apparently giving her underlings last-minute instructions.

"Check."

Diane looked over at him. "Apparently Marie won't be going. Want to change your mind about the Buckscent?"

"No. Remember, I'll probably be gone at least a day if Angela's info is accurate. I'll check in with you once I reach their destination, and again when I start back. But the rest of the time I'll have the phone off to save the batteries. Also, expect a call when I get back on this side of the border tomorrow evening, or the next night if there's a problem with the suppliers," Lee added, reaching for the door handle. "This run might take longer, since I think it's off-schedule because of our big order."

"Got the digital camera with the zoom lens?"

"Yes, Mother," Lee whispered, patting his other shirt pocket, where the tiny camera was stowed. Diane had brought it along with her on stakeout and he'd be using it to photograph the Mexican suppliers, along with any other incriminating images he could collect.

"Be careful," Lee said, then opened the door and slipped outside, using the vehicle for cover. There was a moderate breeze, coming from the southwest. He was safe for the moment from the skinwalkers' strong olfactory senses.

Diane nodded. "You, too."

He'd already planned his route and moved back toward the north where there was a low ridge, actually a high ditch bank, that ran east and west on the north side of the property. He could use that as cover, run swiftly to the east of the house, then enter the arroyo that the wolves would undoubtedly use to cover them as they ran south.

Lee knew how to move quietly, and with no visibility problems at all was able to get almost even with the house before the wolves trotted toward the arroyo. The animals moved quickly in single file, led by someone other than

Stump or Angela. Lee figured it was one of the pack members that made the deliveries.

He stopped and watched them jump down into the arroyo. Moving rapidly now that he was screened from Marie's sight by the house, he proceeded to the arroyo and peered inside. The steep-sided water-carved ditch was around ten feet wide and half that deep, the bottom hard-packed sand. It was still a few months before the rainy season, such as it was, and travel would be easy.

Crouching down low, he walked quickly down the arroyo. Turning the corner of a narrow bend, he saw the disturbed ground where the heavy animals had leaped into the channel. The tracks led south, and when he got closer he could see by the distance between tracks that they'd picked up the pace. Knowing he'd have to run to keep up, Lee began a quick jog. He'd be depending on his night vision and excellent hearing to keep from coming upon the pack accidently. Lee knew he could run a marathon, if necessary. Focusing on his breathing, Lee continued south, keeping a sharp lookout for any sign that one of the animals had jumped out of the arroyo.

Once every fifteen minutes Lee would stop, listen, and examine the tracks to make sure the wolves were keeping their steady pace. There was one long, relatively straight stretch of arroyo where he nearly caught up to the pack. Ahead he saw the last animal in the pack, a male with its tail up high, trotting along as if it could run forever. Lee estimated they were moving at about five miles an hour. Lee slowed his pace.

Once Lee noticed a fence line ahead he stopped running and moved slowly. This was probably the border, and this close to communities he expected to encounter border guards in vehicles or on foot.

Crouched low, he saw headlights coming from east to west. Flattening, he hugged the ground just behind a gentle curve in the arroyo as a spotlight searched the ground in front of him. An SUV changed speeds and fishtailed slightly as it passed through the sandy bottom, then the vehicle, belonging to the U.S. Border Patrol, continued west along the dirt track that paralleled the fence.

Lee rose up enough to look out and spotted the wolves. Apparently they had been crouched down as well, hiding in a narrow tributary to the arroyo that branched off to the right. Farther down the arroyo, where it passed through the fence, were coils of barbed wire that reminded Lee of war movies he'd seen. Tumbleweeds and brush clogged the wire, making the barrier seem even more impenetrable.

The fence was taller closer to the communities to the east, Lee knew, but here it was only around four feet high. The wolves cleared it easily, one at a time. Now in Mexico, the animals ran back toward the arroyo.

Lee waited, noticing that one wolf had remained behind just on the Mexican side, watching the arroyo and the road. It looked like the one that was Angela, and he wondered if she was looking to see if somehow he'd managed to follow them. She must know that he or someone working with him has been watching Frank's Automotive.

For a moment, Lee thought she had seen him in his hiding place. She looked in his direction for perhaps thirty seconds, sniffing the air. Finally another wolf came up to her and snarled. She turned and ran down the arroyo to catch up with the rest of the pack, while the other, larger wolf nipped at her heels to speed her up. Lee followed, hurdling the fence without breaking stride.

Almost two hours later, a quarter mile from a metal-roofed building among a cluster of low hills, the wolves walked into a dense thicket of fifteen-foot-high mesquite. The plants branched at the trunks and had already begun to leaf out for the season, making visibility in and out of the grove nearly impossible.

It would be getting light soon, so Lee stopped, still east and downwind of the wolves, and applied sunscreen to his head, face, and hands. He drank half of a small bottle of water, ate two granola bars, and waited for people to emerge from the thicket. They were now far enough from the border to change back to human form.

Hopefully, the building with the corrugated metal roof was where they met their contact. A well-used five- or six-year-old pickup was parked by the building. Near the house were an outhouse, an old farm tractor and cultivator slowly rusting to oblivion, and a water pump and tank. A thin wisp of smoke coming from a stovepipe suggested that someone was awake inside the house.

The Navajo gang must have been resting up from their lengthy journey, because they didn't come out of the thicket for an hour or so, until the sun started to come up. Lee had moved by then, finding a shaded hiding place in another, smaller mesquite grove farther uphill. He was within a few hundred yards of the house, the only visible structure around, and he had the camera out. Now that they were in human form again he could take a few incriminating photos.

Stump came out of the thicket first, wearing a thin desert-camouflage jumpsuit and tan shoes. He had one of the backpacks slung over his shoulder. The big Navajo looked around carefully, then turned and said something. Angela came out in similar garb, her long hair tucked inside a cap, followed by the three delivery men—including Long-hair—and Raymus, who was carrying a gray pack, different from the others, which were greenish black. Their clothing was so well matched with the terrain that they could have probably remained hidden from view even in broad daylight.

Lee knew it was all just for show. The Mexican suppliers had no idea they were dealing with skinwalkers who didn't need camouflage clothing to avoid being seen and stopped by the border patrol.

He watched through the camera's zoom lens as Stump walked up to the door of the building, knocked twice, then whistled loudly. The door opened quickly and an old man in a baseball cap stepped out, smiling, and patted him on the shoulder. They talked animatedly for a minute or so—a good thing, because their conversation would cover the faint click of the camera and Lee had been worried that the skinwalker's sharp hearing would pick up the sound.

Then Stump waved for the rest of the Navajos to come up to the building and they all went inside.

Lee waited, and within five minutes a tall Mexican man in a broad-rimmed hat appeared at the rear of the building carrying a shotgun. He walked over to a shady spot against the building and stood watch. Lee had expected a guard to surface and had stayed behind cover.

Within an hour the old man came outside with another young Mexican man wearing a brown leather jacket. The outside guard handed his shotgun to the old man, then joined his younger companion in the pickup. As they drove off, the old man went back inside. Lee put the camera back into his pocket. Hopefully they were going to pick up the turquoise and silver, not groceries.

It had been a long, hot day hiding in whatever shade he could find. Once it was finally dark, the pack left the house, following the same route to the mesquite thicket where they'd changed before. After shape-shifting, they hurried to the border and crossed the fence over to the U.S. side. But there they suddenly became unpredictable, stopping and reversing direction, sniffing the ground, and obviously looking for footprints. He had tried to avoid leaving a trail, but knew his scent had remained and might still be detectable.

With the sky clear of clouds and a full moon out, Lee knew he had to keep his distance and stay downwind. He moved slowly in stops and starts to avoid running into the animals by accident, especially with less cover for his extra height.

Right now he was crouched low behind a creosote bush, watching carefully for signs of movement after having lost track of them momentarily. He could hear the sound of a vehicle, no doubt the border patrol, off in the distance somewhere, though he hadn't seen any headlights. The wolves were probably crouched low to the ground just as he was, waiting for the vehicle to leave.

The engine sounds faded at long last. The unit either had gone into an arroyo, had gone behind a hill or thicket, or was finally far enough away. It was an opportunity to move on.

Lee walked slowly along the eastern rim of a small wash, looking ahead and down. If the wolves were hiding, this would be a likely spot for them. He'd have to be extra careful if he didn't want them to detect him first.

A hundred yards down the shallow ditch he discovered their trail in the sandy bottom, leading away from an evenly spaced row of tall creosote bushes. The pungent scent of these plants was apparent in this area, though now Lee was beginning to wish he'd brought along the Buckscent after all. Several depressions along the sandy sides of the arroyo indicated that large animals had lain there recently, hunkering down to avoid being seen. He breathed a sigh of relief. Now he was back in the hunt.

Lee stopped to examine the tracks by the depression, and confirmed that the marks were fresh and headed in the right direction. Then suddenly he realized that there were only five depressions, not six.

Instinct and an almost supernatural reaction time saved his life. Out of the corner of his eye he saw a dark shape looming somewhere to his left. Diving in the direction of the attack, Lee evaded the powerful jaws of the massive animal as it hurled itself over him, grazing him roughly as it ran down his back.

Lee ducked his head and rolled over onto his feet, spinning around and grabbing his pistol. The wolf, a male with a gray backpack, which meant it was Raymus, turned in his length and snarled, lowering his head and baring his fangs as hair stood up on its back. The pack fit along the contours of his sides, and obviously didn't restrict his ability to maneuver and attack.

The animal held back, curious now as it picked up Lee's unique scent. The snarl turned into an evil grin, and Lee knew it wasn't going to run, despite seeing his pistol.

A shape-shifted skinwalker kept his or her human consciousness, so it knew what the gun represented, but this man-monster was counting on Lee's hesitation to fire. Lee knew that resorting to his gun now would practically guarantee his death. The noise would alert the others, and taking on a pack of wolves out here in the open could be suicidal.

Lee faked a shaky hand as he kept his pistol aimed at the tensed-up beast. Meanwhile he slipped his other hand down for the commando dagger in his boot sheath. The instant Lee jammed the pistol into his jacket pocket, the wolf came in low and fast.

Expecting the attack, Lee rose up and kicked the wolf in the side of his head just below the left eye, turning to his left as the animal brushed by him, like a bullfighter evading the horn.

The animal yelped, spinning around behind Lee to catch him before he could turn. Lee jumped straight up, but the wolf caught his boot in his jaws just enough to send him off balance, and Lee fell onto his side. Lee barely got to his knees before the yellow-eyed beast lunged forward again, teeth bared, angling for his throat.

Lee fell back, bringing his dagger up as the animal landed on his chest. The dagger sank in deep, and Lee yanked the blade forward. Raymus yelped again, kicking hard to pull away, and Lee let go of the handle as the wolf fell off of him. The creature rolled over onto his back. Lee rose to a crouch, took out his pistol, and waited.

The wolf's eyes were still open, but the creature wasn't moving anymore. Blood flowed rapidly from the beast's chest for a moment, then stopped. Unless he could shape-shift now, the creature would die. Raymus's eyes glazed over, something impossible to fake.

Lee studied the area around him. The pack was probably still upwind, but if he was wrong about that and they picked up his scent, they'd come after him, particularly after they found Raymus.

He put his pistol away, pulled his dagger from the dead skinwalker's chest, then ran quickly south toward Mexico, trying to stay downwind and careful to avoid leaving a prominent trail.

Thirty seconds later and a quarter mile closer to Mexico, Lee stopped, flattened behind a creosote bush, and waited, checking the action of his Beretta. He heard a low bark, then a mournful, long-drawn howl. They'd found Raymus.

After that, it was silent again, and all he could hear was

the rattle of a few dry leaves stirred up by the breeze. Reaching into his front right trouser pocket, Lee pulled out his backup .45 auto, thumbed off the safety, then placed it into his jacket pocket for easy access. He wouldn't have the opportunity to reload if they all came at him at once.

Lee looked toward the border, knowing that he had to decide on a strategy quickly. If they managed to surround him or attack in a group . . .

Ten minutes went by, and he wouldn't have seen them at all in the dark if his eyes had been those of a normal human. They were moving parallel to him, behind a long line of brush less than a hundred yards away.

Holding his Beretta rock-steady, he aimed toward an opening in the brush in their direction of movement. He couldn't decide if he should open fire, uncertain whether they knew his exact location or not. Yet, the closer they got, unmolested, the greater the chance one or more would get past his gunfire and tear him to pieces.

He heard engine noise behind him just then and noticed that the wolves had stopped, frozen in place. Turning his head slightly, he located a border-patrol vehicle, headlights blazing, approaching along a dirt road just north of the border.

Lee jammed his pistol into his holster, then jumped up and turned, sprinting in the general direction of the vehicle at top speed.

They had a night scope, just as he'd hoped. In a matter of seconds a spotlight was directed in his direction, and there were shouts. *"La Guardia, alto!"* He recognized the words "Halt, Border Patrol." When he ignored them the vehicle picked up speed, trying to cut him off before he reached the fence. The spotlight operator tried to capture him in the beam, but he was moving too fast to track easily.

Lee knew he had the speed necessary to make the border. Going full tilt, arms and legs pumping like a machine, Lee cleared the border fence just as the spotlight caught up to him. He continued running, slowing to Olympic sprint speed for the next half mile. Spotting an arroyo, he came to a stop and jumped down inside the waist-high channel.

Breathing hard, Lee looked back toward the border, where the patrol vehicle had now come to a stop. Out of their jurisdiction now, the U.S. officers had given up on him and were looking back in the direction he'd come from, hoping to find others who might have remained in hiding when he broke cover.

His tactics had worked. The pack would have to leave the area now, or be spotted. Their packs looked too unusual for them to risk detection. Still he waited, pistol ready. They might also decide to circle around the border patrol and come back into Mexico after him.

Diane had been able to catnap during the daylight hours after she realized that Marie probably wasn't going anywhere. But it was dark again now and she felt dead tired. Only the adrenaline from the excitement of knowing the wolf pack would be returning before sunrise kept her alert.

After taking a sip of water—she'd been trying to limit her fluid intake for obvious reasons—Diane picked up the night scope and scanned the house, garage, and yard, then slowly turned in a circle, verifying that no people or animals were within view. It was incredibly boring, but most law enforcement was similar. Hours, days, and sometimes weeks of safe, routine investigation, research, and study, interrupted by seconds and minutes of intense action, stress, and danger. With a nightwalker as her partner it had been one hell of an adventure.

Hours went by, and Diane took frequent bites from the high-energy junk food they'd picked up on the journey southeast from Albuquerque. Knowing she couldn't risk going outside and walking around to loosen up, Diane had tried to compensate by stretching her legs and arms alternately, hoping to keep them from cramping up. Though it was June and she was in the southern part of the state, it was cold outside. Despite that, Diane decided to keep the windows down at least halfway so she could listen.

It was nearly four in the morning, very dark now after the full moon had set, when Diane saw movement along the ditch and a big wolf popped into view. The animal, wearing a bulging backpack, stood there motionless, watching the house, which had been dark since midnight.

Diane reached down without taking her eyes off the animal and brought up the scope. From the angle Diane could see that it wasn't a male. "Angela, you're back. But where are the others?"

Lowering the night viewing device, Diane checked out the larger viewing field available to her unaided eyes and noted that Marie had just come outside. The woman stood by the front door for a moment, then motioned for the Angela wolf to come forward.

Angela trotted over quickly, then stood steady as Maria unfastened the backpack and set it down beside the entrance. Angela remained beside Marie like an enormous German shepherd on sit-and-stay, watching the ditch from which she'd emerged a few minutes earlier.

Diane looked along the ditch line, then toward the other side of the property, then finally glanced around behind her own car and into the fields on either side.

Turning back, Diane saw another wolf wearing a backpack scramble out of the ditch. It trotted over to Marie without waiting for a signal, then stood while its load was removed and stacked beside the other bag. Marie turned and said something to the Angela wolf, and the animal lay down on the ground.

Diane watched as Angela's fur began to disappear and her human body began to emerge from the canine form. Skin and flesh seemed to grow outward, expanding. The morphing took almost five minutes, Diane estimated. Then the nude young woman stood and faced Marie.

Marie asked the questions, it appeared, and Angela answered quickly. Marie reached out and slapped Angela suddenly, and the younger woman flinched, raising hands to defend herself. But Marie shouted something, and slapped Angela harder. Angela held out her hands in submission, then turned, picked up the two backpacks, and went inside the house.

The other wolf lay down, as if ready to morph back into human form, but Marie kicked it sharply and it yelped before standing again. "Trouble, huh? I bet Lee had something to do with this," Diane muttered.

Within the next hour two more wolves returned, and each time Marie would remove their load, then kick them around, not allowing them to morph back into human form despite their yelping and squirming around, tails lowered. Diane noted that Angela was still inside, but no lights had been turned on.

Finally the big wolf returned—Stump. Marie ran forward as soon as she saw him climbing over the ditch bank. He was carrying an additional backpack in his teeth.

Marie grabbed the extra backpack, then kicked Stump in the hindquarters, hustling him toward the other males, still standing there by the house.

Bending down quickly, Marie took off the backpack, then stood and looked toward the ditch. She remained motionless for perhaps a minute, then turned, looked toward the house, and ran over to the wall, grabbing a rake. Whirling around, Marie started cursing, beating the male wolves across their backs with the handle. The animals yelped and whined, rolling and ducking from the beating, but none of them ran away. Finally Marie screamed, "Angela, get out here!"

Angela skulked back outside, fully clothed, keeping her distance from the others, who were whining and showing their undersides in submission now.

"Take these inside!" Marie yelled, pointing to the backpacks. "And you worthless shits . . . get inside." She moved toward the wolves, kicking at them as they fled into the house, tails between their legs.

"God. It's like a Walt Disney version of hell." Diane shook her head slowly as she saw Angela carrying in the backpacks, followed by Marie, who slammed the door behind her. In a few seconds the lights went on inside.

Diane waited, watching along the ditch bank and around the fields for any sign of Lee. After an eventful half hour, her heart rate was definitely beginning to pick up speed.

Suddenly her cell phone beeped. "Shit! Scare the water out of me, will you?" Diane groaned, picking up the receiver.

"Hi, it's me," Lee said softly, the sound on the receiver faint. "I'm okay. Have all our animal friends returned yet?"

"Five so far. But they got their asses kicked by the head bitch. That have something to do with you?"

"Yeah. The sixth wolf won't be coming back. I'll meet you at five-thirty a mile north of your current location, then tell you about it."

"What about our friends?" Diane asked, looking back toward the house.

"They'll probably be leaving soon, but don't worry. We

know where they live. I've got to hang up now and cover the rest of the ground quickly if I'm going to beat the sunrise. I'm running low on sunblock. Call if something comes up." Lee's signal went dead.

Just before dawn, Lee met Diane beside the road north of the Silver Eagle house. She reached out and unlocked the door as he came up from the shoulder, and slipped onto the seat.

"Welcome back, Lee. You look like crap," Diane said.

"Glad to be here, or anywhere, for that matter. Where's the water?" Lee took the bottle she offered him and drank greedily, emptying the container.

"More?" Diane turned around in the seat, and reached between the cushions, grabbing another bottle from the rear floorboard.

"Thanks." Lee opened the cap and took a sip. "Thank God for cell phones. I didn't want to come back the same way I left, not after my encounter with the wolves. I'll risk the border patrol any day. What are our friends doing now?"

"Marie and the others left the house about ten minutes ago. I'd backed off down a side road so they wouldn't pass right by me on the way out."

"Just head back north and we should be able to pick up that tracker again. It's out of range by now, right?" Lee sat up straight, took a deep swig of water, then fastened his seat belt.

As Diane drove, Lee quickly gave her a synopsis of what had happened since they'd parted, then waited for her report.

She told him quickly about the nonevents of the past day and a half, then caught him up to date on the details of the wolves' return and Marie's reaction.

"Angela must have told her what happened to Raymus. Marie beat the crap out of them, knowing they'd heal when they morphed back into humans. If she'd broken their bones or cut them up later they would have been of no use to her for quite a while." While he was talking, Lee found a box of granola bars and started eating one.

"We know where they're headed, right? Back to Albuquerque by the same route?"

"It's the shortest distance. I guess we'll find out," Lee said, closing his eyes. "Wake me up when the signal kicks in again, okay?"

"Okay. Glad you made it back, Lee. How tough was it?"

"Tough enough. I just hope they haven't made me. I still don't know if they got lucky spotting me or if Angela found a way to tip them off without risking her own tail."

"Can't trust a skinwalker, Lee. That's what you told me."

"Yeah, I did. Words to live by."

# CHAPTER 14

Elka drove through section B of the hospital parking lot. In the E-mails she and Bridget had exchanged last night she'd given the key phrase that determined which prearranged meeting locations they'd use.

She glanced casually at the parked vehicles for the recognition signal. Bridget's vehicle would have the sun visor down with a postcard fastened to it.

Elka knew where Rogers was staying at the moment and had already come up with an alternative strategy for getting to the target. Now that it was obvious that she was in the area, law enforcement and government security agencies would make it difficult for her to get close. But Bridget, looking no more dangerous than a high-school cheerleader, might be able to make the lethal move.

Unfortunately Bridget had announced, with another key phrase, that she'd been unable to kill Officer Nez. Perhaps the opportunity would come up later, but now another target had priority.

Elka was eager to speak with Bridget again in some form other than code phrases in made-up conversations. They hadn't had contact for a week now and there was a lot of information that needed to be exchanged, including the reason for Bridget's failure to kill the Navajo vampire.

The parking lot was full at eight in the morning, with many outpatients visiting the attached clinic, so Elka surmised that Bridget might have been circling, trying to find a place in the B section. Turning down the next row, Elka saw what she was searching for. The third vehicle, a small Chevy sedan, had the proper signal.

Bridget, wearing one of those long-billed caps she'd seen on young mothers pushing baby carriages from here to Santa Fe, was sitting in the driver's seat reading a paperback novel. New Mexico was such a sunny place that her sunglasses, and Elka's, didn't look out of place.

Daylight had been chosen as the time to meet in order to throw off Officer Hawk/Nez, who must have pointed out to the other law-enforcement officers that her group was most active at night. Nez and Lopez had undoubtedly been informed of her presence in New Mexico.

Elka drove past slowly, lowering her own sun visor but making a point of not turning her head while she watched Bridget.

Continuing on to the end of the row, Elka paused, checking in the rearview mirror to confirm that Bridget was on the move. Knowing the girl would be following closely, Elka drove to the end of the parking lot, waited until the traffic was clear, then pulled out and drove south. Bridget followed, hurrying to close the distance to about five car lengths.

An hour later, after driving around the city to insure that they weren't being followed, Elka pulled off the highway at the south end of a community named Corrales and drove east down a dirt road lined by tall trees. She'd already scouted out the place and knew there'd be plenty of shade this time of the morning. The few flat-roofed houses she saw were set well back from the road, so they would have plenty of privacy to talk.

Stopping beside a wire fence that formed a property line between houses, Elka was able to safely roll down her window. She watched in her rearview mirror as Bridget's vehicle approached.

Bridget pulled up even with Elka, stopped, and rolled down the passenger-side window so they could talk. "Nez never showed up," Bridget said quickly. "I could tell he hadn't been there for several days. Maybe I can track him down after we take care of your priority target. I read Nez's mail and got the FBI woman's new address."

A white van with no markings came out to the street from a driveway across the street, and the man behind the wheel watched them curiously. "The government must know I'm in the area, because they just increased security on Rogers, so let's continue this back at my place. I'm staying at 7800 Montgomery NE in Albuquerque, apartment 1017. Follow me if you want, just remember to break off if you spot a tail. If we get separated, maintain strict security—no calls, just E-mail."

Elka rolled up her window and signaled Bridget to move on. Once the girl's car was down the street, Elka looked over and saw that the man in the van had pulled into the street and was driving away. Elka continued east, circled the block, then drove back to the main road, moving slow so that Bridget could keep her in sight. Soon Elka saw Bridget's vehicle about a quarter mile back.

Anger boiled inside her. Bridget had just lied to her. The American girl had been looking in her direction while speaking, but she'd never made eye contact. A sure sign when dealing with Bridget. Maybe she just didn't have the guts to kill someone, even when big money was involved. Overall, Bridget's loyalty was questionable at best. It had only been the promise of money that had kept the girl from running off once they'd separated to come to the

U.S. Relying on Bridget from this point on would be a mistake.

She'd driven less than a mile farther when blue and red lights began flashing from the dashboard of a black SUV coming up fast behind her. Elka noted a speed-limit sign on the right side of the road which read 25, then looked down at her speedometer. "Shit. I'm only going a little over thirty."

Taking a deep breath, Elka slowed and pulled over to the graveled shoulder of the road. Above her to the right were the high banks of an irrigation ditch that probably functioned as an flood levee, and beyond that trees and a few houses. The sun was high enough that it wouldn't be shining directly into her side window—one less worry.

In her rearview mirror she could see only one uniformed officer in the shiny vehicle and he was on the radio, probably calling in the tag number of her rented car. Farther back down the road she noticed that Bridget had pulled over to the side. Bridget was an excellent thief, but still hadn't had very much training in tradecraft. Staying in the area under these circumstances wasn't a very good move.

Bridget hadn't really bonded to the family in the six months she'd been around. That alone made her an undependable ally. But after the loss of Jochen and the others, she'd really needed the girl's help to complete this final act of retribution. Maybe now that Bridget had missed out on Nez, for whatever the reason, she'd have the incentive to do her part in the next phase of the operation. After all, partial payment for her services was bound to look better to Bridget than coming out of this empty-handed. If there was one thing Bridget knew, it was the value of money.

Elka removed the pistol from her purse and placed it under the seat. She sat up slightly, adjusted her hair, then practiced an apologetic smile. She could pass for thirty, was in excellent shape, and had on a tight turtleneck sweater. Men often gave her a second or third look, so chances were that she'd be able to charm the man into a warning if she flirted.

She hoped her change in hair color and colored contact lenses had altered her appearance enough that he wouldn't recognize who she really was despite her German accent. It was doubtful that a cop from a small town would have looked closely at any flyers, assuming they'd been distributed in the area in the first place.

Elka watched the officer in the side mirror. He was writing a ticket attached to a small clipboard as he approached, which also meant he couldn't quickly draw his sidearm. Careless and complacent. Her weapon was within reach, less than two seconds away. If she had to shoot, he'd eat a bullet by the time he realized she even had a gun.

"Good morning, ma'am." The fortyish black-haired man smiled from behind the dark glasses. "Please turn off your engine." His gaze went quickly from her face to her breasts, then back up. A microphone on his uniform front, below the left epaulet, was connected to a tape recorder in his pocket, and his gold badge indicated that he was a member of the Corrales Police Department. "Driver's license, please."

She handed him the phony operator's license, which was for the state of Rhode Island. In her experience, it was easier to fake a document that was most likely unfamiliar to the person who'd be examining it.

"You're a long way from home, Mrs. Henderson," the officer said, looking at the license casually before placing it beneath the clamp on his clipboard.

"I just love your beautiful state, and the people have been so friendly. Was I speeding? The speed limit is thirty-five, isn't it?" She smiled widely, taking off her sunglasses for a moment so he could see her beautiful brown contact lenses. Putting them back on, she unfastened her seat belt and turned toward the door, parting her legs slightly.

"It's twenty-five, Mrs. Henderson. But you're obviously not from around here, so I'm going to give you a warning—this time." He looked at her again, very closely, his eyes narrowing. His mouth opened slightly, and she saw his arms tense up as he realized his hands were full. He knew who she was!

Elka reached down below the seat with her right hand slowly and he followed the motion with his eyes instead of watching where her left arm was going.

She grabbed the back of his collar with her left hand and slammed his throat against the window frame. She held him there, pinned against the car. He gagged, eyes bulging and arms thrashing about as he tried to grab his pistol. His uniform cap fell onto her lap. With the heel of her right hand she jabbed upward, catching him under the chin and snapping his head back. There was a mushy crunch.

She supported the officer with her left hand to keep him from slumping down as a vehicle with a woman and an infant in a car seat passed by. Hopefully it would look obscene rather than deadly. Behind her she could see Bridget's car still beside the road, but the street was clear otherwise.

With her left hand still on his collar, Elka lowered him as far as she could before letting him drop to the ground. Quickly she opened the door, picked up the dead officer by the leather belt and collar, and shoved him onto the backseat. Her sunblock would give her a few minutes' protection, but here beside the road in broad daylight, being seen by a passerby was potentially as dangerous as direct sunlight.

Already feeling heat on her hands, Elka grabbed the police officer's clipboard, which held her driver's license and the ticket he was writing. She scanned the ground around her car. Spotting his pen, she picked it up quickly and jumped back into her vehicle. When she tossed the clipboard onto the seat beside her she could see a flyer beneath the ticket he'd started to write. The flyer, in color, included a close-up photo of her at the Dallas airport.

Rolling up the window and thinking how glad she was that she'd learned to read people so well, she glanced over and saw Bridget passing by slowly, staring, her eyes wide open. "Keep going," Elka mouthed, motioning with her hand to urge her along.

Bridget picked up speed and drove on. Elka started the engine, checked behind the police vehicle for oncoming traffic, then pulled out quickly, accelerating nearly to the speed limit.

She had to do something about the dead officer in the back right away. If any taller vehicle, like a truck, passed by and the driver or a passenger looked down, the body on the backseat would be clearly visible.

Elka slowed and took a side road—another residential street in a nearly rural area with houses on large lots. At the next intersection she turned again, looking for a spot where one of the large, old trees shaded the road. She drove on past several upper-middle-class houses with green fields around them, then passed over a large irrigation ditch. Two large trees—she thought they might be cottonwoods—were on either side of the road. Pulling over to the right, Elka parked in the shade.

Getting out quickly, she reached in the back and rolled the dead officer's body onto the floorboards, then spread her extra jacket over him as much as possible, covering his upper torso. It would have to do. She still had at least another twenty-minute drive through the city back to her apartment, and traffic was heavy with many people still on their way to work. If anyone came up and looked in, they'd spot the body immediately. It was too risky. She'd have to dump the dead policeman.

Elka cursed her luck and decided to head away from the city. Bridget would be waiting at the apartment when she finally caught up to her, assuming the girl didn't bail on her now. But it was quickly becoming clear that she'd have to think of a whole new strategy—and maybe a new target as well—to get what she wanted.

# CHAPTER 15

Lee had done the driving for the past two hours. He looked away from morning rush-hour freeway traffic toward the horizon, then checked his watch. The sun was rising above the Manzano Mountains and Diane was just stirring on the seat beside him.

The ring of Diane's phone woke her up completely and she answered it with a surly voice. "Good morning, sir," she said, mouthing the word "Logan" and sitting up, her tone changing in an instant. "We've made some major breakthroughs but I'm still in transit. I could give you a summary now and E-mail the rest in two hours."

Listening to her supervisor's response, Diane looked around, quickly orienting herself by noting the relative distance from their location to the Sandias and Manzanos. The closer the Sandias, the closer to Albuquerque. Then she saw the downtown area several miles to the north. "We're about ten minutes out of the city." Listening again, she nodded, then glanced over at Lee again. "Meet at the Truman gate again? We can be there in . . ."

"Fifteen," Lee said.

"Fifteen minutes if the traffic down Gibson cooperates," she replied. "Yes, sir, we'll be there."

"What's so urgent?" Lee asked as soon as she hung up.

"That vampire woman, Elka, may have killed a Corrales cop. It all happened about an hour ago, apparently." Diane looked closely at a van Lee was passing as he moved toward the left-hand lane on the freeway. The Gibson exit was only a few minutes farther north.

"Full vampires can't take more than a few minutes in the sun, even with major sunblock. What the hell is she doing outside this time of day?"

Fifteen minutes later Lee and Diane sat down in folding chairs across the table from SAC Logan in the same guardhouse they'd visited before. Traffic was moving along slowly outside, predictable this time of day, but it was just a dull rumble with the door closed.

"Okay, here's what happened this morning. A Corrales police officer in an unmarked vehicle pulled over a female in a Chevy sedan just after 9 A.M. The officer called his dispatcher, gave his location, then waited until the plate was run. It's an airport rental. Then dispatch lost contact with the officer. Backup was sent, and the officer's vehicle was found, but nothing else—no cop, no speeder."

"There must have been a witness or else a video camera in the officer's vehicle," Diane offered.

"Exactly. The investigating cop played back the video and from the description I heard the woman driver broke the cop's neck with her bare hands, then just threw him into the backseat. She picked up his clipboard and pen, then drove off in a hurry. And, get this—she looked back at the unmarked SUV and the camera got a good shot of her. It looks like Elka, though she was wearing dark glasses and maybe a wig. The woman must be as strong as hell to do what she did."

Lee nodded, noting silently that Elka had left her car for only a few seconds. "Anything else?"

"Apparently another sedan drove past just after the perp threw the cop's body in the backseat. It slowed for a second, but was waved on by Elka. The officers are trying to get a tag number on that vehicle," Logan added.

"That's it?" Diane asked.

"Just about. The Corrales police got a call about fifteen minutes after the officer's vehicle was located. Another civilian who had apparently passed by just before the officer was killed, or during the attack, saw the officer with his head inside the perp's driver-side window. He was behaving strangely, according to the witness," Logan concluded.

Diane nodded. "You suppose Elka will be going after the drivers who saw her kill the Corrales cop? Or at least the second one who must have gotten a good look at her."

"While driving around with a body in the back of her car?" Lee shook his head. "I think Elka will want to get rid of the body and the car instead of worrying about a witness."

"Maybe she'll just toss the body into a trash bin or an irrigation ditch."

"She's obviously a pro, and knows the consequences of taking out a police officer. She'll go to ground as quickly as she can if she has any common sense. We're getting bulletins and color photos out now, and the entire state has been alerted, especially up and down the valley," Logan said. He reached into his jacket and pulled out two full-color flyers, giving one to each of them.

"The ex-CIA man, Rogers. He's been told?" Lee asked, looking at the photo of the vampire woman casually.

"Yes, almost immediately. And if the IDs from the motel staff where Rogers was staying in Los Alamos are accurate,

Elka was even a guest there until all the extra security arrived and the ex-spook moved out. They remembered her accent, which tipped the scale on a positive ID," Logan said. "I've already been in contact with the Secret Service but you two watch your backs as well. We just don't know for certain where she'll strike next."

"Everyone knows to be especially vigilant at night?" Diane added, glancing over at Lee.

"Yes, but it didn't help the Corrales cop that much, did it?" Logan crossed his arms across his chest. "Now tell me what you were up to last night that has Officer Hawk smelling like a gym locker."

Bridget was driving south, now across the river in Albuquerque's North Valley. Elka had killed a policeman—a very stupid thing to do for any number of reasons. Usually Elka was very smooth with men, so the only reason Bridget could think of for killing the officer was that Elka had been identified.

To make matters worse, Bridget knew that many American police units carried video cameras. The Corrales officer's vehicle had probably had one as well. If she hadn't thought of this and taken the videotape when she fled the scene, Elka—and anyone associated with her—would become the object of an intense statewide search.

It would be too risky going to Elka's apartment now. If Elka's photo had been shown on TV, one of the tenants or the rental-office clerk might lead the police to the apartment she'd rented on Montgomery Avenue.

She couldn't go near Elka now without making certain it was safe. Getting caught would mean going to jail, and in the lockup she'd have no access to sunblock. The first time she was forced outside, she'd go up in flames like a

105-pound Fourth of July sparkler. The real problem was that Elka's survival instincts were taking second place to her desire for revenge, but she wouldn't be pulled into that kind of craziness. Her own safety and well-being were tops on her list. Retribution at any cost was nothing short of suicidal and Bridget wanted no part of that.

She pulled over into one of the parking spaces beside a restaurant on Fourth Street and turned off the engine. No sense in wasting gas while she evaluated the situation. As Bridget replayed her meeting with Elka and the killing of the officer over in her mind, she suddenly realized that her own vehicle would probably show up in the tape as well. It would be dangerous to assume her vehicle tag hadn't been recorded. She had to get rid of the vehicle immediately, or at least switch plates.

But she was a vampire, and even in the minute or less it would take to get into somebody's car or remove the rear plate, she could burn to a crisp. She'd be better off finding some quiet, shady spot where she could park among other vehicles. An apartment complex would do fine, one with carports. She'd just have to make sure she didn't get somebody else's spot and attract attention.

Then Bridget remembered Agent Lopez's address—an apartment. It was worth a look. A new plan started to form in her mind as she started the car engine.

Less than an hour later Diane and Lee arrived at her apartment in the small complex in Albuquerque's Northeast Heights, weary, hungry, and both in need of a bath.

Diane climbed out of the car quickly, moving ahead of Lee a few feet to unlock the door. As he followed her up the sidewalk he took the opportunity to look around, especially alert for Elka now. Ahead on the sidewalk a young man in a business suit was carrying an infant strapped into a car seat as his wife, girlfriend, or whatever hurried along behind him, digging through her purse and grumbling about the car keys. She was wearing one of those real-estate-agent jackets, so it wasn't hard to guess where she worked.

In one of the parking slots beneath the facility's carport a pretty blonde who either was ditching high school or looked young for her age was putting on lipstick in the rearview mirror of her car. The girl glanced over and smiled, then went back to the makeup. He didn't remember having seen her before, but maybe it was because he and Diane were usually elsewhere by this time of the morning.

"You need a shower more than me, so I go first," Diane said, taking a quick look around her apartment when they stepped in to make sure it hadn't been disturbed.

"You first? Where is the logic in that? I thought Logan was going to spray me with disinfectant." Lee chuckled as he closed and locked the door. It smelled a little musty in here, but at least he knew they were relatively safe.

Diane kicked off her shoes, removed her jacket, then started to unbutton her blouse. Looking up, she saw Lee watching and turned red. "Sorry, still not used to having a man around," she mumbled, then walked into the bedroom.

Out of his view now, she answered his question. "Here's my unshakable reasoning. You ran to Mexico and back, crawled around the desert for the good part of two days, then went hand-to-hand with a wolf. Obviously you're going to get the bathroom all filthy and muddy and it will take hours to get it clean again. I can be in and out of there in ten minutes. Besides, you can get breakfast started. You think you make better coffee than I do, and you've got to be hungrier than me."

"That's the truth," Lee yelled as he heard the bathroom door close. He was already in the kitchen area.

"What's wrong with my coffee?" Diane yelled back, getting the last word before the water started running in the shower.

As Lee added coffee to the small percolator, he thought about how much he was getting used to spending time with Diane.

Not much more than forty minutes later Lee walked back into the kitchen area. A fresh coat of sunblock, clean clothes, and the .45 in his pocket made him feel invigorated and at ease. He'd developed the ability long ago to go without sleep for days at a time. Diane was buttering the French toast he'd begun earlier while sipping on a mug of coffee. He picked up his own mug, topped it off again, and took a long sip.

"Well, we know from what Logan told us that Elka was watching Rogers. I'd say that tends to rule out you, me, or the President as targets, wouldn't you?" Diane asked, handing him a plate with six pieces of French toast and several pieces of microwaved bacon.

"Hell if I know." He took the plate, then joined her at the table, handing her the maple syrup. "Muller apparently communicated with her during the time he was in New Mexico, but we have no way of knowing how much, if anything, she knows about us. Elka might be on somebody's payroll right now. Paul Rogers must have made a lot of enemies when he was a case officer in the Company. Even when Muller and his people were after us they kept their focus pretty much on the job at hand."

"If she's not here on a personal vendetta, that means her target has to be Rogers or the President."

"Rogers is ex-CIA. Anybody in the Middle East who's been a target of the Agency could have hired her. Or maybe she's just out for revenge. She was watching him, not us. Then again, what we did had some lethal consequences that led to the death of her husband, brother, and his wife. So we may be on her list somewhere, but unless there are more in her family the CIA doesn't know about, it's just Elka now."

"And now that her presence in known, her plans could change," Diane said.

Lee nodded; then, after a moment's pause, he spoke. "For the next few days, in addition to our work on the Silver Eagle case, we need to keep an eye out for anything that might indicate that there's a link between what happened to Muller and his people and the President's visit. We have to make sure the President is protected. As for Rogers . . ."

Diane nodded. "He has his own stepped-up security and, as a CIA case officer, should know how to protect himself at some level. The only problem is, a vampire is many times more dangerous than a simple trained assassin. And we can't tell him what he's dealing with."

"Agreed," he said. "I recommend that we press your SAC to recommend that the President cancel his visit or send someone else in his place. But there's a problem with that too."

"If Elka is really targeting the President and is tailing Rogers just to create a diversion, she'll make her move later on in some other state, or D.C., and we—well, you—won't be around to counter her special abilities," Diane said.

"Yeah, it puts us in a tough situation. Then again maybe she's doing all this just to smoke us out," Lee suggested. "Muller could have told her all about us before he died. What if it's personal, and everything else is the diversion?"

"I hadn't thought of that. Meanwhile, we have this other little matter to deal with—skinwalkers and cop killers."

"I know." He glanced at his watch. "Guess we'd better

finish up here and head for the office. We're going to have to spring the trap, and for that to happen, we'll have to convince Silver Eagle to change their delivery plans." Lee swallowed the last bites of French toast, washed it down with coffee, then sat back while Diane continued to eat.

"You don't have to wait for me," Diane said. "Start cleaning up and loading the dishwasher and I'll join you in a minute. Then make that call to the local state police office and let's see if we can get the ball rolling."

As soon as they arrived at their downtown jewelry business Diane made a call to the Silver Eagle number, with Lee listening in case something was said in Navajo in the background. Stump answered almost immediately, and Diane looked over at Lee, who shrugged. They'd both been expecting Angela to answer.

Diane requested an additional set of matched stones for squash blossoms and was told that they were already separating the order placed two days earlier. They should expect a delivery later in the day and to have the cash ready.

"There's a complication I think you should know about," Diane said before Stump could hang up.

"We don't like complications. You'll only get what you can pay for. Don't make me have to tell my boss about this," Stump grumbled.

"It has nothing to do with money." Diane looked over at Lee, who held up his hand, palm first, to remind her to wait and let Stump think about it for a few seconds.

"Get to the point then," Stump pressed.

"An officer from the state police department called us this morning as soon as we arrived at our business. He had all kinds of questions about some illegal activity in the local jewelry wholesale business, and because we're new in the business he wanted to know if anyone had approached us about making deals under the table. I think you're being investigated. Is that going to be a problem? We don't want to have the stuff delivered, then as soon as we open our wallets a SWAT team kicks in the door," Diane added.

Lee smiled.

"Shit. Think they're watching *your* building?"

"I doubt it, they can't have anything on *us*, not unless one of your people rolled over on us and, even then, nothing has changed hands yet. It may have just been routine because we *are* new. But let's try to come up with something without talking about this on the phone. If they get suspicious and bug our telephone line, then we're *all* screwed," Diane emphasized.

There was a pause while Stump was obviously speaking to someone else. But he must have had his hand over the mouthpiece, because they couldn't hear anything. Fifteen or twenty seconds went by, and then he spoke again. "At nine tonight be where you were when we first met. Then we can arrange a place for the delivery. Bring the cash with you," Stump added.

"I was hoping to get this done earlier. How about this afternoon instead?" Diane responded.

"Nine tonight or never."

Diane shrugged and Lee nodded reluctantly.

"Fine. But no goods, no money," Diane replied.

There was another pause. "Just be there. And don't bring any company except for your partner. We won't be alone." Stump hung up.

Lee and Diane both hung up. "There goes our hope of goading them into a shootout during daylight. Had it gone down that way, we could have put them out of business forever," he said. "I wonder if they want to make the transaction in the parking lot at Cabezon's? We can't risk a fire fight in a crowded place like that."

"If they're paranoid now—and they have good reason to be—they'll probably bring the stuff in a separate vehicle. Once they confirm that we're alone, they'll send us to another location to conduct business. They'll probably have some of their people watching us too. I'd guess some isolated location, with some of the watchers shape-shifted," Diane answered.

"It'll make it a lot harder getting any backup close enough to be any help. If some are in wolf mode, they'll have a better chance of getting away too. Our people aren't likely to shoot what they think is just a big dog unless it attacks us or them."

"So we'll have to take the responsibility ourselves, even if the animal rights groups are going to hear about it," Diane said. "We can't just shoot those who are in human form without provocation. Any ideas on how to set them into a frenzy to make sure they get hostile?"

"No sweat." Lee smiled, knowing she'd know exactly what he meant.

# CHAPTER 16

Less than an hour went by before they received another call. Lee picked it up. "You recognize my voice?" Stump snapped.

"Yes. Recognize mine?" Lee replied, pressing the button on the speaker so Diane could listen in.

"Smartass. We won't be meeting with you tonight."

"Why not?"

"It's crowded in that neighborhood today. Check the news. We'll meet at the same place and time tomorrow night instead."

Stump hung up.

"All the law enforcement roaming around the area must have bothered them. The Corrales patrolman was killed within a mile of that restaurant," Diane said. "And he's probably thinking about our phone being bugged. He didn't want to name another meeting place. Notice how cryptic he was?"

"It's all for the better, I guess. The President is still coming in tomorrow for the ceremony at the base," Diane added, "and the search for Elka has moved farther south, closer to the airport and base. This change of plans by Silver Eagle will give us the opportunity to humor Logan and spend some time out of the office searching for any sign of Elka Pfeiffer."

Lee nodded. "In a metropolitan area with nearly a half-million people, there's only a slim chance that we'll come across any of the skinwalkers. Hopefully by the time we make our last move on the Silver Eagle pack, the President will be safely on the way to Washington, Texas, or wherever he's going next."

After coordinating their efforts with other law-enforcement officers in order to eliminate duplication of efforts, Lee and Diane cruised through all the city neighborhoods within rifle reach and sight lines of the airport. Diane went door to door to question people at home while Lee checked out those businesses where he could go inside, out of the sun. No one reported having seen a stranger in the area matching Elka's description.

Later that afternoon, the Corrales police officer's body was discovered in the Rio Grande bosque north of Corrales. Then, around five-thirty, as downtown parking garages finally emptied for the day, Elka's car was discovered by an attendant. Both sites had immediately been inundated with personnel from several agencies, so Lee and Diane stayed clear.

A building-to-building search began in the downtown area, but Lee doubted Elka was huddled somewhere in an office or the shadow of a building. Three cars had already been reported stolen in the area, and one had probably been taken by the vampire woman.

"Well, if Elka Pfeiffer has a partner, all she would have had to do was call and arrange for a meet in the underground parking area. Or there could be a fourth stolen car that hasn't been discovered missing yet. Security cameras in the garage don't show any problems, apparently, but they didn't cover the entire level, just the entrances and exit. There're lots of possibilities," Diane said.

"She could be anywhere, and once the sun sets, in about a half hour, Elka will be free to roam. Your suggestion to Logan that base security bring out their night scopes to check for a sniper tonight was a good one," Lee said.

"What do we do next? Silver Eagle is on hold until tomorrow," she said. "We could always check with the hotel and motel desks in the metro area and see if anyone recognizes Elka."

"APD and the sheriff's department have people working on that, supposedly. Why don't we pay a visit to the CIA man, Rogers? Maybe he can tell us something he doesn't even know he knows about Elka and the rest of her terrorist group."

"I'll call and find out where he's staying at the moment, then let him know we're coming." Diane made a quick call to the Bureau's local office, then contacted Rogers at the number she was given—a local hotel.

They were headed south on I-25, less than a mile away from the new high-rise hotel just northwest of the airport, when an ambulance, sirens wailing, flew by on the northbound section of the freeway. The emergency vehicle was escorted by two police cars, following close behind.

"Oh crap, Diane. You think something's happened to Rogers?" Lee glanced in his rearview mirror. "There are two hospitals in that direction."

"There's a police escort, and that's unusual. Hang on, I'll call."

Diane listened to the phone ring, then finally someone answered. "Okay. We'll be there in a few minutes," she answered in a clipped tone, then turned to Lee. "Rogers was just attacked, but apparently he escaped injury and is back in his hotel room. I'm speaking to one of the security people."

"See if you can find out who's in the ambulance," Lee pressed, taking the freeway exit east, then turning onto the street where the hotel was located.

"Right. If it's Elka, then she won't be hurt for long."

"Damn, he hung up." Diane started to redial, but had to stop and hang on as Lee made a quick turn into the motel's parking lot. A police car with emergency lights flashing was blocking a row of vehicles and an EMT vehicle was beside it. "Never mind, we're here."

Diane got to the sidewalk first, stopped, and held out her badge as two security people in black jackets came forward, blocking her way to the ground-floor hotel room behind them.

Lee noted the men were both over six-four and as solid as rocks. They were also on high alert. Both had a hand on the grip of their weapons when they saw him right behind Diane.

"Paul Rogers. He's inside and okay?" Diane asked. "I need to ask him about the perp. Where is she?"

"How'd you know it was a woman?" One of the guards, an older man with gray around his temples, took a step forward, his eyes narrowing.

"The flyers," his partner muttered, putting a hand on his shoulder.

"Where did it happen, and what did she do?" Lee wondered why Rogers wasn't dead if Elka had been the attacker.

"That Pfeiffer woman jumped him under the breezeway leading to the restaurant," said the young, black guard, who looked ex-military. He pointed to a covered area between two buildings which led into a restaurant.

Two EMTs were picking up their gear while police officers strung yellow crime-scene tape around the section of covered walkway. "The woman wrestled our client to the ground, screaming and calling him a traitorous bastard. They squirmed around so much neither one of us could get a hold on her."

Diane looked at Lee curiously. "That doesn't sound like Elka to me."

"That's the name Rogers . . . the client used. He recognized her right away," the older guard answered.

Lee shook his head. It still didn't make sense. "What happened to the perp? She was hurt, right?"

"While they were rolling around she grabbed Rogers's gun. He managed to turn the muzzle around, and it went off. She was gut-shot," the black man said. "The ambulance is taking her to the university medical center."

"Stay close, she may have a partner," Lee said, then motioned toward Diane as a bright light came on. "Time to leave," he added, turning away. There was a television news team on the scene now, and neither one of them could afford to show up on a local broadcast.

"Let's hope we get to the hospital in time." Diane nodded, stepping away quickly.

"She looked pretty far gone to me," the older guard called out, but Lee and Diane were already hurrying for his car and didn't respond.

Lee pulled out onto the street as Diane adjusted her seat belt and reached down into her jacket to verify that she still had her big lockback knife. "If that really was Elka, why didn't she kill Rogers? She had to be holding back."

"Yeah, unless it really wasn't Elka, despite what the security said. A vampire, male or female, can kick any normal human's ass in hand-to-hand. There's no way he could have twisted a gun around in her hand so she shot herself. Either she's playing some kind of game, or we have the world's biggest coincidence."

"We don't believe in coincidences." Diane nodded. "Think we can get there before Elka, if that's really her, heals herself?"

"I'm working on that." Lee had already reached the freeway ramp, and was now accelerating up onto I-25. The hospital exit was less than three minutes away, so the ambulance was already there.

Diane was on the cell phone again, trying to raise someone at University Hospital who could alert additional security. It was completely dark now and Elka would be much harder for a mortal to locate if she managed to get away from the lights.

"I'm parking in the emergency area," Lee said as they roared east up Lomas Avenue, weaving back and forth between lanes as he fought drive-home traffic. "Damn, I wish I had my department unit right now."

Barely missing a red light, Lee cut across traffic and screeched to a stop by the emergency-room entrance. He jumped out and ran toward the double doors, going slow enough not to give away his speed capabilities, but faster than most humans could move. Diane was somewhere behind him.

Lee came to a quick stop inside, almost colliding with an orderly pushing a wheelchair across the small emergency room lobby. "Excuse me, where did they take the woman who just arrived?" he asked.

Diane entered just then, her badge in the air. "FBI. We need an answer now!" Lee was already moving toward the double doors that had the words EMERGENCY ROOM painted upon them.

"Hold on!" A stern-looking Chicano woman in her forties stood up from behind a counter just to the right of the entrance. "Two officers are already inside with the patient. Wait right here," she insisted.

Diane got right up in her face. "Two aren't going to be enough when she wakes up." She reached down over the counter and pressed the button that released the lock.

There was a loud thud that shook the wall, then the clanking ring of metal.

Lee was first through the door. One APD officer was lying on the floor, clutching at his chest, his legs moving in slow motion as he groaned in agony. The other was face-down, blood running out onto the tile floor from his head. A nurse in scrubs was screaming, trying to support a doctor who was down on his knees, gagging. Stainless-steel tools and pans were all over the floor.

A heavy wooden door had been kicked open so hard it had splintered, the glass and wire panel in the middle shattered. Beyond was a dimly lit corridor and stairs leading up.

"Where does that go?" Lee shouted, grabbing a woman in scrubs with a stethoscope around her neck.

"Laundry, storage areas, staff lounge," she answered. "You're not allowed . . ."

"Neither is she." Diane stepped on through, moving carefully for a few steps until she was clear of the slippery glass and debris on the waxed floor.

"Have security cover every exit. The woman has a gun!" Lee yelled back at the emergency-room staff still on their feet as he followed Diane up the flight of stairs.

"She grabbed one from a cop?" Diane whispered as Lee came up beside her.

"I thought I saw an empty holster. Even if she isn't armed, the civilians need to stay out of her way," Lee whispered as he moved quickly forward.

Diane nodded. "Once the story gets around about her taking out two cops from her gurney, that should reinforce their caution."

Lee and Diane continued down the hall, hurriedly checking inside an empty linen storage area, a laundry full of churning machines and three sweating employees, and a staff lounge with two women in scrubs playing cards.

A loud boom, metallic rather than from a gunshot, came from somewhere ahead. Lee ran forward, taking a corner so fast he bounced off the wall on the other side of the hall. Someone was standing in a half-opened door at the end of the passage. It was Elka, barefooted but still in bloody sweatshirt and jeans. She raised a hand in his direction.

"Gun!" Lee yelled, diving to the floor as a bullet ricocheted past him and struck the end wall.

Diane poked her head around the corner, pistol leading the way. Elka fired again, then dove out of sight down a set of stairs.

Lee rose to his knees, his pistol pointed in the direction Elka had gone. "You okay?"

"I'll cover you. Go!" Diane called.

Lee ran to the doorway leading downstairs and hugged the wall. Glancing over, he noted a large dent in the metal door near the latch. So much for keys. Hearing the vampire wrecking crew at the bottom of the stairwell, he took a half step forward and peeked over the edge, ducking back just before Elka, at the bottom, fired two more rounds up the stairwell. The bullets struck a lighted Exit sign on the ceiling, shattering the bulb and darkening the hall even more—theoretically.

There was another loud thud, and then a loud electric bell went off—an alarm.

Diane came running up and actually slid three feet before coming to rest opposite him. They both looked down at once.

"She went outside!" Diane shouted.

Lee looked down below the front sight of his pistol. At the bottom of the flight was a barred door with an alarm and a sign that read EMERGENCY EXIT, ALARM WILL SOUND WHEN DOOR IS OPENED.

Lee took the flight down in two steps, stopping at an open window beside the door, which led down still another flight of stairs. Glancing out the window, he saw that the stairs led to the roof of the ground floor. Beyond that was a section of the parking lot reserved for doctors and staff. "She didn't take the stairs, she went out onto the roof."

Diane joined him, breathing hard. "Is she back in the shadows there against the wall?"

Lee looked. "No, but there are some imprints in the roof gravel. She probably jumped over the parapet and down to the pavement."

"What now? She could be long gone."

"This is on the south side of the building. Take the stairs down, then make sure she didn't cut back into the building. Check the parking lot and see if she's trying to hot-wire a car. But be very careful," Lee said, putting away his pistol and climbing up onto the window frame. "I'll meet you outside."

Diane started to speak, but he launched himself over the metal frame and dropped down onto the roof with a crunch, bending at the knees to reduce the shock. Like stepping off the curb, he thought, then glanced down from the roof at the nearly full parking lot, illuminated by floodlights for the night-vision-impaired.

Seeing nothing that got his immediate attention, Lee moved toward the parapet, then suddenly heard crunching gravel above and behind him.

"Crap!" Lee dove back toward the window. He felt a stinging pain in the back of his right leg at the same instant a boom sounded above his head. Lee rolled onto his back, trying to bring his pistol around and up.

A woman cursed, and then a revolver appeared over the roof edge above him pointed down in his direction. There was a click, then another curse. Fighting the numbness in his leg, Lee aimed, but held off firing when the hand disappeared.

Lee stood, shakily, and heard footsteps fading across the

roof above. Clambering up onto the window ledge, he leaped up and grabbed hold of a drainpipe, then pulled himself on up to the roof. He saw movement out of the corner of his eye just as Elka dropped out of sight below the roof level.

Limping across the roof as quickly as he could with a bullet wound in his calf, Lee came to the spot where Elka had disappeared. The revolver she'd been using was lying on the roof. The click he'd heard suggested she'd run out of ammo and explained why she'd left it behind. About fifteen feet below was a van. A big dent in the vehicle's roof showed where she'd jumped. In the distance, probably a hundred yards or more, he could see Elka running rapidly across the parking lot.

Lee thought about jumping down, looked down at his bloody pant leg, then decided to watch where Elka was going instead. Crossing a side street at a run, the woman disappeared down an alley and out of sight.

Lee moved back across the roof and, finding that his leg had already stopped bleeding and was healing rapidly from the inside out, climbed back down to the porch roof, then inside the hospital again.

Ten minutes later, after finding Diane and directing officers to the area where Elka had last been seen, Lee was back in his own vehicle with Diane, checking alleys and side streets in an ever-increasing spiral search. City officers were combing the entire uptown area now.

Lee knew Elka would probably break into a home or business and, undetected, steal some clothes and hole up for a while. The hours of darkness were the perfect time for vampires, and Elka was a predator with an entire city of victims to stalk. But who was her real target, and what had happened with Rogers less than an hour ago? He wasn't sure if he'd just been lucky, or if Elka was carrying out part of some greater plan.

. . .

Lee and Diane soon left the block-by-block search up to the officers already involved and decided to interview Rogers. While he was driving, Diane dialed up the CIA man's hotel room. Grumbling to herself, she quickly made two other calls.

"You mean that nobody knows where he is?" Lee demanded as Diane finally put away her phone.

She shrugged. "Either that or it's a cover story being given to everyone right now, especially the press. According to the Albuquerque Police Department, Rogers said that he'd call in later, then drove off with his own security people. Logan said he'll have Rogers give us a call as soon as he checks in. I think Rogers believes that someone tipped off Elka."

"Elka probably hung back and watched him leave Los Alamos. His motorcade involved at least three vehicles, and those big Suburbans are hard to lose. It would have been a cinch to follow him here. His security has plenty of muscle, but I doubt they're used to working against a professional like Elka."

"Logan's going to fax me a photo of the person who saw Elka kill that police officer, though he said it really doesn't show much. The license plate was stolen, so that wasn't much help either."

"So maybe Elka does have a partner. That's something else we'll have to deal with."

"Speaking of dealing with things, how's your leg?"

"The bullet passed right through. Don't let all the blood mislead you," Lee smiled. "I'm just glad that was her last bullet. Another hit might have made it very inconvenient."

"Like in your heart? You're lucky the weapon she grabbed was a revolver and only had six rounds."

Lee nodded. "How are the officers she attacked doing?"

"Both are expected to live, but Elka really manhandled them. Which raises the question, why almost kill them and not Rogers?"

"Maybe he'll be able to give us an idea." Lee was driving west toward I-25, having intended on heading south again to the hotel where Rogers had been. Now he decided to go north instead and began looking for the next exit.

"When we talk to Rogers we'll find out exactly what happened between him and Elka," Diane said.

"Let's go home, check out the fax, then we can both clean up and have something to eat. Afterward we can figure out our next move while we're waiting for the call," Lee suggested. "I gather from your side of the conversation with Logan that the President still isn't going to cancel his visit."

Diane shook her head. "No. But they're going to keep his security extremely tight and close the ceremony to everyone except base personnel, invited guests, and a few members of the press. At least the ceremony is going to be in broad daylight on the loading apron right beside a gate and those participating will come by vehicle directly to the site. I just wish we had some idea what Elka was planning."

They arrived at Diane's apartment building shortly thereafter, but before Diane could open her door, Lee reached out and touched her arm. "Wait, let's look around before we get out. We have more than one enemy looking for us now."

Diane turned her head, studying the area. About a third of the parking spaces normally occupied were vacant. "Seems normal for this time of day. People going out for dinner, a movie, dating."

"Don't see anyone waiting in their vehicles—except us," Lee said, checking everything outside within his view. "Isn't that a light on in the apartment, though?" He looked closely, seeing what appeared to be flickering lights on the living/dining area window curtain.

"In our—my apartment?" Diane ducked down lower to see out the windshield toward the second story. "Looks like the TV is on. It wasn't like that when we left." She reached down and felt for her pistol, checking the side mirror to make sure nobody was coming up from behind.

"Thieves don't usually evaluate the loot before taking it, do they?" Lee opened the door slowly, keeping an eye on the apartment windows. The bedroom was dark, and nobody was visible inside that he could spot. "Don't close your door. We want to do a silent approach. It might just be a snoopy landlord."

"Nobody is supposed to have any key except me. I had a deal with management." Diane slipped out her door, bringing up her pistol and keeping a sharp eye around them.

"I'll go up first," Lee said.

"It's my place."

"I'm harder to kill."

"That's true. Okay, just this time." Diane stopped, letting Lee get a few steps ahead. She'd provide cover and watch the windows.

"The freaking sound is on. The damn burglar is watching the news," Diane whispered.

Lee nodded but kept moving silently up the stairs. When he reached the door, he saw no signs that the entrance had been forced, but the match that had been placed in the upper jamb of the door was gone. Whoever was inside, or had gone in and left leaving the TV on, either had a key or was an expert locksmith.

Instantly thinking of Elka, he turned and mouthed the word to Diane, shrugging to make it a question. She set her jaw as she brought her pistol in line with the door, then nodded.

## CHAPTER 17

Lee switched his pistol to his left hand and slowly turned the knob. It moved freely. Nodding to Diane, he turned it completely and lunged forward, muscles coiled enough to break the deadbolt free if necessary. The door flew open with barely a sound and he dove across the dimly lit room, vaguely aware that someone was sitting on the sofa in front of the TV. Rolling and coming to a crouched position, Lee swung his pistol up. "Don't move!"

Seated on the sofa in front of the television, looking over at him with her hands up and an anxious expression on her face, was an attractive long-haired blonde barely out of her teens, dressed in tight jeans and a baggy sweatshirt. "Don't shoot me, Officer Hawk. Or should I call you Lee Nez?" Her voice was a bit shaky, but the words came out as if they'd been rehearsed.

"Who the hell are you?" Diane said, peering around the door. Her pistol was aimed at the young woman's head.

"I'm Bridget. You must be Special Agent Lopez—Diane in the card you sent Officer Nez in Las Cruces."

Diane stepped forward and closed the door, locking it with her left hand while she kept her handgun directed toward the woman seated on the sofa. Then Diane flipped on the light switch. Bridget was clearly visible now, even to her.

"I'll check out the rest of the apartment," Diane said.

Lee nodded, but kept his pistol and eyes directed toward the young woman while Diane checked the other areas of the apartment. She returned within the minute, indicating with a thumbs-up that the place was clear. Diane's weapon was still out, and she pointed it toward Bridget again.

Lee spoke. "I noticed you in a car outside this morning when we left, Bridget, putting on makeup. You're wearing a lot of sunscreen and it smells like the brand I use. Does that mean what I think it does?"

"That all depends, Officer Nez. Agent Lopez *does* know what you really are, doesn't she?" Bridget smiled sweetly, looking and sounding more confident now.

Lee looked at Diane, who shrugged. "A state policeman?" she asked, not lowering her weapon a centimeter.

"You know he's more," she answered, not taken in by Diane's evasion. "I'm speaking of the undead, Nosferatu—vampires." She smiled, showing that her hands were empty as she stretched and yawned, trying to appear at ease, though Lee thought he could see nervousness in those blue eyes. "I've been waiting all day for you two to return. I turned on the television so I wouldn't surprise you and get myself shot. I managed to stop myself from raiding your cupboards and refrigerator, but I'm really hungry now. If I can have something to eat, I'll tell you what's going on."

Lee didn't move, though he finally smiled. "What are you doing *here*, Bridget?"

"I'm supposed to be helping Elka Pfeiffer kill her enemies, including you, Officer Nez. She was going to pay me a *lot* of money. I could probably get a bonus for killing Agent Lopez too. But after seeing Elka kill that policeman this morning—I decided there were limits to what I'd do for money."

Bridget gestured toward the kitchen table. "My pistol

and ammunition are over there, well out of reach for even someone as fast as me. My purse is there too, but all I have in it are makeup, my phony ID and billfold, car keys . . . stuff like that. There's a fax in your machine with my picture. It was taken by a police camera, so you can't tell for sure it's me, but it is."

Diane took a few steps toward the table, but Lee kept his eye on the innocent-looking young woman. No vampire was innocent anymore, not even the decent, moral ones.

"There's a fax from Logan here, and her fully loaded .380 handgun along with an extra clip containing four rounds." Diane examined the contents of the small, black leather handbag, laying them out on the table. Then she turned to look at Bridget. "Where's your knife, Bridget?"

"You mean the one I carry in case I have to cut off somebody's head—if I'm attacked by an enemy who happens to also be a vampire?" Bridget sat up, then bent down and lifted the hem of her pant leg up enough to reveal a flat, long-bladed dagger in a soft leather case taped to her ankle. "But you could shoot before I could pull it out, so relax."

"Where's Elka, Bridget? We came across her at a hospital not long ago." Lee moved to the side of the window and looked outside. For all he knew, Elka could be within fifty feet.

"Was that her I heard about on TV? There was a report of someone being attacked at a motel by a woman who went berserk. I understand she was taken to a hospital, then escaped from the emergency room." Seeing the answer on their faces, she added, "I should have known that was Elka. "She' s been freaking out like that from time to time lately."

The young woman looked down at Lee's pant leg, where there was a hole and dried-up blood. "It looks like you've been shot, Officer Hawk . . . Nez. Did Elka do *that*?"

"Yeah, at the hospital. But getting back to her current location . . ."

"I really don't know where she is. I haven't seen her at all since she killed the officer this morning and, just so you know, I wasn't involved in that at all. The police video used to lift the photo on that fax you received proves that," Bridget said, gesturing to the table. As she started to get up, Diane tensed slightly.

"Sorry. I understand you have no reason to trust me. Want me to get rid of the knife? It's my only weapon now."

Bridget reached down and slowly eased the blade out of the holster with her thumb and forefinger, then tossed it gently to the floor. It stuck in the carpet. "Ooops."

"You starting to relax a bit now, aren't you?" Lee said, taking the knife, then sitting in the chair across from her.

"Finally. I sat outside in that car nearly all day, worrying about the possibility of being attacked by you two and having to defend myself. Believe me, the last thing I want is a fight. The past few months have been scary enough." Bridget looked down at her hands, and told them about being forced to become a vampire, then how she'd used her skills as a thief to help the group.

"I was never given a choice, not from day one. They would have killed me if I hadn't obeyed them." She looked at Diane and Lee, tears in her eyes.

"Now that I'm away from Elka and the rest of them are dead, I've got the chance to start living my own life again without being afraid. I've decided to go for it. Elka's on her own. I'm putting myself in your hands." Bridget folded her legs up beneath her on the sofa and leaned back, crossing her arms over her chest, then smiled self-consciously as she wiped the tears away from her eyes with her fingertip.

Diane took a step forward, lowering her pistol to her side, but keeping it firmly in her grip. "Interesting story. But you said you'd come to New Mexico to kill Lee—Officer Hawk—and some other people as well. You want to tell us more about that now, Bridget?"

After Diane had gone outside, checked out Bridget's car, and moved it away from the apartment complex in case it harbored a tracking device, they all worked together to fix dinner. Soon the three of them were seated at the table, sipping iced tea and eating lasagna.

By then Bridget had told them about her earlier meeting with Elka, about the death of the police officer in Corrales, and about their decision to split up and go in different directions.

Then Bridget confirmed much of what Lee and Diane knew already about the activities of the terrorists in New Mexico, and Jochen Pfeiffer's death.

"The pieces are all coming together now," Lee said. "But one thing just isn't clear to me. Who is Elka after? Rogers? The President? Me? Someone else? And do you think she'll change her plans now that she's the subject of a statewide dragnet?"

Bridget took a small bite of garlic bread, then pretended to gag. "Garlic bread? No, no, no!"

Lee chuckled, but Diane shook her head and rolled her eyes. "Lee already pulled that one on me."

"Vampires have a unique sense of humor." She took a sip of iced tea before continuing. "In answer to your question, Elka told me it was personal—for her at least. So, no, I don't think she'll back off."

"It was personal for her, but not for you?" Diane pressed.

"All I wanted was the chance to make enough money so I could stop being a thief and never again have to risk getting caught and going to jail. She promised to pay me for killing you, Officer Nez, and more if I helped her kill Paul Rogers. But if it really was her at the motel, then something's seriously wrong. That incident just doesn't make sense."

"You think she may be mentally unstable?" Lee asked.

"I'm no shrink, but I wouldn't doubt that for a minute. She's changed a lot since the Plummers, Muller, and Jochen got killed. When Jochen was captured by the Iraqis and locked up in prison, she was determined to trade the plutonium that was hidden here in New Mexico—stuff that you took and hid elsewhere—in exchange for his life. But that plan ended when everyone she cared about got killed. She's been alive for two hundred years but in two weeks all her family and close friends were dead. Grief does weird things to people."

"And now . . ." Lee pressed.

"The last time I talked to her for more than a minute we went over her plan, but I know she didn't tell me everything. She doesn't trust me—that's why she offered me money and my freedom if I helped her out now. It was her way of insuring I'd stick around. But again, she wasn't really giving me another option, though it may have sounded that way. If I hadn't agreed to her terms, she would have turned on me. I'm no match for her."

Bridget looked at Lee, then Diane. "Elka said Rogers was her main target, but she was lying about that, or maybe she changed her plan. If her target had really been the CIA man, she could have snapped his neck like a pencil. But to wrestle with him, then let herself get shot . . . that just doesn't sound like Elka. The cop she killed was just doing his job and she broke his neck like he was nothing."

Diane's cell phone rang just then and they all jumped. Bridget started giggling and Lee couldn't help but smile. Diane scowled at them both, then stood and walked away, speaking in low tones, obviously remembering how good vampire hearing was.

"Is she going to tell whoever it is about me?" Bridget asked, hearing Diane close the bedroom door.

Lee shrugged. She looked vulnerable now, but he didn't know if she was playing him or not. Bridget was innocent-looking and attractive, and undoubtedly knew how to use both of those attributes to her advantage. Remembering Angela, he decided to be extra careful with this particular vampire. Though everything she'd told them so far seemed believable, the best lies were 90 percent truth.

"A couple of questions. Where did you get the pistol, and why are some rounds missing from the second clip?" he asked.

Bridget rolled her eyes. "I followed a guy home from a sporting-goods store, then, when he left the house, broke in and found the pistol. There were two clips, but one wasn't fully loaded. I fired a couple of shots into a hillside later on just to get a feel for the weapon."

Lee thought she might be lying about the gun or bullets, but why? Had she shot someone and they just didn't know about it yet? He looked at her skeptically, letting her know he wasn't buying the story.

"I understand you not trusting me yet. Maybe you never will. But you can return the pistol to the owner and prove I'm telling you the truth. Anything to give me back my life. I promise I had nothing to do with the death of that police officer and I won't try to hurt you or your girlfriend, partner, or whatever she is. I just want the chance to disappear."

Bridget looked around the apartment as if someone

were listening, lowered her voice, then continued. "For my own safety—and you know why—I'll have to try and escape if you take me to jail or someplace like that. All it takes are a few minutes in the sun and I'm toast."

Diane came back into the room and Lee's eyebrows rose in question, not knowing if Diane wanted to speak in front of Bridget. "Something I should know about?"

Diane nodded. "A confirmation from the source on Elka's attack. She came out from the restaurant and lunged at him from beneath the shade of the walkway, wrestling him to the ground before the security guards could intervene. During the attack she kept screaming that he'd killed her husband and family. She grabbed Rogers's .38 from the holster—but he managed to twist the barrel around and she accidentally shot herself in the side."

"And Rogers wasn't even hurt?" Lee asked.

"He was scratched and his hair was pulled, but thinks he'll get off with just a few bruises," Diane replied.

"Elka was playing with him," Bridget said firmly. "She's strong enough to crush his fingers like they were Cheetos."

"Obviously. So what happened then?" Lee prodded Diane.

His partner continued. "Elka lay there groaning and clutching her side until the EMTs arrived, along with two squad cars. Then they took her away in the ambulance we saw. One more thing. Elka called Rogers by the name he'd used as a CIA case officer."

"Stands to reason," Lee said.

"Rogers admitted that Elka came to him a few months ago to get the Agency's help in freeing her husband. Rogers promised Elka he'd help, then bailed on her. Of course he didn't word it that way. But reading between the lines, my bet is that he was the one who compromised Elka's husband. A short time after that, he got out of the CIA and started working for the DOE as a security consultant. A real fast-track deal. Tomorrow the President is going to be shaking his hand and patting him on the back for service to his country."

"The Peter Principle. Being promoted to your highest level of incompetence," Lee grumbled.

"Never heard of it." Bridget shook her head.

"Before your time." Lee smiled.

Diane and Lee exchanged glances. They hadn't had the chance to discuss what to do about Bridget, much less how much to trust her—if at all. And although well-nourished vampires didn't need much sleep unless they were healing an injury or starved, Diane was yawning almost constantly now.

"You talked to Rogers quite a while, Diane. He open up to you a little? I'd always heard that the CIA and the FBI were mortal enemies, fighting over turf, funding, prestige." Lee was just making conversation now, not wanting to discuss anything really important in front of Bridget until they'd decided what to do about her.

"That's true enough. But maybe Rogers is less paranoid now that he's no longer on the Agency's payroll. Or more likely, he needs any ally he can find," Diane replied.

"He no longer has power over so many lives," Bridget said softly. "Elka said he was a manipulator. I guess it takes one to know one."

Neither Lee nor Diane replied, and the three of them sat there for a few minutes. Finally Lee spoke. "Bridget, I suppose you know Diane and I are going to have to discuss exactly what to do about you."

"I wondered when you were going to bring that up. But like I said, I'm not turning myself in or anything like that. I came to you, Officer Nez, because you're the only one who can really understand my situation. You both know why vampires can't allow themselves to be taken prisoner and locked up," Bridget replied. Her voice was firm, but Lee saw uncertainty and what could be fear in her eyes.

Diane smiled. "Trust is something none of us here offer or accept easily. Let's take it one step at a time. Would you mind going into the bedroom for a while so Lee and I can have a little privacy?"

Bridget thought about it a moment. "Well, okay. I don't have any other place to go at the moment." She walked toward the bedroom door, then stopped and looked back at Lee questioningly.

"We won't call the cops or the FBI on you. You have my word," Lee said.

"That's because you *are* the cops and the FBI." She shrugged, then turned, stepped into the bedroom, and closed the door.

Lee motioned for Diane to join him at the table. "Reminds me of the ancient curse that goes 'May you live in interesting times.'"

"You've got that right. Now, let's get to the point," she said, her voice low, almost a whisper. "What do we do about Blondie?" She brought out her notebook and pen, writing down one suggestion.

He nodded. Vampires could hear too damn well not to take this extra precaution.

# CHAPTER 18

"Last time we left someone alone, they turned into a panther," Diane wrote.

Lee nodded, then added, "Bridget came here on her own and put herself at our mercy. That says something."

"When I moved her car I couldn't find anything inside that would contradict what she'd been saying." Diane put down the pen and looked up toward the bedroom door. Lee had positioned himself beside her so they both had a wall to their back and could see across the room.

He picked up Bridget's pistol and examined it carefully, whispering this time instead of writing. "Loaded, and looks functional. She claims to have stolen the pistol, but she's also fired it more than once, supposedly just checking it out. I got a feeling she wasn't telling me everything about this pistol."

"You think she used it on someone?" Diane's eyebrows rose.

"Unless a body turns up somewhere, we won't know, will we? Maybe I just misread Bridget. If she's really a professional thief, chances are she's not a killer, at least not intentionally. Thieves don't want confrontations. It's bad for business," Lee answered.

"True, and she had the skills needed to break into here. That required picking two good locks."

"Becoming a vampire must have made her a formidable thief, all things considered."

"Yeah, I agree. Vampires would make great burglars. They're quiet, fast, strong, and can jump like frogs," Diane noted as she looked through Bridget's purse again, examining each item, such as the lipstick, to confirm they were not some spy device or weapon.

"Gazelle, deer, graceful cats. Not frogs," Lee corrected.

"I could have said fleas." Diane smiled, examining the purse itself.

Lee picked up the pen and wrote so she could read at the same time. "Let's keep Bridget here for now but watch what we say around her. If she's setting us up for Elka, then we can make Bridget our bait. But this bait can bite back so we have to be ready for anything."

Diane nodded, then stood, folded up the paper, and stuffed it into her pocket. "Let's confirm with Bridget that Elka doesn't know where we live, what we're doing right now, or how to find us. And look for any sign of lying or deception. If Blondie wants to get away from Elka she's going to have to cooperate with us and tells us all she knows about Elka's plans. We aren't going to baby-sit for free."

Lee walked over to the bedroom door and tapped lightly. "Bridget, we have a few questions for you."

Just then Diane's cell phone rang.

Bridget opened the door and peeked out. Lee motioned with his head for her to come out as Diane walked back toward the kitchen area. Although Diane's telephone conversation was too low for even a vampire to hear clearly, he'd managed to make out that the call was about Elka, so the caller was probably Logan.

He smiled at Bridget. "Let's go to the sofa while she's

on the phone. I need to ask you a few more questions about Elka."

Lee sat in the chair across from her, not too close. He wanted her to feel comfortable with him. If what she'd said about her background was true, he suspected she'd developed some serious skills as a con artist—many young runaways like her had been forced to play a role in order to survive.

"I know you said something about this before, but think carefully—is there any way that Elka could know or learn about this apartment? Or that you're here? Assuming you're not trying to con us, of course."

Bridget looked up at Diane, who had just come back from the kitchen.

"I'm not trying to trick you or set you up. I decided to turn myself in to you when I realized there was only one other choice. I could either help kill people and risk being killed myself, or put myself in the hands of a 'good' vampire—if that's what *you* really are." Bridget looked at Lee, but instead of validating that, he simply waited.

Bridget took a deep breath and continued. "When I spoke with Elka this morning I told her that I knew where Diane lived, but I never gave her the address. And since I got the information when I picked the lock on Lee's mailbox a few nights ago, there's no way she could know."

"You're very handy around locks," Diane said acidly.

"One of the things I did for Elka and her family was help gather information about people."

"People who were to be killed?" Diane challenged.

"Or compromised. But I didn't hurt anyone directly."

"How do you two stay in contact? Cell phones?" Lee asked.

"Sometimes, but not on this trip. Elka was worried about being monitored. We use code phrases on E-mails to set up meetings, but crucial information, like names and addresses, are only passed face-to-face."

"You have a laptop, then? Where is it?" Diane asked. "I didn't see it in your car."

"It's under the spare tire in the trunk. I can give you the codes we use, I suppose, and how we get in touch," Bridget said.

"Keep telling Lee all you can, but I'm going to have to go out for a while," she said, reaching for her jacket. "Logan wants to meet me at Elka's apartment—the address Bridget gave us earlier," she told Lee. "She wasn't there, of course, but apparently there's some evidence he'd like me to examine."

"Anything about me?" Bridget asked, her tone betraying her uncertainty.

"Not that he mentioned. You've never been there, right?" Diane asked.

"No, she gave me the address just before we separated in Corrales. After the officer was killed I decided it was time for a change in plans. There was no way I wanted to become linked to his death—or yours either. So I came here. You know the rest."

Diane nodded.

"I'll stay here with Bridget. Call if you need something," Lee said to Diane. "You might want to get that laptop out of her car on the way back, though."

"Okay. Stay safe. I'll be back as soon as I can," Diane said, then let herself out.

Lee went to the window and watched until Diane drove away. Locking the door, he walked back to Bridget, who had remained on the sofa.

"You two are more than partners. I can see the way you look at each other," Bridget said. "Elka's husband, Jochen, who was killed by the Iraqis—he wasn't a vampire. Did you know that?"

Lee shrugged. "I figured as much, him being an assassin and going into a country with so much sunshine. What else did you find out about them during the time you were together?"

"Well, I was treated like hired help, so they never told me much more than I had to know to do the jobs they gave me, and one of them always went with me. Elka is . . . was the leader, and until recently has always been really cold and analytical."

She stopped, then abruptly changed the subject. "Have you and Diane ever thought about making her a vampire?" Bridget asked.

He was thinking about how to answer that when the telephone rang. Lee walked over to the wall unit. It probably wasn't Diane or one of their supervisors, Lieutenant Richmond or SAC Logan. They would have dialed his cell number.

"Yes." Lee decided not to identify himself. He'd forwarded all his business calls here and was using two different names in addition to his real one. He couldn't afford a slipup that might cost a life.

Lee recognized Stump's voice. "We've decided to move up the delivery time. Bring the cash and meet me on the east end of the bridge closest to our last meeting place. Be there in a half hour or the sale is off."

Lee's thoughts raced. The Silver Eagle skinwalkers were throwing him a curve ball. Had Angela talked, or were they just paranoid after Raymus's death? Stump was still being cryptic, as if the call was being monitored. It was, of course.

"Can you give me an hour? I'm way up in the Heights,

and the money is in our office downtown. We weren't planning on delivery so soon, and your call was forwarded to our home." Lee needed to stall until Diane returned. They were planning on taking the skinwalkers down hard and the plan called for her backup.

"Forty-five minutes. Or no deal."

"That might be enough time. One more thing," Lee added.

"Now what?" Stump grumbled.

"Which side, north or south?" He knew that Stump was referring to the Alameda bridge, closest to Corrales, but there were really two bridges side by side.

"Just go under the eastern end. We'll find you." Stump hung up.

Lee turned and noticed Bridget had been listening. It was expected, especially because she probably didn't trust them very much yet either, for good reason.

"Sounds like cop work. Nothing about Elka?" Bridget crinkled her nose, a flirting gesture that could have disarmed most men, even a hardened policeman.

"I've got some cop work to do tonight." Lee checked his pistol and spare ammunition automatically. He left his backup .45 and commando dagger untouched, not wanting to give out too much information to the young vampire on the sofa. He also scooped up her pistol and ammunition from the table, but left the knife. Unless he took the entire silverware drawer with him, she'd still have a weapon anyway.

She saw what he was doing but didn't protest. "And Diane's not going to be here either? Don't I get a baby-sitter?" she teased.

"That would probably only complicate matters. Stay here and avoid any chance of being seen. Got that?"

"You *are* going to trust me," she said, surprised.

Letting her think whatever she wanted, Lee used the cell phone and cryptically let Diane know about Stump's call. He gave the time of the meeting, and the location of the bridge as the one closest to where she grew up. Bridget had no way of knowing where Diane had spent her childhood and that extra precaution seemed like a smart move at the moment.

Diane was now at a security command post on the base. She'd have to travel all the way across Albuquerque to back him up, but she'd be there. He hurried to the door, knowing he had to move fast to get back and forth across town, even during this time of night.

"I'll be here when you come back, probably," Bridget said, standing and walking across the room toward him.

"Probably?"

"Well, if I were to go, then you wouldn't have the problem of trying to figure out what to do with me or who to tell."

"True," he said, then paused for a long moment. "Whatever you decide to do, Bridget, stay out of trouble." He added, "I'd hate to be the one who has to kill you later on," then stepped outside quickly. "Lock the door." He hurried down to the car, keeping a sharp eye out for skinwalkers or vampires. As he reached into the backseat for his bullet-resistant vest, he smiled. His life was becoming more and more like a horror movie.

As he drove south down the freeway toward the downtown area, Lee remembered that the Silver Eagle skinwalkers knew where his office was, so it was possible they'd be waiting for him there instead.

Lee strongly suspected he was being led into a trap. The skinwalkers were changing the way they worked, and that was a bad sign, but he still had to play things out. All he had now was evidence of their smuggling operations, and he needed more. He called Lieutenant Richmond and told him about the meeting at the Alameda bridge, asking for heavily armed backup, but requested that the officers use a silent approach to avoid tipping off the Silver Eagle smugglers.

When he arrived downtown he circled the block twice, looking into every dark alley and doorway before stopping at their business. To break the pattern he parked in front and went in that entrance, avoiding the alley completely. He was in and out in five minutes with the cash in a small metal briefcase, now dusted with a powder that would show up under ultraviolet light, and carrying a tiny digital audio recorder in his button-down shirt pocket.

I-25 was only a few minutes away from their office location, and at this time of night Lee had no problem making good time northeast on the freeway to the Alameda exit. Off-Interstate traffic was heavier than he expected going west on Alameda Boulevard, but he made it to the river five minutes ahead of schedule.

Lee slowed the vehicle and pulled into a parking lot just south of Alameda where it approached the newer, wide concrete bridge. No other vehicles were there this time of night, but he'd seen the recreation area filled with cars early in the morning and on weekends. There were trails and bicycle paths that paralleled the river here, and access to the bosque and the Rio Grande.

He looked at his watch, then called Richmond again. A few officers would be in the area soon, but hadn't arrived yet. Lee asked that when his backup arrived the officers hold their positions beside the two intersections east and west of the river for at least five more minutes, then advance on foot. He wanted to make sure money and contraband changed hands first, and, if possible, get something recorded that would provide evidence for murder charges.

It had sounded very plausible, but Lee knew that the scent of the officers, even at a distance, would alert the skinwalkers, and that was why he'd really made that request. As he stepped out of the vehicle with the briefcase, he checked the direction of the wind. There was a slight breeze coming from the west, which served him well because he was on the east side of the river. The skinwalkers, unless they approached from behind, wouldn't be able to catch his real scent until just the right moment, which was part of his plan.

Lee knew he had been too far away the other night to be recognized by sight, but the wolves had picked up his real scent, the scent of the man who'd killed Raymus. Marie wouldn't let him walk away tonight.

The absence of other vehicles didn't necessarily mean he'd beat them to the meeting place. Lee walked west out of the parking area and onto a narrow asphalt path. On his left, a small, permanently flowing canal ran parallel to the river. He looked ahead to where the path continued beside the canal as both passed beneath the bridge. It was clear except for a little graffiti on the bridge pillar to his right.

There was a noise somewhere to his left and Lee saw a beaver scuttle into the canal from the bank. It swam off south with the current.

Lee passed beneath the bridge. Not far in the distance, the path made a ninety-degree turn back to the west to parallel the bridge on its north side. Lee decided that Stump had probably meant the old structure. The old Alameda bridge, now painted blue, was a narrow wood and steel structure that had been left intact just north of the new one. It now served as a pedestrian walkway and for people on bicycles or horses.

Lee turned on his recorder, then continued over the

hill, actually a long, high levee. Once across the top, he continued down the pathway and through a steel gate used by the parks department to restrict vehicle access to the bosque. Now he could see three people standing beneath the bridge about halfway to the river, which rippled quietly fifty feet behind them.

They probably didn't realize that he could see them already despite the darkness, so he had the opportunity to evaluate the situation. Stump was recognizable by his bulk even if Lee couldn't see his face. He wore a black trench coat like in some old gangster movie, and his sawed-off shotgun was visible in his right hand. The second person was one of the delivery guys, but not Long-hair. He was holding a pistol half out of his jacket pocket. It would have been invisible to a mortal even up close.

Angela, wearing a windbreaker and jeans, was standing beside a large duffel bag, which rested on the sand at her feet. She didn't appear to be carrying a weapon, and instead of watching Lee, Angela's eyes were directed toward the grove of giant cottonwood trees to the north.

Stump elbowed her, muttering something Lee couldn't quite make out. Immediately she focused in Lee's direction. Lee glanced out of the corner of his eye and saw the muzzle of a wolf down low beside the trunk of one of the trees. Angela had just sent him a warning, intentional or not.

Lee was having second thoughts about his hasty call for backup to the lieutenant. Any help was supposed to approach from both sides of the river. It had been too late to send officers along the riverbanks themselves, up and down the bosque from north and south.

The obvious direction of escape for the skinwalkers would be to the left and right along the wooded bosque, and in that environment Lee would have the advantage over any police officer. None had his speed or night vision, and he knew that any fleeing skinwalker would assume animal form the moment they had the time. The problem would arise if the Silver Eagle pack split up when the shooting started.

His and Diane's original plan had been flexible, but it had been based upon the original meeting time and the necessity of provoking violence. Tonight had quickly become a pull-it-out-of-your-ass operation. However, Lee felt very confident that his scent would incite the skinwalkers into a fight.

The instant they reacted, as skinwalkers always seemed to do without much thought, they would be taken down hard. Their guns would be his biggest problem, because bullets traveled much faster than fangs and claws, and only his torso was protected by the vest, now underneath his jacket.

*"Yáat'ééh,"* Lee greeted, then stopped. "That our stuff in the bag?"

"Could be. You have the money?" Stump grumbled.

Lee held out the briefcase. "Could be."

There was a low growl, then the sound of rustling leaves to his right. Lee turned his head and saw three enormous wolves less than fifty feet away, watching him intently. Angela had betrayed him after all.

"Those your dogs? I think the parks department requires leashes. You could get a ticket." Lee used the position of the briefcase to conceal his other hand, which now held his pistol.

Wishing Diane were here beside him and at the same time grateful she wasn't, Lee forced himself to look away from the wolves and at Stump, his biggest danger from this direction. He took another step toward the three humans, watching how the big Navajo was holding his shotgun.

As stupid as it sounded, he was going to have to force a fight and hope they didn't shoot him up too badly. "Where's Raymus?" he said loudly, turning to look at the wolves, which were circling around behind him. The female was undoubtedly Marie and her teeth were bared.

"Quit trying to bullshit us, cop. We saw you and your woman on TV!" the man with Stump and Angela yelled sarcastically. "Didn't you cops get our message last time? How many more have to die before you back off?"

Lee remembered that they'd been within sight of a camera crew over at the hotel where Rogers had been attacked, but he'd believed that they'd been far enough away. That mistake would cost him now, but on the good side, he wouldn't have to force a confrontation.

"You're all bark and no bite, delivery boy," Lee said. "Who killed the two officers anyway? Stump did the shotgun work, obviously, but which of you gutless dogs emptied your magazines on them *after* they were already down? Besides that sick puppy Raymus, of course." Lee looked over at the Marie wolf. The bitch's hair was standing up along her backbone. It was a wonder she hadn't attacked already.

"Trash talk is still trash, cop. You're not walking away, and there's not going to be any quick death for cop number three. Those two guys died in a hurry, but we're going to eat *you* alive," Stump said with a sneer.

"Oh, you think I came *alone*? My partner's up there waiting for my signal to send down the troops."

"Yeah, right. We've been here an hour and the place is deserted. Our partners here"—Stump pointed toward the wolves with pursed lips, Navajo style—"have been sniffing around. Just us and one walking, talking chew stick."

Angela was anxiously watching the others now, not him, and she hadn't shown a weapon. Unless she got the chance to shape-shift, it didn't appear she was going to be any help tonight to anyone. At least he finally knew she hadn't betrayed him.

Lee fought the distraction. Angela was just here for herself, and she wouldn't make a move to help him unless it was clear he'd already won. Lee needed to focus—and stall. Another two or three minutes and his backup would start moving in.

One of the wolves snorted, maybe Long-hair, and he knew they were now downwind enough to detect his nightwalker scent—the scent of the one they knew killed Raymus. They froze, their nostrils working overtime.

Lee knew this was his only chance. Stump and the loudmouth with the pistol couldn't shoot without hitting their own. He swung around, hurling the briefcase at the big female just as she made her move. She had to dodge before she could leap, and by then he was in a crouch, his pistol out and on target.

Lee fired two shots into her chest. The big bitch yelped as the bullets struck, but she managed to bowl him over as she slammed into his upper body.

Lee fell onto his back, concentrating on holding on to his pistol. The attack by the others was fierce, but skinwalkers just didn't have the natural instincts of the creatures they'd mimicked.

Instead of striking at his arms or legs wherever they could make contact, the two skinwalkers kept straining to grab his throat, getting in each other's way as well. They rolled around on the sand; it was like wrestling two bears at once. He managed to free his weapon for a second and shot one below the eye, pushing it away with his other arm as it suddenly relaxed.

Lee rolled up to a squatting position and twisted around just as the remaining wolf made a grab for his head from behind. A small-caliber gunshot rang out and the animal jerked, hit along the spine.

Someone cursed and Lee realized that the skinwalker

had been shot by Angela. Lee dove behind Marie's animal form and rolled, firing at the closest man. The man went down from two rounds in the chest; then Lee rolled again in the opposite direction, nearly avoiding a shotgun blast. Most of the buckshot struck the ground beside his outstretched leg, but a few caught his thigh and pain shot through him like hot needles.

"No, you idiot. Don't you know what he is?" Angela yelled, pointing a small .32 auto at Stump and firing right into the surprised man's chest, causing him to drop his shotgun. "Bitch!" Stump yelled, grabbing her pistol hand.

Lee could hear her fingers crunching under the pressure, but Angela hung on to the weapon. "Shoot him, shoot him," she screamed.

Lee tried to get a bead on Stump's head, but he kept Angela between them as he tried to wrench away the pistol. Stump punched her brutally in the face with his free hand and her head snapped back.

Lee shot Stump in the thigh and the butt and he grunted, but the bullets didn't stop him. With a mighty yell, Stump finally swung Angela around like a rag doll and the pistol in her hand went off as he tore it free. Angela sagged and he let her drop to the ground.

Lee squeezed the trigger twice more. The first round caught Stump in the center of his chest and he dropped the handgun, collapsing to his knees. There was no second shot. The action remained open on an empty chamber.

In a split second Lee had his backup .45 in his hand. Stump made the mistake of reaching for the shotgun and Lee shot him in the chest again. The man fell forward onto the sand.

A quick turn of his head showed that everyone was down. Lee found his pocket recorder, luckily still intact and in his pocket, and turned it off as he stepped quickly over to Angela, who was groaning, her hands clutching her bloody abdomen.

"I tried to help, Uncle."

Uncle? What was she talking about? Navajos sometimes gave others these titles as signs of respect, but it sure as hell was an odd time for that. "You did fine, Angela." Lee got down on his knees beside her, checking to see how badly she'd been hit. She'd been gut-shot and was losing a lot of blood. He thought about the cell phone in his jacket, if it still worked, but even the best medical care would probably be too little, too late. The only thing that might save her now was vampire blood.

Lee looked up the trail leading to the road and couldn't see anyone, though there were plenty of sirens bearing down. If Diane was coming at all it wouldn't be much longer, and the police were probably running in his direction from both east and west. It was now or never.

Lee pulled out his boot dagger and slid the blade across his wrist just enough to open a vein. His arm felt warm as blood began to flow across his skin. He pressed his wound gently into hers, then applied pressure with his other hand, hoping to slow her own blood loss.

"What are you doing, Uncle?" Angela said softly. "I'm going to die. You can't stop it. Had I been shot while in wolf form, I could have shape-shifted back into a human and healed myself, but my luck's run out."

"My blood can heal. I'm different from other people, you know." Lee looked into her eyes and for a second imagined he saw Annie in there someplace. Was his memory of his lost wife so faded now that Angela's image had taken her place? Or was there a real connection? Angela had called him uncle . . .

Angela had her eyes closed, and he examined her features without having to confront those demanding eyes.

They weren't like Annie's. His wife had been kind and gentle, but this woman was hard and manipulative. Yet the cheekbones, the lips, and the shape of the chin was so familiar.

He waited, watching Angela's wounds. There seemed to be no change, but it had been only a short time, and she was, after all, a skinwalker, not a normal human by any stretch of the imagination.

Angela opened her eyes. "Lee? Is that your real name? I *have* to tell you something . . . You've always looked at me so strangely, haven't you? Like I'm someone you've known before."

Lee nodded. He was starting to see the connection now, and it made his heart beat a little faster. He concentrated on keeping his blood mixing with hers, but now he couldn't take his eyes off her face.

"I didn't recognize you at first, not when I first saw you over by Fort Wingate that night. But later I remembered a photo my mother had of you and her sister." Angela smiled. There was a trace of blood on her lips now.

"Connie! Was that your mother?" Lee knew the truth. Connie had been Annie's little sister and had attended their wedding. He hadn't seen her since Annie's burial, but remembered reading about her death a few years ago in a car accident. Annie and Connie had looked a lot alike, and Connie had had children.

"Yes. You're my uncle, Lee Nez. But you should be eighty years old by now. I've seen some very strange things and I've become something . . . evil. But what creature are you . . . so strong and quick?" Angela's voice was nearly gone. Unless his half-vampire blood started healing her soon, she'd die.

It didn't matter what he told her now. If Angela lived,

she would be part vampire and know the truth anyway. If she died . . .

"I'm a nightwalker, Niece."

Angela was shivering. Lee held her as closely as he could, trying to transfer some heat. But he had to keep his blood in contact with hers if there was a chance at all.

She was barely able to whisper. "I've heard stories. The one who made me an animal said that if we drank the blood of a nightwalker we might become immortal. But Marie laughed . . . said that was a lie. Skinwalkers only have a few years, so we must take what we want quickly." Angela smiled. "I wanted you, even . . . my uncle."

Lee could hear someone running down the hill and he looked back. It was Diane, followed by another two officers, and he raised his arm to signal where he was.

"Look out!" Diane shouted, and Lee realized someone was coming up from the opposite direction.

As Lee reached for the .45 in his pocket, two shots rang out, then a third blast nearly shattered his eardrums.

Finally he had his pistol out. Stump was standing there, an ugly mess, the shotgun sagging to the ground at his feet. An angry wound had appeared in his forehead, and it was amazing he was still on his feet. Diane fired again and the big Navajo dropped to the sand. His feet twitched for a moment, then stopped.

Lee turned back to Angela and could see her eyes had lost their light, glazing over. "Good-bye, Niece." He eased her body down onto the sand just as Diane ran up, gasping for air.

"You okay? It looks like a massacre," Diane managed. "Sorry I was late." The officers with her began to examine the downed skinwalkers.

Lee could see more officers coming over the hill right now.

"Well, things did get out of hand quicker than I expected," Lee said.

"You tried to save Angela?" she whispered, seeing his wrist, now healing up quickly on its own.

"Yeah. Guess my blood won't work on her kind," he whispered, looking around to make sure the other cops weren't within hearing range. He covered her up with his jacket. "She saved my ass, I owed her one."

"She wasn't completely bad . . ." Diane reached over and touched his arm.

"Guess not, but I'll never know if she did it for me or for what she wanted." Lee saw flashlights along the bridge and the lights from a squad car, and realized more cavalry was about to arrive. He put his pistol into his pocket, then wiped the blade of his dagger on his pant leg and placed it back in his boot sheath.

"If it makes it any easier, try and remember that she stood with you tonight, Lee." Diane nodded, then turned to look around at the wreckage of humans and the shape-shifted animal forms three had been trapped in as they died. "You get anything on the murdered cops?"

"Enough on audio to show they were responsible." Lee showed her the recorder, then played back a few seconds of speech to verify the device had done the job. "We can close the case now—except for the missing gang members we're going to have to explain away. At least the Silver Eagle pack won't be killing any more cops."

"The international aspects of the smuggling operation will have to fall in someone else's lap now that our cover's blown. Think this'll put the presidential visit on page two tomorrow? The politicians would hate that." Diane waved to the officers coming in their direction. One was Lieutenant Richmond.

"The threat to the President still exists if Elka is still

out there somewhere in this community. She can make headlines on her own. I wish I knew what she had in mind. You're no closer than we were earlier tonight to tracking her, right?" Lee asked.

"No, not really. Maybe our houseguest can give us some suggestions," she whispered, seeing Richmond draw closer.

"If she's still there," Lee said softly.

# CHAPTER 19

Hours went by at the crime scene beneath the old Corrales bridge on Alameda, with Lee and Diane going over the details for Logan and Richmond. Lee, who did almost all the talking, had to hide his healed-up wounds and introduce some fiction, omitting his attempt to save Angela by turning her into a vampire. At least Diane didn't have to corroborate what had actually happened before she'd arrived, and the recording Lee had made satisfied both of their supervisors.

Angela was identified as the newest member of the gang, and both Lee and Diane reported that Angela had become their informant after they learned she'd witnessed the killing of the first undercover officers on the case.

The wolves were identified as trained wolf-dog hybrids belonging to the Silver Eagle gang. Lee explained that they obviously intended on killing him and ripping off the buy-money. The duffel bag didn't contain any of the smuggled Mexican silver or turquoise, only some dirty laundry.

While Lee and Diane were being debriefed, state police officers and local Bureau agents raided Frank's Automotive and the gang's house in the North Valley. Officers recovered thousands of dollars' worth of smuggled silver, turquoise, and other jewelry-making supplies, along with more weapons and over two hundred thousand dollars in cash.

Word was sent to Las Cruces, and other state police officers and Bureau agents were scheduled to visit the smugglers' base near the Mexican border. Mexican authorities would be informed about the suppliers but what they chose to do after that was strictly up to them.

Lee and Diane believed that ballistics would identify at least some of the weapons on the scene or confiscated on the raids as those used to kill the state police officer and Navajo tribal cop. That evidence, when combined with the recorded confrontation and dialogue Lee provided, would be enough to end his and Diane's involvement in the investigation.

When they finally arrived at her apartment complex, Diane was nearly dead on her feet. Lee was starting to tire as well, but they both kept careful watch as they left the car.

"There's something you need to be aware of," he said. "Leaving Bridget alone in the apartment with a phone could mean that she's already contacted Elka."

"You really didn't have another choice. Do you think this'll draw Elka to us?"

"If Bridget's on the level, we'll be safe. If not . . ."

As they climbed the stairs to the apartment he made it clear that both of them wouldn't be able to go to sleep around Bridget at the same time. "We need to have eyes in the back of our heads now," Lee said softly.

"The TV is on," Diane whispered as they reached the door. They could see the flickering of colors on the curtain. "Doesn't Blondie ever sleep?"

Lee whispered back, "But there's no sound. Let's play it safe. It's us," he called, loud enough for anyone inside to hear.

"Come on in." It sounded like Bridget's voice. There was the sound of the lock mechanism, and then the door opened from the inside. "I'm still alone." Bridget showed her face in the darkness. "How about you two?"

"We weren't followed," Lee said.

They slipped inside and Diane locked the door behind them. Then she turned on the lamp. "Not everyone can see so well in the dark, people."

Bridget was in Diane's robe, and her hair looked a little damp. "I hope you don't mind, Diane. I borrowed this after taking a shower. My clothes were getting a little funky."

Lee quickly checked the bedroom and the bathroom, his hand on the butt of his gun. As he looked in the kitchen area he noted that Bridget's knife was still on the table where he'd left it. Finally he relaxed. Sensing Bridget's gaze, he glanced at her. "Don't take it too personally. I always check the apartment when I get in."

"Vampires are paranoid. I picked up on that right away once Elka sank her teeth into me and I became part of her family," Bridget said.

Diane looked at her oddly. "That's how you became a vampire then—a bite on the jugular?"

"No, of course not," Bridget said, and chuckled. "It was one of those palm-slicing exchanges. Like young boys becoming blood brothers, except for keeps."

Bridget looked at Lee's clothes, apparently just noting the blood on his jacket, pants, and sleeve. "Yours or somebody else's?" she asked in a shaky voice.

"A little of both, I suppose," Lee mumbled, then turned away and walked toward the kitchen area. "Anybody want coffee?"

"Not me," Diane replied. "Just a shower and a little sleep. We need to be out looking for Elka around the base area by the time the President arrives in town."

"You want your robe back?" Bridget reached for the cloth belt that held it in place and started unfastening the knot.

"No!" Diane said abruptly.

Lee laughed and Bridget smiled broadly.

"I mean, no thanks," Diane said. "I have another old one in the closet that will suit me just fine."

"I was just teasing. How'd I do, Lee?" Bridget turned to see his expression.

Lee shook his head. "I see nothing, I hear nothing."

"Bridget, you're about my size, so you ought to fit into my slacks and blouses. Go ahead and see what you can find to wear while I'm in the shower." Then Diane caught Lee's eye.

"I'll take a shower when you're through, Diane," he said, trying to figure out what was on her mind. "Then we can work out the sleeping arrangements."

Lee lay motionless on the living-room chair, resting but not sleeping, and taking occasional, refreshing sips from a juice glass containing the last of his current supply of pig's blood. Revitalized somewhat, he knew that if someone either moved or tried to enter the room he would hear them.

Eyes closed now, he focused his hearing and could detect two separate breathing patterns, one from the sofa just ten feet away where Diane was asleep, and from the bedroom the faint, deep breaths belonging to Bridget.

Diane had made it clear that either she or Lee had to be close to the only entrance to the apartment, and he'd agreed. Elka was out there somewhere, and if she managed to find them the door was the only quick way into or out of the place. One of the chairs from the dining set had been wedged under the knob to slow anyone down, even a vampire. Climbing in the second-story window would require a long ladder or rappelling down from the roof, then breaking through the glass, also a noisy operation.

It was Diane's apartment, so she got the sofa and he settled on the easy chair. Bridget still couldn't be trusted enough for either of them to risk falling asleep beside her, so she occupied the bed.

Bridget said she understood, and offered to keep the bedroom door closed so they'd feel safer. The door hinge squeaked a bit, so Lee knew he'd hear it when she came back out into the living-room area.

Lee opened his eyes, noting that sunlight was beginning to creep in around the sides of the window curtain. The room was just as he'd left it, and the exit door locked and chained, the chair still wedged under the knob.

Bridget was the last to wake up. The young vampire, a pleasant expression on her face, came over to the table where Lee and Diane were having breakfast. She was now wearing eye shadow, blush, and lipstick beneath the sunblock, details that had been missing before.

"How did you sleep, Bridget?" Lee asked, putting down his coffee mug. He'd quit worrying about the rounds Bridget had fired from the pistol he now had tucked under the seat of his car. No bodies had turned up except for those he already knew about, and none that had died by gunfire.

"Very well, I even slept on my back and didn't have to worry if I snored. I feel so free I've decided to wear a little more makeup. Elka has taught me not to attract any more attention than necessary when on a job, but now I'm unemployed, I guess."

"What are your plans now?" Diane asked, her tone more businesslike than friendly.

Bridget looked at Lee, then back to Diane. "So you're really going to let me walk away?"

Diane nodded. "We've had the chance to talk about it while you were in the other room. Just don't give us any reason to believe you've started breaking any laws, okay?"

"But we need you to stay here in the apartment until the issue with Elka is resolved," Lee added. "Which brings up a question we've been trying to answer since last night. Is there anything that Elka said to you that can help confirm her target? Think hard, Bridget. I know she *told* you it was Rogers, but is it possible she's after the President or someone else in addition to Rogers?"

"Let me try to recall her exact words. May I?" Bridget gestured toward the coffee. "Elka said she was paying me to help her punish Rogers and the others who'd been responsible for the loss of her family."

"And Lee was mentioned specifically?" Diane asked.

"And you, Agent Lopez—if you tried to get in the way. Rogers was the main target because he'd recruited Jochen in the first place, then bailed on him when Jochen got caught."

"'Punish' was the term she used? Not 'stab,' 'shoot,' 'blow up,' 'assassinate,' or anything like that?" Lee pressed.

"No, she said 'punish' two or three times," Bridget said.

"To me that sounds like she meant Rogers, not the President," Diane said.

"And Bridget was supposed to kill me. So Elka's main target is Rogers," Lee said.

"But that logic falls apart when you look at what's happened, Lee," Diane argued. "Elka's attacked Rogers already, and she failed to give him anything more than just a few bruises and scratches. Logan confirmed that again last night when I met with him and the Secret Service. But at the hospital she nearly killed three people, not including us, and broke down two or three steel doors getting away. She's as strong as an ox."

Lee suddenly stood up. "Oh, crap. I get it now."

"You get what?" Diane asked.

"Nobody wants to be scratched by a vampire, or scratch one either. Remember that comment Bridget made last night about blood brothers?" Lee asked.

"Elka wants to punish the CIA man by turning him into a vampire?" Bridget asked. "That would just make him harder to kill."

"No, easier, and he'll die in a particularly horrible way," Diane said, suddenly understanding. "She must have mixed her blood with his when they were wrestling around in that shaded walkway."

"Yes, and he's probably feeling better right now than he has in his entire life—strong, alert, and very hungry. But he doesn't *know* he's a vampire," Lee said.

"And his security will probably keep him inside until his meeting with the President. But the moment Rogers steps out of the car at the airport he's going to get a faceful of New Mexico sunshine. He'll turn into a ball of fire. Talk about being punished." Diane reached for her cell phone. "We've got to warn him."

"That does sound like Elka." Bridget nodded. "Originally, I think she planned to shoot him while I created some kind of diversion. But what she did makes sense now, in a perverse way, and this way of killing him has given her hours to make her escape. It's like a bomb that no explosives dog can detect. She may already be out of the state—unless she wants to watch Rogers go up in smoke."

"It's a spectacular way to punish someone, and there's no way a forensic team will be able to establish what happened, so she'll get away with murder. It'll go down as another one of those spontaneous-combustion stories you see between the covers of supermarket tabloids."

Diane raised her voice to the person on the phone.

"Have him call me, Special Agent Lopez, *before* he steps outside. This is absolutely critical and concerns the woman who attacked him yesterday. We know she's going to strike again. He needs to stay indoors and out of view until he speaks to me personally." Diane rolled her eyes, obviously on hold now. "His security people are idiots," she said, glancing at Lee.

"No, I can't wait and have him call me back," Diane insisted. "I'll stay on the line while you get him." Diane waited, getting angrier by the second.

"Shit, shit, shit. He's going to die," Diane said, disconnecting the call. "He's been at some security briefing since six this morning. Maybe we can get over there in time to stop him from going outside." She hurried to find her jacket, placing the holster and pistol on her belt while she moved around the room.

"Where is he now?" Lee asked. His jacket already on, he put on his baseball cap and dark glasses.

"He stayed in base quarters last night, then went to a secure area before dawn," Diane explained. "The security man I spoke to wouldn't even call him to the phone. He said they'd been getting crank calls all morning because of the presidential visit and he'd call me back later once I was 'cleared.' That asshole is going to get Rogers fried."

"We'll never make it there in time. All he has to do is step outside for a minute or two," Lee reminded. "Try and get Logan on the phone. If he can send somebody to detain Rogers, we have a chance. I hope Rogers uses sunblock. At least that would give him a few minutes to save himself."

Diane nodded. Logan was on speed dial, so the call only took a few seconds. Diane started to explain, got interrupted, then motioned to Lee. "Turn on the TV!"

Bridget got there first. The set came on quickly, and they could see a live broadcast from the Albuquerque Sunport. In the background was Air Force One. Stairs attached to a truck were already in place and the main exit door to the giant aircraft was open. Armed guards were stationed by the exit and at the foot of the steps, where a reception area had been roped off and a podium was already in place.

"The President arrived early," Lee said flatly. "The security guy was bullshitting you."

Diane nodded to Lee. She'd moved over where she could see the TV screen. "You have to keep him from stepping out of his vehicle," she nearly yelled into the phone.

The camera remained focused on the entrance to the aircraft with the viewing field large enough to include the ramp at the bottom as well. "Turn up the sound a little," Lee whispered, and Bridget reached over to a knob.

". . . the local dignitaries scheduled to welcome the President to the Land of Enchantment are now making their way to the reception area," the reporter announced.

"Get Rogers back inside!" Diane yelled.

There was an off-camera shout and the camera suddenly shifted to the left. People were scattering in every direction. A man in a suit was literally burning up, screaming and thrashing around in unimaginable pain. His clothes remained relatively untouched, but his face and hands shot out smokeless flames like blowtorches. A security man in a black jacket tackled him and tried to roll him on the concrete. "My God, my God, a man is on fire!" the announcer yelled.

Men came forward in ones and twos with their jackets and tried to smother the flames, but by then Rogers's body was dissolving away, turning to ashes.

The camera turned quickly again, out of focus for a few seconds before capturing the image of Air Force One. Amid a chorus of shouts the guard at the aircraft door was helping an attendant close up the aircraft's main hatch.

Below on the runway the driver of the truck containing the ramp was already moving away.

There was the roar of aircraft engines starting up and the sound drowned out everything else. The camera shifted back to the spot on the concrete where Rogers had died. All that remained was a pile of men's dark suit jackets, an empty suit, and two shoes lying alone with the socks half in, half out. Someone was spraying them with a small fire extinguisher while guards hustled dignitaries back to the motorcade of black vehicles. Chaos had been replaced with automatic responses based upon training and rehearsal.

The television camera shifted back to Air Force One, which was starting to roll across the concrete toward the runway.

Lee stepped over to Diane, who was shaking her head, unable to look at the TV anymore. "Well, Rogers wasn't using sunblock, that's for sure. I should have guessed what Elka was doing," he said softly.

Bridget was as pale as a . . . vampire. "Is this what will happen to me?"

"Learn from what you just saw, Bridget," Lee said. "Elka is over a hundred years old, isn't she? Being smart has kept *her* from this fate. It's more than luck. Rogers didn't have a clue what he'd become, and his self-important attitude contributed to his death. You know what you are, and why becoming a vampire has to be such a secret."

They stood around, thinking about what had just happened and what they might have done differently. Finally Diane spoke again. "Logan is going to call me back once things have calmed down a bit. He's going to want to know *why* I was so certain that Rogers was in danger. He's going to ask me how a man could burn up and still not set fire to the clothes he's wearing."

"Stick to the notion that you believed Elka had infiltrated

the base somehow and was going to take a shot at him while all eyes were on the President. Because Rogers had betrayed her husband, you concluded that Rogers was the primary target all along," Lee said. "Put your own spin on it, but make sure it fits the known facts, at least as mortals see them."

"And I can explain her first contact with him at the hotel, when she attacked him, as her way of letting him know she was here and coming for him later. To put the fear of God in him, so to speak. Maybe she gave him a message that he didn't mention to anyone else," Diane said, the idea taking shape in her mind. "It'll work."

"Excuse me for butting in, but how will you explain his reaction to sunlight and the way he burned up without heating anything else around him?" Bridget was a little less pale than before.

"She won't," Lee said. "There's no explanation that works." He looked at Diane. "Maybe you can suggest that it must have been an undetected chemical in his aftershave or suntan lotion that finally reacted. Or point out that Rogers was overweight, under a lot of strain, and may have just spontaneously burst into flames from some biological imbalance. It doesn't matter what theory you run past him, just as long as you don't suggest he'd become a vampire without knowing it. Let somebody else bring that up and be laughed into silence. The idea is that you have no idea."

Bridget nodded. "I'll have to remember that. Have you seen other vampires die this way?"

Lee nodded somberly. "And, believe me when I tell you, the memory stays with you for as long as you live."

# CHAPTER 20

The shock of Rogers's spectacular death passed quickly for Diane, but Bridget sat motionless on the sofa, riveted to the television screen. Regular programming had been preempted with a special report and commentators and hurriedly provided "experts" were still speculating on what had happened to Rogers.

Within fifteen minutes Diane's cell phone rang. Lee, who was working on his final report concerning last night's events, looked up as she answered the call. Diane nodded to him, confirming that it was Logan. Lee half listened, but Diane had a good handle on the necessary ignorance required under such bizarre circumstances. Within three minutes the call ended.

"Federal law enforcement is bringing in a forensic team from somewhere back East to examine the remains. What do you think they'll find, Lee?" Diane asked.

"If they had let the state Office of the Medical Investigators look at the ashes and compare test data it would have become obvious that Rogers and the bodies over near Fort Wingate a few months ago all shared the same cause of death—burning due to an untraceable accelerant," Lee said.

"I remember you said that when a vampire ignites like

that it's due to some kind of biological oxidation that doesn't conduct heat to anything but vampire tissue. You think they'll see the connection?" she asked.

"Eventually, if the feds listen to what the local experts tell them. You might get another call, too, or maybe me, because I'm Navajo. But I'll just play dumb like before," Lee said.

Just as Lee was getting up to pour himself more coffee, the apartment telephone rang. It was Lieutenant Richmond, so Diane, who'd answered, gave the phone to Lee.

"Lee, I want you to write up the report about Rogers and the German terrorist group before you complete the final paperwork on the Silver Eagle operation. Make sure to express your opinion on Rogers's death. You see that on TV, right?"

"Yes, sir." Lee decided not to comment about the change in timing that kept them from getting to Rogers before he stepped out into direct sunlight. Richmond would have had no input in that decision.

"Now, getting to the main reason for my call—a woman who refused to identify herself called the local state police office, asking to speak to you specifically concerning the German terrorists. She mentioned Elka Pfeiffer."

"She's not still on the line, is she?"

"No, and that alone was enough to make me consider that she's not another crackpot. She asked the switchboard operator to contact you and ask that you make arrangements needed to take her return call. She said she'd call back in an hour. Then she hung up. All we could get was the number of an Albuquerque pay phone."

"Interesting. Her call was recorded. Can you play it back to me? Maybe I can identify her." Lee motioned Bridget and Diane over to the receiver, then put the phone on speaker so they could all listen.

"I'll transfer the call back to our operator."

Several seconds went by, then a woman with a German accent came on the line, speaking briefly as Richmond had described, then hanging up.

"That's Elka," Bridget whispered, her face pale again.

Richmond got back on the line just then. "Recognize the woman, Lee?"

"Her voice sounds familiar, but I can't place it right now. When she calls back, give her this number." Lee looked over at Diane, who nodded her approval.

"You want me to set up a trace?"

"Exactly. Get Logan to okay it if it'll speed things up. The Bureau has more juice," Lee answered.

"Good thinking. Keep me posted," he said.

"At least she doesn't know where we are, apparently," Diane said.

"What do you think she wants? Me?" Bridget said, her voice shaky.

"Elka may be fishing for information. How could she possible know you've contacted us? I'd think she's more likely to assume you've just taken off for good. And now that it's light outside, her own movements outside a vehicle are restricted," Lee pointed out.

Unless, he thought, Elka already knew where Bridget was, and this was just a signal for Bridget to proceed with whatever plan they had cooked up to get rid of him. Rogers was finished; perhaps he and Diane were next. The one glitch with that theory was that it assumed Bridget would hear Elka's call and there was no way Elka could have been positive that would happen. Maybe Elka had infinite faith in Bridget's abilities as a con artist. And if Bridget was setting them up, there was no denying she was good at her job. They *had* lowered their guard around her somewhat—a remarkable thing, really, considering that they knew Bridget had fired her pistol after stealing it and they had no evidence to support her claim that all she'd done was a little target shooting.

"It doesn't make sense for Elka to call us unless her business isn't finished here," Diane said. "Otherwise she would have stolen a car and been miles from here by now. Do you know what other identities she uses?" Diane asked Bridget, watching her reaction slowly.

"No, and I don't know where she's stashed her travel documents or her cash. We keep those details a secret even from each other. That way if one of us gets caught we can't give away information we don't know."

"That makes perfect sense," Lee said.

Bridget said nothing for a moment, then, in a thoughtful voice, added, "Maybe Elka's still here because this time she doesn't care if she gets caught."

"You mean she's not planning on making an escape?" Lee asked.

"Well, I told you how she's acted since Jochen and the others died. This was going to be our last job, and she was going to pay me off so I could be on my own once it was over," Bridget said. "Then again, she could be playing us for fools. Think of what she did to Rogers."

"Death by cop is a choice a lot of disturbed people are taking these days, if that's really what she has in mind. The only problem is, Elka could be very hard to kill," Diane said.

"It's possible she's tried to contact me recently. There's my laptop. Shall I check my E-mail?" Bridget asked.

"Go ahead." Diane brought the small unit out of a desk drawer, where she'd kept it after bringing it inside earlier this morning, then hooked up the phone line to Bridget's machine.

Five minutes later, Diane at the keyboard, they discovered three very recent E-mail messages from an Internet address Bridget said belonged to Elka. They all said the same thing, in English: "I miss hearing from you, please write."

"Well, unless that's some code you're keeping from us," Lee said, looking at Bridget, who shook her head, "we'll have to wait and see what she wants when she calls me."

The phone rang twenty minutes later. "Hello, this is Officer Hawk," Lee said, pushing the speaker button so they all could hear.

"We've never met, Officer Hawk, but you've seen my work, I assume?"

It was the same woman recorded earlier, accent and everything. Bridget nodded, confirming it was Elka.

Lee knew that other law-enforcement people, including Richmond and Logan, would eventually hear this conversation as well, so he didn't want to say anything that would compromise Bridget or himself as being vampires. "You must be Elka Pfeiffer. I've seen your photograph. It's good to be able to put a voice to a face. Too bad you missed the chance to kill your old CIA handler when you had the opportunity. After seeing how you shook off that bullet wound and later kicked open the hospital doors, I wonder why you weren't able to just break his neck like you did with the Corrales police officer."

"Being thorough, Officer Hawk? And making sure you don't give out any information that might come back at you?" Elka was mocking him, but her voice seemed weary and strained.

"You sound tired, Mrs. Pfeiffer. And now you'll never be able to kill Rogers. You did come to our state looking for revenge, didn't you?"

"Revenge is for amateurs, Officer Hawk, but it was satisfying to see that CIA bastard get what he deserved. I'm so glad it's finally . . ." Her voice trailed off, as if she had something more to say, then changed her mind.

"Why are you calling, Elka? You know you're never going to be able to get to me. I'm the hunter now. This is my state and I know every hiding place, night or day. You're all alone, but I have many friends and allies," Lee said.

"I just wanted to hear your voice, Officer Hawk, before I go. You and that FBI woman are responsible for what happened to my brother *and* my friends. When they died, any chance of saving my husband's life was lost." Elka's voice was wavering a bit now, showing more emotion.

"They were killers who knew the risks and paid the price for their crimes. You, too, will be facing death or imprisonment sooner than you think if you decide to stick around," Lee replied. He looked at his watch. A trace had already had time to go through, he thought.

"My family was well suited for our work, Officer Hawk, and you as well for yours. I'm not sure about Agent Lopez though. Is it in her blood, like it is with you?" Elka was being cryptic now, fishing for information. If Diane had become a vampire, it would be easier to explain how they were able to defeat Elka's family.

"You'll find that out for yourself, Elka, if you stick around," Lee said.

"Perhaps," Elka said. "I'll be in touch—one way or the other." She hung up.

"Why did she stay on the line so long?" Diane asked immediately. "She had to know we're tracing the call."

Bridget shook her head. "She was either using a public phone or her cell. Elka would never let you track her down so easily."

Lee's cell phone rang before he could reply.

It was Lieutenant Richmond. "Lee, she called from a private home in Placitas, according to the information I have. We're getting together a team and will rendezvous at the Foothills shopping center a mile from the location. The home address is 303 Juniper Trail. Meet us at the rendezvous site."

"Agent Lopez and I are getting ready now," Lee confirmed, then disconnected the call. "They have a location."

"She's not going to be there," Diane said, shaking her head in disbelief.

"I'm not so sure. If she's suicidal or hoping to get one last shot at us, literally, she'll be waiting. Get loaded for bear, Diane. She wants a confrontation, so let's give it to her." Lee grabbed two additional ammo clips from a drawer in the kitchen.

"I hope you both get out of this alive, I really do, but I'm not going to stick around," Bridget said, her voice steady. "In spite of what Elka is, she did value me more than my biological family ever did, so I don't want to be around when she dies—or either of you, if the worst happens."

"Will you be taking off right away?" Lee asked, putting on his raid jacket, gloves, and cap, then checking his handheld radio. Diane was ready now too, it seemed.

"No. I'll wait until dark. So, depending on when you return, I may still be here. But I wanted to say good-bye now, just in case we don't see each other again." Bridget started to give Diane a quick hug, then changed her mind and made it a handshake. She then kissed Lee on the cheek. "Good luck."

Worse-case scenario, Bridget already knows where Elka is because they planned it that way," Diane said as they hurried north on the Interstate. "Maybe she'll show up, join Elka, and try to kill us."

Lee shook his head, not taking his eyes off the traffic. "My gut feeling is that she's for real. Several times she had the opportunity to make a move against us and she hasn't. But, having said that, you noticed that I didn't give her the address and did my best to make sure she didn't overhear it on the phone."

From their northeastern location in Albuquerque it took less than twenty minutes to arrive in Placitas, an eclectic community of old settlers and crackpots, former hippie communes, and a few modern cookie-cutter housing developments extending up into the foothills of the northern end of the Sandia Mountains.

Diane took another look at the map section she'd folded out to read as Lee drove east up Highway 165. "There's the shopping center on the left. Looks like we beat the crowd."

As they passed by, Lee could see several SUVs and pickups that appeared to belong to civilians, plus one county sheriff's vehicle parked at the end of the lot farthest from the businesses.

"There's a small subdivision to our right up ahead. I can see some new houses among the pine trees. According to your map Juniper Trail is the second road coming up. It makes a half circle, then comes back to the highway farther east."

"What's the plan?" Diane asked. "Other than go up to the door and knock?"

"Why not? If she's taken over somebody's home, there could be hostages," Lee said. "And if we wait outside, the FBI and everyone else will show up. We need to immobilize her as quickly as possible, then make sure she doesn't have the chance to heal herself. With Logan looking over our shoulders, we can't exactly decapitate her. Second-best option would be several shots to the head and heart, enough to literally destroy either organ."

"We're playing it her way, though, Lee. She's a vampire, so calling during the daytime is also pressuring you to risk being caught outside. Elka doesn't know you're only a half vampire and can stay outside much longer than she can. If she's looking for a confrontation, it's meant to be inside that house—and soon."

"Okay. It's a trap, we know it's a trap, she knows we know it's a trap. The cards have been dealt. We now have to play them out," Lee replied. "I just hope she's not planning on setting off a bomb or something like that."

"There's the house up ahead, I think." Diane pointed down the street, then looked over at Lee. "I forgot about bombs, until now. Thanks for bringing it up."

"Hey, what are friends for?"

Right up against the side of the mountain was a large three-story wood-frame and stucco home with a steep metal pitched roof and several fireplaces. Balconies extended out from two upper-story rooms, one, probably a bedroom, which looked out across the valley to the west. There were no vehicles in the driveway or at the curb.

"How'd she get here?" Diane wondered aloud. "Walk?"

"Maybe she came over from another street, or is already long gone. We still have to check out the house." Lee looked up and down the block and around the curve where the street looped back toward the highway. An expensive-looking SUV was in the driveway on the opposite side of the street two houses down.

"How's this for tactics?" Lee suggested. "If she's still inside, Elka will be expecting normal law enforcement to surround the residence and assault all the entrances simultaneously—unless contact is made and a hostage is spotted. Let's just rush the door we least expect her to have covered. I'll go first, you cover my back."

"We're wearing our vests, but don't give her a clear head shot or we're screwed," Diane replied, her expression grim.

"I'll go in first and you cover me while we sweep the house. I'm probably as fast as she is, if not faster." Lee pulled up in the middle of the driveway, almost touching the double garage door with the bumper. If her car was inside, she'd have to move his first in order to flee by vehicle.

"She entered through the front, probably kicked it in," Diane pointed out as they both exited the car, her on the side facing the main entrance. Lee, coming around the rear of their vehicle, could see the heavy carved wooden door slightly ajar. The doorjamb was shattered. There was an alarm system, even one of those little signs stuck into the ground announcing the security. If the alarm had gone off, they certainly hadn't been notified by radio.

"Follow me," he whispered, running around the side of the house. The house was xeriscaped with different shades and textures of gravel, Southwest shrubs, and flowers, but there was also a flagstone walk that led around back. Lee stayed on the flagstones to avoid the crunchy noise. A narrow, covered walkway between two wings of the house led through a glass door into what looked like a library or home office. Nobody was visible inside.

Lee tried the knob, but it was locked. He stepped back and kicked the door right in the center of the clear panel. It was Plexiglas, and broke loose around the edges of the doorframe, falling back onto the carpet in one piece.

Diane caught up with him just then, and directed her pistol toward the exit into a hallway as Lee stepped through the opening into the office. A chair was wedged against the knob of a narrow office door, probably a closet judging from the location. He could hear tapping and muffled speech within.

He took a quick look around. Elka wasn't hiding behind the desk, and except for the closet, there were no other places to conceal herself. The curtain was askew.

Lee had to use quite a bit of force to yank the chair away from the closet door. Huddled together on the floor inside were a man and woman, bound and gagged, in their nightclothes.

While Diane kept watch on the hall, Lee cut the couple's bonds with his dagger, then helped them to their feet and out of the closet. The couple, Hispanics in their early fifties, took off their own gags.

"Anyone else here besides you?" Lee whispered to the man.

"Just that bitch who did this to us," the woman whispered back harshly before her husband could speak.

"Go down the street to a neighbor's house and get inside. More police are coming," Lee whispered, turning the woman toward the opening he'd created in the door. They left immediately, slipping through the damaged door without comment.

Lee joined Diane in the short hallway leading to the rest of the house and took a quick look around the corner. It was dark, at least for nonvampires. Ahead was a longer hall leading to a central area, possibly a den or the living room.

Halfway down the hall on the opposite side Lee could smell scented soap. The open doorway probably led into a laundry room. He tiptoed down the carpeted hall, keeping his pistol pointed toward the doorway. Diane was crouched low on the opposite side to the hall, covering the far end of the hall and the central space beyond.

Using hand signals, Lee indicated that he was going to check out the scented room. In a heartbeat he was crouched by the entrance. He took a quick look, ducking back before a trigger could be pulled. It was obviously a laundry room with updated appliances and other high-end features, but there were no humans or vampires hiding inside.

Lee turned and looked at Diane, shaking his head. Advancing to the end of the hall, Diane covering him, Lee looked out into a large den or family room. An enormous television and bookshelf filled most of a flagstone wall, and on the opposite side of the room was a large sofa unit and several easy chairs. In the center of the floor was a standard pool table, and in the corner a wide stairway with oak steps circled up to a wide landing with a dark railing. At the base of the stairs was another door, leading to the garage based upon its location.

"I was hoping you two wouldn't wait for the others to arrive. After all, you're probably the only ones who know how important it is to *really* kill me," Elka called down the stairwell from one of the upper floors. "You'd better hurry. If you don't kill me before the others arrive, I might just surrender to someone else and let them take me to jail."

Lee and Diane exchanged glances as she moved forward, even with him now. There were two more floors, based upon the windows they'd seen when driving up, but the voice had been faint. She could have been on the third floor, but had to have been close to the stairwell to hear them at all.

"I heard you release the Moras. They seem like such a loving couple. I hated putting them in the closet, but I didn't want them to get in the way when you two arrived," Elka said.

Lee moved up the stairs quickly. At the top of the landing was a huge living room with a big fireplace. In one direction was an open area containing a dining table, and beyond, a shiny, expensive kitchen. At the opposite end were a glass wall and sliding doors leading out to a balcony overlooking the valley to the west.

"Up here, children," Elka called from the third floor.

Lee glanced up the stairwell, but no one was visible. Taking very light steps, he inched upward. Once his head was just above the level of the third floor, which was hardwood, Lee stopped and looked around cautiously. Down the hall on his right was a set of double doors, possibly the master bedroom.

In the opposite direction was another, almost identical hall, but with three open doorways, one on either side, and a third at the end. That room appeared to be almost empty except for the edge of a barely visible metal contraption that reminded him of exercise equipment. Moving off the stairs, he flattened himself against the wall of the hallway containing the open doors and waited, keeping his pistol ready. He wasn't worried about the closed doors at the moment.

Diane, fast but not nearly as quick or light on her feet, came up now, took a look, then stepped off the stairs and took a position against the opposite wall. She was crouched, pistol ready, covering the open doors ahead of them.

He waited for her to catch her breath.

"You're pretty light on your feet for a human, Agent Lopez, but I can tell the difference," Elka said. "Until now I didn't know that Nez *hadn't* turned you."

Lee and Diane waited, not saying a word. Two minutes went by while they listened, trying to detect any movement that would verify exactly where she was. Lee thought she might be in the second room down, but he couldn't be certain.

"You know why I killed Rogers, don't you? He was the worst kind of man—weak, a user. I let him shoot me, then scraped him with my bloody fingernail. Fool, he was so grateful I was shot and not him that he probably never even noticed what I'd done. Did you see it? He went up in flames like the *Hindenberg*." Elka laughed. This time her voice was strong and steady, full of purpose.

They waited for Elka to speak again and it didn't take long. "I could be gone by now, you know. I *was* going to retire. But I just had to try and see if I could get you too, Nez. Even if I don't, it won't really matter that much. I've had a good, very long life. And I still won. I've already killed the man who destroyed my family."

Lee heard a vehicle pull up outside, then maybe two or three more.

Elka heard them too. The hardwood floor creaked slightly, and then the tip of a pistol barrel appeared beside the doorjamb at waist level. Diane had been looking in just the right direction. She fired one shot, hitting the pistol close to the muzzle and knocking it out of Elka's hand.

Lee ran forward and dove into the room, coming to his feet in a roll with his pistol up just as a figure in a blue jumpsuit ran through an adjoining door into the end room. He followed Elka at a run, thinking she wouldn't expect immediate pursuit.

Elka flashed across the brightly lit exercise room, enhanced by two wide, nearly ceiling-height windows on each of the exterior walls. Diane fired from back down the hall as Elka passed across her sights, missing Elka by a few inches and striking the wall between windows.

The tall, red-haired vampire drew a backup pistol from her pocket and fired two shots as she ducked behind what looked like a juice bar on casters. Lee dodged, firing back. He missed Elka but a blender exploded on the counter and the window behind the bar broke, cascading down to the floor like a waterfall of glass.

Diane appeared beside the hall door, low to the ground, straining to locate Elka. Lee moved forward again, pistol aimed at the bar. If Elka poked her head out, she was dead.

"Cover me!" he shouted. Lee jammed his pistol back in the holster and dove into the room.

Elka risked a quick look and Diane snapped off a shot. The bullet missed, taking out the biggest remaining sliver of the six-foot-high window.

Lee rose from the floor and charged like an offensive tackle, striking the bar with his shoulder and pushing it toward the window. Elka grunted from the impact and stuck her pistol out, firing blindly. Bullets erupted from through the wood panel, and Lee felt the impact of one striking his vest. He churned forward, driving with his legs and shoulder, forcing the bar all the way to the wall. Elka screamed as she crashed into the window opening, but Lee kept pushing.

Diane arrived just then and jammed her shoulder into the bar, adding to the pressure, forcing the bar forward. Elka lost the contest, slipping on the glass-littered carpet. She toppled out of the window backward. The portable bar followed her down the outside of the building, taking part of the window frame with it.

Lee looked out and saw Elka hit the gravel just before the bar did. The heavy piece of furniture struck her on the head and upper body before shattering into pieces.

He felt his neck getting warm and ducked back inside out of the direct sunlight. He'd lost his cap in the other room.

Elka tried to scream, perhaps, but her head had been sliced open by the impact of the bar top and the cry came out muffled, as if her mouth were half full. Then she lay still and silent, apparently unconscious. Four officers in blue raid jackets ran up, aiming their assault weapons and pistols at the woman. No one fired, but they kept their distance, waiting and watching, apparently respecting what they'd all heard concerning Elka's resilience. Finally someone yelled, "Medic!" Still, nobody moved any closer.

Within seconds Elka's head began to darken, her hair shriveling into black coils. Then came smoke. Everyone below took a step back. Suddenly the wounds on her face burst into flames, spreading quickly. There was a loud moan, more like a rumble as she began to thrash around wildly; then the sound died abruptly. Lee stepped back, deciding it was time to find his cap, but Diane remained at the window for a moment.

"All clear," she shouted down to the officers, then turned back to Lee, who'd found his cap. "You sure you're wearing enough sunblock?"

He nodded. "I'll find a way to stand in the shade, though."

"Let's try to do the debrief inside, just in case. I've seen enough roasting flesh today to last me a lifetime." Diane looked at him anxiously.

"You think Elka really thought she could kill me—us—before the rest of the officers arrived?" Lee asked her. "She sure didn't go out of that window easily. Hell of a fighter."

"We may never know for sure what was really going through her mind. But she couldn't have gone far on foot. You notice she wasn't even wearing a hat? Maybe she did plan on surrendering—taking her chances later with a jailbreak once the sun went down," Diane said with a shrug. "All in all, I don't think she was really suicidal."

Five hours later Diane and Lee drove away from the crime scene. "If we hadn't taken out Elka, we'd be on suspension for not waiting until backup arrived and coordinating efforts with them," Diane said.

"If we hadn't played it like we did, we probably wouldn't

have been around to have this conversation," Lee countered, driving west toward the Interstate from Placitas.

"Yeah, and Elka might have gotten away. Considering the ski mask and gloves we found in her jumpsuit pockets, and the motorcycle hidden behind the house, escape was a definite part of her plan. She'd have gone up that forest service road and disappeared long before a search party arrived."

"I think she planned on jumping from the second-story balcony. That's where the motorcycle helmet was sitting," Lee reminded her. "But I wasn't about to suggest that to Logan or Richmond."

"At least they have something to be happy about. After the human-torch video and the shortest presidential visit on record, catching and killing an international terrorist at least brings New Mexico back into the win column. They're already discussing the obvious connection between the way Elka and Rogers died, but they'll never be able to prove anything conclusively. The best forensic experts won't be able to help either. Vampire tissue loses its unique structure when it goes up in flames, right?"

Lee nodded.

"I guess we can finally start breathing normally again," she said. "Let's close down our business operations and write up those reports while we still remember what we told them last night," Diane added, leaning back in her seat and closing her eyes. "Wake me up when we get there, okay?"

Hours later, Lee and Diane left the FBI office downtown, having turned over their business records, supplies, and inventory to the bean counters and filled out their final written reports. Copies were ready for Lieutenant Richmond, who was scheduled to pick them up later.

"The sun's been down almost an hour now," Lee said. "You think Bridget will still be at your apartment?"

Diane was in the passenger seat topping off her pistol clip with fresh rounds while Lee drove. "I'm not sure. There's something not quite right about her, you know?"

Lee's cell phone rang. "Crap."

"Now what?" she muttered.

He grabbed the phone from atop the seat cushion. "Yes?"

"Officer Hawk?" It was Iris, the night dispatcher from the Las Cruces state police office.

"Yes, Iris. What's going on?"

"Something weird, Officer Hawk. I just got a call from the Cruces PD. The landlord at your apartment complex entered your apartment to check out complaints of a strong odor and found a body inside. A Native American or Hispanic man with his head cut off."

"Decapitated? In my apartment?" Lee noticed Diane looking at him closely.

"That's what I said, Lee. And he'd apparently been shot several times. From what we've been told, the man has been dead two or three days. His body and his head were both in your bathtub."

"Has Cruces PD been able to ID the body?" Lee suddenly knew who'd killed the man. "Bridget," he mouthed to Diane, who was staring at him now questioningly.

"They found a New Mexico operator's license for a San Juan County man named Clarence Atso. But we don't have a confirmation for sure. The body's in pretty bad shape," Iris replied.

"Clarence Atso? We've been looking for him. Does Lieutenant Richmond know about this yet?" Lee asked, noting Diane's eyebrows going up at the mention of the skinwalker's name.

"He's my next call. You'll probably be hearing from a

Cruces detective within the hour, but they'll have to go though channels."

"Thanks for the heads-up. I'll be contacting Richmond myself later," Lee added, then ended the call.

"Clarence Atso was found dead in *your* Las Cruces apartment? Bridget went there too, didn't she?" Diane shook her head. "Maybe they were both looking for you and found each other instead."

"And Bridget thought it was me, so she shot him and cut off his head. She *did* try to kill me," he said slowly. He hadn't wanted to believe that. Actually, he'd hoped like hell that he'd finally found just the opposite—a vampire who had kept their sense of right and wrong despite the lure of power they'd inherited along with the nightwalker curse. It would have meant actually having an ally who shared his fate, living in that dark world his human companions would never really know.

"Bridget got the wrong Navajo. But now what do we do with her?" Diane still had her pistol in her hand. She looked at it for a moment, then jammed the weapon back into the holster.

"You know what we would have done had we found Atso first. The way I see it, she ended up doing us a favor," Lee said.

"And Atso *was* there to kill you, so there's justice in how he died," she said quietly. "But what really sucks is that she's been lying to us all along."

"About that, yes." He took a deep breath then let it out again. "Let's see if she's still there, then play it by ear." Lee slowed the vehicle, realizing that the apartment complex was just a block farther down the street.

"Act normal?" Diane said.

"Yeah. But be ready for anything," Lee said, pulling into one of the parking slots close to the building.

Diane looked up at her apartment window. "Lights are out and the TV doesn't seem to be on. Maybe Bridget's really gone now. She had to know the body would be discovered within a few days. It's summer, and dead things get ripe even in an air-conditioned apartment."

They stepped out of Lee's car, looked around carefully one more time, then climbed the stairs.

"Let me go first," Lee insisted, taking the key from her hand.

"You've seen too many old movies, Lee," Diane whispered.

"And I want us to be around to see them again on DVD." He unlocked the door, then eased it open, peering inside, his hand on the butt of his pistol. "Looks okay." He flipped on the inside light for Diane's benefit, then walked quickly toward the doors leading to the bathroom and bedroom.

Diane followed, locking the door behind her before checking out the kitchen area.

"Nobody here but us," Lee announced, stepping out of the bedroom.

"There's a note on the table," Diane said, picking up the single page. "Want me to read it?"

"Sure."

Diane looked at the paper for about ten seconds.

"Out loud!"

Diane laughed. "Okay.

" 'Guys, I'm taking a cab to the place where I've stashed some money and new ID, then I'm outta here. I heard what happened at Placitas and I'm glad to hear you two are okay. Thanks for giving me a chance to get my life back again. I promise I'll do better this time.' " Diane paused, then added, "She signed it 'Me.' "

Diane looked over at Lee. "Lose a life or two, save one—maybe. It's up to her now."

Lee nodded, then sat down on the sofa. Leaning way back against the cushions, he looked over at her through weary eyes. "It's been tough lately, hasn't it?"

"You look dead tired, Lee. I never thought I'd see it. You okay?"

"Yeah. I'm not physically tired. It's just that being a nightwalker gets to me at times. I'm tired in spirit, if you know what I mean. What I really need is a change of pace—a new outlook. What do you say we clean up and go out for some dinner? Maybe a place with some music."

"You mean like a date?" Diane replied, smiling.

"Kinda like that, yeah."

"I don't dance, but I do know a little restaurant in Old Town that has a fine guitarist. No country-Western, but some great Spanish classical music."

"Sounds good."

Diane looked at the clothes she was wearing. "We dressing up or down tonight, Lee?"

"*You* own a dress?" he teased.

"Not since college, smartass. How about something that coordinates with the essential law-enforcement accessories?" Diane struck a modeling pose, opening her jacket enough to show her handgun.

"Fashionably dangerous. My kind of woman."